The Princess Witch; Or, It Isn't As Easy To Go Crazy As You Might Think

Part Two Blue Tara Trilogy

Book Two Princess Tara Chronicles

By Michael Ostrogorsky

Blue Parrot Books
Seattle

Blue Parrot Books Paperback Edition

Published in the United States By

Copyright 2019 by Michael Ostrogorsky

All Rights Reserved

ISBN 978-1-0878-0126-1

First Blue Parrot Books Edition

Table of Contents

The Princess Tara Chronicles are dedicated to the Hyacinth Macaw Parrot Princess Tara, my favorite witch. And yes, she really is a witch. I should know.

Special mention to the Blue and Gold Macaw Parrot Aboo, Princess Tara's sidekick. Princess Tara is a hard act to follow, but rest assured, Aboo will get his place in the spotlight.

Special thank you to my editor, Helen O. Jones, for catching my mistakes.

Introduction

I must finally have gone over the edge to totally batshit crazy. There could be no other explanation. No other explanation for why the cannibal warlock Hamatsa's procurer of bodies, the svelte seductress Kinqalatlala, stood before me with her razor-sharp hand stabbed through my chest while her tongue pushed into my mouth. No other explanation for why I stood frozen in shock while blood streamed down my legs. My blood. No other explanation for why my girlfriend Jean lay unmoving and unconscious on the pavement. No other explanation for why a tall naked muscular Amazonian goddess with glowing crystalline blue skin and only one eye and one breast let out a screech that threatened to burst my head.

Well, wait. There could be one other explanation. I could be dead. I couldn't discount the possibility that I might be a new resident in the spirit world. Crazy or dead. This day was not going well.

Prologue

When I awoke from my dream I stood safely on the U Dub's, University of Washington's, Red Square. My girlfriend Jean stood at my side. Well, we didn't stand directly on the red brick that gave Red Square its name. We stood on the outstretched blood red wing of the King of the Birds, Garuda. A wing that stretched across the horizon. The blood red wing stretched down to the pavement from the bird's massive glowing golden body that filled the sky above us, turning night to day.

I took Jean's hand and we jumped off the wing onto the brick pavement. I could barely contain my joy at seeing Jean alive and standing next to me. I could barely contain my joy at finding myself, and Jean, alive and well. As well as could be expected after our tussle with the cannibal warlock Hamatsa one hundred and forty feet in the air on top of the red brick monoliths in the middle of Red Square.

Washed in the golden glow of Garuda's massive body, Jean looked to me to be a statue of a Greek goddess. Her long flowing brunette hair, her mournful brown Slavic eyes, her ruby red lips, even her pale Seattle skin, shined brilliantly bathed in the light emanating from Garuda's golden body. I pulled Jean to me and kissed her.

Chapter One
Part One

I am beginning to think that my act of kissing my girlfriend is the cue to my parrot, a huge hyacinth macaw named Princess Tara, a parrot who just happens to be a witch, with a coffee addiction, a witch named Blue Tara, to let out one of her head popping mind numbing screeches that signals her bending time and space. In this case, bending time and space between the U Dub's, University of Washington's, Red Square and my apartment in the old Saint Charles Hotel in Seattle's downtown Old Ballard neighborhood. Blue Tara's habit of bending time and space between two points, first, the point she's standing at, and second, the point she wants to be standing at, is nifty magic she possesses to transport us instantaneously from the first point to the second. One moment we're standing in the U Dub's Red Square, a humongous golden feathered god with a gleaming white eagle's face and blood red wings that span the sky above us. The red brick of Red Square below us, strewn with countless bodies. Dead and decapitated bodies. Black clad Deportation Police ghouls. Laxsa. Warriors of the spirit world. Zombies. Undead. Whatever word you prefer. The headless ones, they truly were dead. The others fortunate enough to still have their heads attached to their bodies, they could be brought back to life by the cannibal warlock Hamatsa with his magic Water of Life. And go on to fight another day for Dear Leader and the New American Order.

Like I said, one moment I'm standing in Red Square. The next moment, I'm standing in my Ballard apartment in North Seattle. And I'm not alone. I found the apartment quite crowded. Me. Jean, my girlfriend. My buddy and old teaching colleague from the U Dub, Mike, Dr. Michael Bulgakov. Adjunct Professor of History. Michael's black cat Margarita, who just happens to be the witch called Black Tara, the Tara of vengeance, one of the twenty-one Taras, a coven of warrior witches led by my Tara, the hyacinth macaw parrot Princess Tara, an exceedingly large cobalt blue feathered parrot with a huge black beak and penetrating yellow-rimmed coal black eyes.

When Princess Tara transforms herself into the witch Blue Tara, she becomes a frighteningly beautiful six foot plus tall musclebound glowing crystalline blue-skinned Amazonian warrior with a battle axe. Wait, that's not completely accurate. She becomes a totally naked frighteningly beautiful six-foot plus tall musclebound glowing crystalline blue-skinned Amazonian warrior with a battle axe and one striking yellow eye and one pendulous breast. Jagged scars mar her face and chest where her second eye and second breast should be.

And we seem to have added to our company on this particular time space bend. Now I found in my apartment along with Princess Tara another macaw parrot, a large flamboyantly colored blue and gold macaw. A blue and gold macaw parrot that looked suspiciously like the one named Aboo who originally steered me to Charlie's Bird Store at Seattle's Pike Place Market, where I first encountered Princess Tara.

We stood staring at each other for a few moments trying to gain our bearings. Blue Tara, my Tara, broke

8

the silence first. "I don't know about anyone else," she said, "but I am starving. How about we order pizza?" She walked to the fridge and peeked inside. "Beer. Yes. I want beer," she stated as she reached in to grab one of my Rainiers. Blue Tara suggesting 'we' order pizza basically meant I should order pizza. Which I did.

I live on the lower part of Ballard Avenue by the marine supply warehouses. The old Saint Charles Hotel is an unimposing turn of the last century two story red brick box. The lower floor long ago had been gutted and converted to self storage. The old hotel rooms upstairs converted to studio apartments, with sun filled floor to ceiling bay windows fronting the street. A few years back as I struggled to achieve tenure at the University of Washington teaching history and archaeology, I enjoyed a small success with the lottery. Enough so that I could give up my pretense of a university teaching career and purchase the old building. I now roast coffee out of one of the storage units below my apartment and enjoy a comfortable income from the storage and apartment rentals.

The old Seattle neighborhood of Ballard suits my temperament. Once a free city of Scandinavian mill workers and Yankee fishermen, the town got swallowed up by a bigger and more rapacious neighbor, the city of Seattle. The eclectic village of unassuming two and three story Victorian red brick and white frame buildings, home to an assortment of artists, crafts people, bars, marine suppliers, restaurants, and coffee shops, boasted an independent streak reflecting the village's Scandinavian and Yankee heritage.

9

I stood in my bay window daydreaming as I looked up the street. Dog walkers, bums, restaurant and bar hoppers scurried up and down the sidewalks. Jean stepped to my side. She set her arm around my shoulder. "A penny for your thoughts," she whispered in my ear, her lips brushing my cheek. Linda Jean was her name, but her friends simply called her Jean. I brushed my hand through her long brunette locks and pulled her to me to kiss her. Reasonably tall, her long brunette hair tied back in a ponytail, she looked athletic without looking like an athlete. She was at that age that was hard to guess. Not young. But not older. Brooding brown eyes matched her hair and gave her a faintly mournful Slavic mystic.

"After what we've been through today, sweetie," I replied, "the price is at least a buck fifty." I could feel Blue Tara's searing yellow eye staring at me. "I know. I know," I acknowledged. "Pizza." I dug my smart phone out of my pocket and looked up the online order form for Ballard Pizza across the street. Although after the last pizza party I thought maybe I should just walk across the street and personally pick up the pizza. I ordered a large Greek pizza for myself, Jean, and Blue Tara. Thin crust. Olive oil base. Heavy on the onions. And a large cardiac arrest meat pizza for Michael, his Tara, Black Tara, and our new friend, the blue and gold macaw sitting on Princess Tara's play stand in the bay window. I clicked the 'Delivery' button.

My eyes turned to admire Blue Tara's taut glistening blue body. "Do you ever, like, wear clothes?" I hesitantly asked her.

"What need have I for clothes when I have such magnificent feathers?" Blue Tara replied, although she clearly wasn't wearing any feathers at the moment. In fact, she wasn't wearing anything at all except her battle axe dangling from a leather belt around her waist.

I walked up to the blue and gold macaw. "Let me guess. Your name is Aboo. You stopped me at the market when I was hell bent on getting a cookie and got me into this mess."

"Hi," Aboo blurted out. He screeched. I nearly dropped my phone as my hands defensively slapped my ears in a futile attempt to muffle the screech.

"Aboo did not get you into any messes," Blue Tara interjected, as she stepped to us. "He just helped you along the way on the path you were already traveling." The thought struck me that a glowing crystalline blue-skinned Amazonian goddess standing totally naked in my bay window except for a battle axe might attract some undue attention from the street below, so I quickly dropped the blinds. "You are addressing Lord Garuda. King of the Birds and Messenger of the Gods," Blue Tara added.

"Garuda? That humongous bird that filled the sky over Red Square and saved my ass? That Garuda?"

"Yes," Blue Tara replied with a grin stretching from ear to ear.

Stunned, I asked Blue Tara, motioning at Aboo, "How can a creature that big possibly fit into such a small package?" The blue and gold macaw parrot perched

11

in front of me by no means was a small animal. In fact, save Princess Tara, he was one of the largest birds I had ever seen. Yet I could not comprehend how the Blue and Gold macaw Aboo and the massive avian god Garuda could be the same creature.

"You are handicapped by your inflexible concepts of time and space," Blue Tara replied. "The constraints on time and space imposed by your reality have no play in my world," she added. "Things that are big can be small. Things that are small can be big. You need to open your mind to the possibilities that there is more to your world than your eyes and your mind alone can show you."

The doorbell rang. I peeked through the blinds. I recognized the pizza delivery guy, a scraggly kid in his teens. I looked at Blue Tara. As a normal American male I couldn't help myself but look at Blue Tara in her gleaming crystalline blue-skinned naked glory. "I better go down and get the pizza," I said. "By myself."

ΔΔΔ

We sat around the dining table and attacked the pizza. I sat at the dining table with Jean, Blue Tara, and Michael. I could see that Michael, sitting between Blue Tara and Jean, struggled to focus on eating his pizza. Aboo perched on Princess Tara's parrot stand with a slice of pizza in his food dish. Margarita lay curled up at Michael's feet chewing on a slice of pizza on a plate.

"So now I've got two parrots?" I asked rhetorically, to no one in particular.

"That would seem to be the case," Michael replied. Medium height. Slightly chunky in all the wrong places. Could stand to spend some time in the gym working out. Short cropped brown hair thinning badly and turning white on the ends. Clark Gable mustache. Standard adjunct professor outfit. Brand label khaki pants. Polo shirt. Sweater vest. All scrounged from trips to Value Village or Goodwill. Michael and I had been office mates back during my U Dub teaching days.

"I've got my hands full with Princess Tara for chrissakes," I blurted out, with a note of exasperation. I immediately regretted my words. I could feel my face flush as I glanced at Blue Tara, her gleaming yellow eye fixed expressionlessly on me. "You want a parrot, Mike?" Michael shook his head. "How about you Jean? You sure your African Grey, what's his name? Corky?" Jean nodded. "You sure he doesn't want a friend?"

"Oh, no," Jean replied. "I've got my hands full with my Corky. And I haven't been much of a mommy to him lately. My roommate is going to kill me. If something else doesn't kill me first," she chuckled. "Thankfully I think the bird is more bonded to my roommate than he is to me."

"Just what I need. Two gods. Two witches in my life," I said dolefully. I looked at Blue Tara. "What form does Aboo take when he's not a bird. . . a parrot?"

"Aboo is Garuda. Garuda is King of the Birds," Blue Tara insisted. "The King of the Birds can take no other form than that of a bird."

13

"About tonight?" Michael hesitantly asked. "Somebody is bound to notice all the bodies and all the heads littering Red Square." He looked at Blue Tara. "Don't you think?"

"Hamatsa suffered a grave humiliation this night," Blue Tara replied. "He will suppress any word or evidence of this defeat to keep the Winalagalis from learning of his failure. He will restore to life the ghouls, the laxsa, with his Water of Life. At least the ones that still keep their heads. The rest he will dispose. The numbers of the laxsa in his service may be limitless. But now we know Hamatsa is not invincible."

"What about the crystal and the magic harpoon?" Michael asked. "And whatever happened to the turndun?"

"All lost, I'm afraid," I replied. "That vixen Kinqalatlala jumped me and smashed the crystal to smithereens. The giant cannibal grizzly bear that attacked us. . . I believe Nanes is the monster's name?" Michael nodded. "Nanes splintered the magic harpoon like the death stick was a toothpick."

"The turndun disintegrated into atoms while I spun the instrument around my head," Blue Tara added. "But the turndun accomplished the desired goal. Lord Garuda is here," she said, turning and bowing toward Aboo. I winced as Aboo screeched in reply.

"Shouldn't Aboo, Garuda, be out calling for the other Taras?" Jean asked. "The other yous?"

"Garuda has already done so," Blue Tara replied. "Now we wait for my sister Taras to join us as we prepare for the final reckoning with Hamatsa and the Winalagalis, the god of war of the north."

I looked around my increasingly crowded apartment. "You mean there's going to be nineteen others like you joining us here?"

"Not all in your place of abode," Blue Tara assured me. "And not all will arrive at once. They must travel from the far corners of this world where they have been scattered over the centuries to join us here in Seattle."

"Can't they all just do that time and space bending trick?" I asked.

"My magic is not a trick," Blue Tara replied with a touch of annoyance. "Not every Tara possesses the same magic. The magic to bend time and space is an art that few have achieved."

"But you said you could teach your magic to me."

"I can try. But I fear you are wedded to a reality that will not allow you to open your mind to the possibility of bending time and space."

"So what do we do next?" Michael asked, to no one in particular, as he walked up to the fridge to grab another can of Rainier beer. "I have classes to prepare for."

"You're kidding? Right?" I replied. "Do you think the goons will allow you to set foot on Red Square again?"

"Your friend is correct," Blue Tara interjected. "He must continue with his life. As must you all. Preparations for the coming gathering of the Taras will take time. Hamatsa has reason to fear us now. He will stay out of our way while he musters his forces. Especially with Garuda on our side. The furies will be powerless against the King of the Birds."

"So we just wait for the Taras to gather and watch to see how Hamatsa responds?" I asked. "But we lost our weapons. The crystal. The magic harpoon. The turndun. We have nothing to defend ourselves with. Besides your battle axe, that is."

"You, my dear boy," Blue Tara said. She reached across the dining table to rub her fingers across my chin. "You will seek the tlogwe."

"The tlogwe?"

"The ultimate treasure. The gift of special powers that the spirits grant those brave enough to enter their realm," Blue Tara elaborated. "But you have need to open your mind. To open your mind to the possibility that other realities exist along with your own. To open your mind to the possibility that you can exist in more than one reality at a time. Otherwise, all is lost."

Great, I thought to myself. *No pressure.*

"And I need to get back to the campus and prepare for my classes," Michael said. "Find out if I've been fired."

"Something tells me you have nothing to worry about," I replied.

"Nothing to worry about?" A frown creased Michael's face. "You mean like busting into the lab? Busting into Special Collections? Littering Red Square with bodies and heads? That kind of nothing to worry about? That's really not going to look good on my resume when I'm begging for a new teaching job at Southern Podunk Baptist College."

"If what Blue Tara says is any guide, and I have no reason to doubt her," I replied, "everything that's transpired on campus will be covered up. You still have the Boas field notes. No telling what other gold nuggets you'll find in there. And you've got Margarita. . . Black Tara. . . for protection." I glanced under the table at Margarita. "I assume Blue Tara can time space bend you back to your office?" I glanced at Blue Tara guzzling a can of Rainier beer. "Better deal than Uber." I handed Michael my truck keys. "My truck is still parked in the visitor parking garage. Just drive the truck back here in the next day or two once you have a good idea what the situation on campus is."

"What is that saying your people have?" Blue Tara asked as she slammed the empty can onto the table. "Oh yes," she smiled. "Do not be a stranger." Blue Tara's mouth fell open. An earsplitting screech rolled out of her throat to engulf the apartment and wrack my head with pain. My beer can slipped out of my fingers, spilling beer across the dining table. Michael and Margarita vanished as Michael reached for his can of beer.

Jesus Fucking Christ, I thought to myself. "Can you at least warn us before you pull your little trick," I griped to Blue Tara. "My head feels like somebody just hit me with a hammer."

"Call my magic a trick one more time and I will trick you right out into Puget Sound," Blue Tara replied, a distinct edge to her voice.

"Sorry," I apologized.

"I need to get some sleep really bad," Jean said, "especially after this beer and pizza. How about we go to bed?"

"What a good idea," Blue Tara replied, standing up.

Jean grabbed my hands, pulling me out of my chair. "I mean the two of us," she admonished Blue Tara. Jean steered me toward the bedroom. I could see a frown break across Blue Tara's face. "We can continue this discussion over coffee in the morning once we're rested," Jean added as she kicked the door shut.

I realized how tired I was as I struggled to take off my clothes. My buttons did not cooperate with my fingers. Jean stripped. She grabbed my belt and pulled me to her. "Let me help you with that," she said. She started kissing me as she pulled off my clothing. We climbed under the sheets. Jean pulled the blanket over us. I started to kiss Jean's body. The bedroom door opened. Blue Tara entered the room and walked to the bed.

"What are you doing?" I asked Blue Tara.

Blue Tara slipped under the sheets with us. "Aboo is asleep on my perch and I do not want to disturb him," Blue Tara replied. "I thought disturbing you might be more fun." She rolled on top of me, sticking her breast into my chest. Her lips found my lips. Her tongue found my tongue.

Part Two

The cannibal warlock Hamatsa seethed with anger following his encounter with Blue Tara at the University of Washington's Red Square. Not even dismembering and eating two female crew members on the flight back to Control in the other Washington could assuage his wrath. Storming into the Control compound in the basement of the Old Executive Office Building, he summoned his slave and procurer of bodies, Kinqalatlala, to his side. Her dark svelte body appeared almost to be an apparition in the dimly lit chamber that was Control. Hamatsa grabbed Kinqalatlala by her neck and forced her to her knees at his feet. "Bow before your master!" he ordered. "Your mission was simple. Stop Blue Tara. Bring the man with the parrot to me."

Kinqalatlala kissed Hamatsa's black boots. "I acknowledge my failure, my master. I accept your punishment."

Hamatsa pulled Kinqalatlala to her feet. He squeezed her throat, choking her. "I should make an example of you and feed you to the furies." He released his hold on her. "Now that blue witch has Garuda at her side and soon she will convene her coven of witches. You must see that does not happen, whatever the cost. You must hunt those witches down and destroy them. And the man with the parrot. I want his head mounted on the wall of this compound. Do you understand me?"

Kinqalatlala struggled to speak. "Yes master. Your wish is my command."

"Fail me again, and I will roast you on a spit in the center of this compound and feed you to my men. There will be no immortality for you. Only darkness and despair. You will cease to exist. Now, get out of my sight!" he exclaimed in a fury. Hamatsa grabbed Kinqalatlala by her neck. He picked her up off the floor and carried her across the room. He flung her out the door.

ΔΔΔ

Kinqalatlala burst into the Deportation Police holding cells with her two special assistants at her side. An unquenching stream of unfortunates filled the cells. Undocumented immigrants trying to make new homes in America. Citizens and activists deemed undesirable by the new regime. People who looked and acted and were different. These and more passed through the holding cells on a daily basis. There the authorities processed and interrogated them. There they disappeared them. Like they say in the movies, dead men tell no tales. The din and commotion of shouts and screams, the bone crunching thud of bodies slammed against walls, the shouted commands of burly guards, ceased the moment these three imposing women walked through the door. A deathly silence gripped the room. Kinqalatlala, her dark skin and svelte athletic body accentuated by her black leather boots, skin tight black leather pants, black leather vest worn over a black sweater, her long black hair flowing over her shoulders, looked every inch a warrior.

The second woman, called Nawalak, towered over Kinqalatlala. An imposing muscular figure of immense size, she exuded sheer strength. The dark canvas robe she wore that dragged behind her across the floor, accentuated her girth and size.

The third woman had no name. Her hair and skin gleamed white as a new Cascade snow pack. An albino, her sunken black eyes terrified anyone who looked at her face. And if her albinism didn't cause her to stand out sufficiently, her wardrobe certainly did. Black boots. Red ankle length skirt. Black sweater hanging down below her knees. Red jacket. White gloves. She wore gloves for a specific reason. She was a lalenox, a living corpse. A zombie that could kill simply by touching.

Kinqalatlala shouted at the guards to clear the facility. They didn't need to be told twice. An anxious murmuring ran through the unfortunate denizens of the holding cells as the guards rushed out the door. The three women walked to the first cell. Kinqalatlala ordered Nawalak to open the cell door. Nawalak grabbed the bars and pulled. For a moment the door resisted. Then the holding cells filled with the grating sound of tearing metal, like fingernails scraping across a chalkboard, as the door sprung open. Five people cowered in the cell. Three appeared to be Latino. The other two African. Three men and two women. They pressed themselves against the back wall as if they were trying to melt into the concrete. Two of the women and one of the men dropped to their knees and tried to pray. Gripped with fear no sounds came out of their mouths.

The lalenox stepped to the three people on their knees. She removed one of her gloves. She placed her hand on each person's shoulder. First the two women. Then the man. Each slumped to the floor. Dead.

Nawalak stepped to the two men still standing and grabbed their necks with each of her hands. She squeezed. Their necks snapped and they too fell to the floor dead. A man standing in an adjacent cell screamed and began pounding his hands on the bars of the cell.

Kinqalatlala stepped to the bars. She put her hand up to her face and looked at her fingers. Fingers became a sharp shimmering steel blade. She thrust her hand through the bars of the cell and into the screaming man's chest. He stopped screaming. His face turned a deathly pale, almost as white as the lalenox. Kinqalatlala pulled her hand out of the man's chest. Blood streamed down his clothes. Grasping the bars of his cell, the man slid to the floor and slumped dead in a pool of his own blood. Kinqalatlala wiped her hand clean on the man's shirt. "Very good," Kinqalatlala told her aides. "I have a job for you. We travel out west to a place called Seattle."

ΔΔΔ

Michael could tell he was losing his Introduction to Western Civilization 101 class. He loudly cleared his throat to try to gain the attention of his students. The windows in the history lecture room on the second floor of the old three story gothic brownstone pile called Denny Hall, the U Dub's history faculty building, had been flung open to greet one of the first warm and sunny spring days that Seattle enjoyed following a long, dark, damp, and dreary winter. After this dismal winter Michael began to appreciate why many of the old buildings on campus had been built in the hauntingly menacing gothic style. Most of the students stared out the windows, or surreptitiously stared at their mobile devices hidden under their notebooks. A few of the students at the back of the room didn't even try to hide their disinterest in the class. "So class," Michael said to the students, relieved to see the clock hanging on the back wall wind down to the end of the period. "I believe I can say that the introduction of coffee to the West by the Muslim world fueled the Renaissance. Before the introduction of coffee, the drink of choice throughout Europe during the Middle Ages was beer. Beer for breakfast. Beer for lunch. Beer for dinner." A couple of the students snickered. "There's a reason this period is known as the Dark Ages," Michael continued. "People went through life stone cold drunk. Have you ever wondered why hundreds of years were required just to build one medieval gothic cathedral? The introduction of coffee radically changed the behavior of medieval Europeans, as well as their attitude. Coffee launched the Age of Enlightenment and the Age of Discovery. People got off their butts and started doing things." The bell rang as a couple of the students laughed at Michael's summation. "Keep that in mind tomorrow morning when you wake up to the smell of fresh roasted coffee," Michael added, to a mostly empty room.

Michael gathered up his lecture notes and books. He stepped out of the lecture room, nodded to the department secretary, Nancy, sitting behind the door to the history department offices across the hall, and headed out of the building to return to his own office in the subbasement of the Suzzallo Library. Once outside in the warm spring sunshine he perked up. A dense pink bloom covered the myriad of cherry trees across campus, and the delectable fragrance of cherry blossoms tickled his nose. Flower beds around campus buildings burst in brilliant color with flowering daffodils and tulips and lilies. Michael loosened the collar button of his Ralph Lauren polo shirt to take a deep breath. Had his hands not been full with his books and papers he might even have slipped off his Nordstrom corduroy jacket. The one with the leather elbow patches. Invigorated by the bountiful scents of spring, his round cheeks ruddy with the infusion of fresh air, Michael decided to take a detour.

Michael took a stroll to the reflecting pond at Drumheller Fountain to take in the spectacular view of Mount Rainier towering to the south. Washington state's tallest peak, as well as an active volcano, the glacier capped mountain shimmered in the sunlit haze that covered the city. A bank of lenticular clouds butted up against the peak. "Such a lovely view," Michael heard a woman's voice behind him say.

The voice seemed strangely familiar. Michael turned to see who was speaking to him. He dropped his books in shock. Panic gripped his face. He stumbled backwards attempting to step away from her. "Kinqalatlala!" he exclaimed. Michael spun around to try to escape but found his way blocked by two other fiercesome women. "A lalenox?" Michael asked stunned, staring at the albino.

"You are correct," Kinqalatlala replied. "Show this man your gloves," she told the lalenox. The albino raised her hands. "As long as those gloves remain on her hands you are safe."

"What do you want with me?" Michael asked worriedly. He felt lightheaded, his face drained of blood.

"What do you think?" Kinqalatlala replied. "Blue Tara. And the man with the parrot. And you can go about your business and live in peace."

"I kind of doubt that," Michael responded.

"I have no interest in you," Kinqalatlala said. "I also have no qualms about killing you if you do not give me what I want."

"You'd kill me? Right out here in the open? In front of all these people?" Michael said, gesturing to the students passing by the fountain. Michael realized that the students passing by the reflecting pond did not seem to take notice of the strange group gathered around him. "They can't see you. Isn't that right? To all of them I'm just a nutjob talking to myself."

"That makes no nevermind to me," Kinqalatlala replied, a wry smile breaking across her face. "In fact, maybe I will start with one of your precious students first, until you give me what I want. Would you like to pick out my first victim? Or do you prefer me to do that?" Kinqalatlala looked around her. She started to walk toward a group of students stopped by the reflecting pond.

"Wait," Michael said. "I'll tell you what you want to know."

"No he will not," said a woman who walked directly to Kinqalatlala.

"What?" Michael asked, as stunned as Kinqalatlala seemed to be.

Kinqalatlala and her two aides stared at the newcomer. Easily six feet tall. A brilliant white face with gleaming white eyes crowned with flaming red hair capping a blood red body. Just as Michael had seen Blue Tara do, she stood on one foot like a parrot, her right foot lifted and placed against her left knee. She wore a red cape draped over her shoulder. She had not two arms, but four arms. She sported a longbow slung over her back, along with a quiver of arrows.

A student passing by stopped and stared at the woman. "Nice bird," he said. "Is the bird yours?" he asked Michael.

"Bird?" Michael replied, totally confused.

"Your red bird," the student continued. "Is that a macaw? Won't the bird just fly off?" Michael stared at the student in bewildered silence. Then he stared at the red woman with four arms. "Beautiful bird," the student added as he walked away.

"I like your bird," a girl walking by added, smiling at Michael.

Michael realized the students did not see what he saw. "You're a Tara!" he exclaimed to the red woman. "The students don't see you the way I see you. They see a parrot. Right? Not a woman with four arms and a longbow strapped over her shoulder."

"She is a witch," Kinqalatlala interjected. "The witch called Red Tara." Pointing to the lalenox, she commanded, "Take her out!"

Before the lalenox could take two steps toward Red Tara, Red Tara whipped off her longbow and nocked an arrow into place. She pointed the arrow at Kinqalatlala's head. "I do not think so," Red Tara said. "I am Kurukulla. I protect the weak from demons and wicked spirits."

Weak? Oh geez, thought Michael to himself.

"You will not harm this man."

"You think you can stop us?" Kinqalatlala asked heatedly. "With your puny bow and arrows? Nawalak!" she summoned her gigantic aide.

Red Tara turned her bow and released the arrow. The point sunk into Nawalak's skull, directly between her eyes. The force of the arrow knocked her backwards onto the ground. She fell with a loud groan and did not get up. Before Kinqalatlala or the lalenox could move, Red Tara nocked another arrow into place. "Do not underestimate what I am capable of," Red Tara replied coldly. "My arrows can not be stopped. Once released, they never ever miss their mark." Red Tara stepped between Michael and the witches, her arrow pointing at Kinqalatlala's head. "Walk away," she told Michael. "I will protect you. Walk away now."

The hell with walking, Michael thought. He scooped up his books and lecture notes and ran from the fountain.

ΔΔΔ

As Michael ran onto Red Square he stopped and turned to see if he was being pursued. He gaped at the brightest colored parrot he had ever seen flying toward him. Brilliant red feathers covered the parrot's body. Green feathers highlighted the bird's wings. A snow white face scored with red zebra stripes accentuated piercing black eyes. A red macaw parrot, called a greenwing macaw by some, flew up to him and landed on his shoulder. "So this is how the students see you," Michael said. Thankfully he saw no sign of Kinqalatlala and the other two witches. Michael craned his head to peer into the parrot's face. "Do you know about Blue Tara?" Michael asked the parrot. "And about Black Tara? My cat, Margarita?"

"You must take me to them as soon as possible," Red Tara replied.

"I don't suppose you do the time and space bend like Blue Tara does?" Michael asked.

"I do not possess that magic," Red Tara said. "My powers reside in matters of the flesh, not in matters of time and space."

"Well, then. I guess I'll take you to Blue Tara the old fashioned way. I'll drive." Michael stopped into his office long enough to drop off his lecture materials and grab the truck keys, as well as Margarita, his black cat. He drove the three of them over to Ballard as fast as possible without getting a traffic ticket. Margarita howled a blue streak at Red Tara, perched on the head rest behind Michael, the entire course of the drive, punctuated by squawks from Red Tara. Michael ignored their conversation to focus on the driving.

ΔΔΔ

"Oh. My. God!" I exclaimed when I opened the door of my apartment to let Michael and Margarita in. "Another parrot!"

"Oh my! Jean exclaimed, rushing to greet Michael. "Wherever did you get a greenwing?"

"Meet Red Tara," Michael replied.

"My honor and my duty have brought me to answer Lord Garuda's call to action," Red Tara said. She spread her wings as she bowed to the blue and gold macaw Aboo perched on Princess Tara's parrot stand. Aboo screeched in reply.

Princess Tara, the hyacinth macaw parrot, had been napping on top of her perch. She let out a head-wracking screech at the sight of Red Tara. She spread her wings and leaped into the air, wings flapping. Halfway across the living room she whirled like a dervish, dissolving into a gleaming blue orb, filling the room with a cloud of blue light. The light coalesced into the crystalline blue-skinned daemon Blue Tara. Seeing Blue Tara, the red macaw screeched. She whirled off Michael's shoulder and landed on the floor in her four-armed red Amazonian glory.

"Greetings Ekajati!" Red Tara exclaimed.

"Greetings to you Kurukulla. Welcome to Seattle," Blue Tara replied as she bowed to Red Tara.

"So this is the man?" Red Tara asked. She stepped to me. She put two of her arms over my shoulders and her other two arms around my back. My body shook when she touched me. An electrical charge of pure sensuality swept through me. Her black tongue flicked out of her mouth and swept across my lips. Like the wicked witch in the Wizard of Oz I felt I was melting. I sensed a sensuality emanating from Red Tara unlike anything I had ever felt before. I wanted to bury myself in Red Tara's body and surrender to her every desire.

Blue Tara grabbed my arms and pulled me away from Red Tara. "We are Taras," she told Red Tara. "We fight the same enemy. But remember this. This man is mine. You will not unleash your magic and your wiles on him. Or you will answer to me. He is not a plaything for you to enjoy."

This is different, I thought. In all my life I had never experienced women fighting over me. But I wasn't

30

sure that having a couple of goddesses fight over me was necessarily a good thing.

"You will focus your energy on Hamatsa and the Winalagalis," Blue Tara added. "Do not ever cross me. Do you understand?"

"Apologies, Ekajati. Sometimes I can not help who I am." She bowed to Blue Tara.

Blue Tara turned to me. She placed her hands on my shoulders. "Do not ever even think about succumbing to Kurukulla's wiles," she demanded. "You do not know what my sister is capable of. You do not understand how she is able to manipulate men like you."

Men like me? I thought to myself. Now I really wondered what kind of shit I'd got myself into.

Part Three

Chicago had Mrs. O'Leary's cow. Seattle had Jonathan Back's glue pot. On the afternoon of June 6, 1889, Jonathan Back accidentally overturned his glue pot while framing one of the booming city's new timber buildings common for the period. He attempted to extinguish the burning glue pot with a bucket of water. Water on a grease fire simply spread the fire. Mr. Back called for Seattle's volunteer fire department. Yet a fairly small city at the time, the volunteer firemen responded quickly but made the mistake of hooking up too many hoses at once. Water pressure failed, and with no water to fight the fire the flames raged through the city's mostly timber structures. The Great Seattle Fire destroyed thirty-one square blocks before the fire finally burned out.

In the rush to rebuild, the city fathers made the decision not to clear out the rubble from the burned buildings. Seattle's founders had established the city on the only level ground at the head of Elliott Bay, mudflats at the mouth of the Duwamish River. The site of an ancient Duwamish Indian village and burial ground.

In response to the Great Seattle Fire, the city fathers ordered the basements of the ruined city to be covered over and new construction of stone and brick to be built on top of the ruins. The old basements and passageways were covered up, sealed, and soon forgotten by polite society busy building the new city. However, a certain segment of the population of the boom town of Seattle thrived in the old catacombs out of sight of decent Victorian society and the law. Smugglers, bootleggers, opium dealers, women of the night, and the few surviving Duwamish Indians who grew up in the old Indian village and refused to leave their traditional home, migrated into the laissez-faire world of the dead under the very feet of the new city to bring the abandoned ruins to life like architectural zombies.

Over the next few years stories of strange goings-on in the dark catacombs filtered up to the streets above. Murders. Suicides. Ancient Indian ghosts. Demons and monsters and cannibals. Polite society often repeated these stories for sheer titillation or to scare the children of the good citizens of the city. Stories guaranteed to catch the interest of a young German archaeologist just starting his academic career in the New World.

After spending the winter of 1896 at Fort Rupert on Vancouver Island, the young German archaeologist Franz Boas stopped in Seattle on his long trip back east to return to his teaching position at Columbia University. In the spring of 1897 Boas found Seattle to be a boom town bursting at the seams with the outbreak of the Klondike Gold Rush. Would-be prospectors and gold miners, and the merchants and con men, and women, who mined the miners packed the unpaved streets of the booming city. Canvas tents and Conestoga wagons set up temporary shops in any space available, even in the middle of streets and intersections. Prospectors who dreamed of gold strikes scurried from tent to shop to secure the supplies they would need in the frozen north prior to booking passage on the overcrowded steam ships docked in the harbor waiting to steam north to Alaska.

As an archaeologist and scholar of civilizations, Franz Boas found the hustle and bustle of the boom town enthralling. He sought out the few Indians still living in the city, quite conspicuous selling old Indian artifacts and baskets on the board sidewalks. Their stories of an ancient Indian village buried under the city sparked Boas' interest. The city's German brewers plied Boas with tales of Indian ghosts and demons waylaying indiscreet prospectors and citizens who stumbled into the old catacombs.

Boas determined to explore the ruins of the underground city. He couldn't believe his good luck when he encountered an old Duwamish Indian woman living in a dilapidated fishing shack on the beach. The old woman turned out to be Princess Angeline, the daughter of the famed Duwamish Chief Sealth, better know as Chief Seattle, the city's namesake, who ceded the land Seattle was built on to the city's founders.

Princess Angeline eked out a living fishing and selling baskets to the Klondike bound adventurers. Bent and wrinkled, in her last days, she walked with a cane wearing her favorite red head scarf and a brown shawl over her squat body. She regaled Boas with stories of the tribe's legends and ceremonies, demons and monsters. Many of her stories and legends revolved around the old Indian burial ground above the mudflats where the city was first established. Encouraged by Princess Angeline's stories, Boas determined to find his way into the catacombs. He was astonished to learn from the old woman that a tunnel existed right behind her shack leading into secret passageways which in turn led into the old ruins. Secret passageways utilized mostly by smugglers sneaking tax free Canadian liquor off ships anchored in the harbor to quench the thirst of the Klondike bound prospectors.

Boas followed the tunnel into the dark and mysterious passageways leading to underground Seattle. Boas found a secret city buried beneath the boom town virtually intact, replete with furnishings untouched by the great fire that burned off the timber buildings above. Boas wandered from basement to basement through underground passageways poorly illuminated by cracks and partially buried skylights in the ceiling.

Astonished, Boas found not a ghost town within the catacombs, but a living buried city. He encountered other explorers and wanderers. Some lost souls. Many just curious, like him. He stumbled across any number of drunks, prostitutes, drug addicts, and opium dens operated by some of the Chinese immigrants flooding to the city to do the work the would-be gold miners refused to do.

Stumbling into an opium den, a couple of drunk sailors accosted Boas and attempted to rob him. Wearing a suit, tie, fedora, and black frock coat, Boas gave the appearance of a wealthy businessman, not the usual denizen of the catacombs. Speaking his native German, Boas pretended not to understand the sailors' demands for money. One of the sailors produced a knife and threatened Boas. Unseen by the sailors, an apparition appeared out of the shadows. Tall, gaunt, pale. Sunken red eyes that glowed in the darkness. Without speaking the apparition stepped to the sailor with the knife and placed a hand on his shoulder. The sailor dropped the knife and collapsed to the floor. Dead.

Boas cried out to the other sailor. "A lalenox! A spirit of the underworld! Do not let the demon touch you. The demon's touch is death."

The second sailor froze in terror. The lalenox stepped to him and touched his shoulder. He collapsed dead as well.

Collecting himself, Boas turned and ran as fast as he could back through the dark passageways, back to the surface and the relative safety of the city streets. Boas retrieved his belongings that he had stashed at the budding University of Washington campus. He hurried to the harbor to wrangle passage on the first ship sailing south. He did not relax until the ship finally raised anchor and steamed out of Elliott Bay.

ΔΔΔ

I discovered that the Taras, blue, red, or black, liked pizza and beer. Lots of pizza and beer. I seemed to become a very good customer of the pizza place across the street. Over pizza and beer Jean and I listened to Michael recount his encounter with Hamatsa's slave and hatchet woman Kinqalatlala at Drumheller Fountain. "Seems like they're coming after us one at a time," I said. "Divide and conquer. We must not give them the opportunity to pick us off. We've got to keep one of the Taras with us at all times."

"Sorry," Michael replied, "but I can't have a four-armed naked woman with red skin coming to my classes with me. Don't think the students would be able to concentrate on my lectures."

"But you said the students couldn't see Red Tara as she really is. They only see a red macaw," I replied.

"You could take Margarita with you," Jean joked. Margarita stopped chewing a slice of pizza on a plate under the dining table to growl at Jean. "She'd be less conspicuous, and your students would probably think more highly of you," Jean added, peering down at Margarita.

Chugging a can of Rainier beer, Red Tara belched. She placed one of her four hands on my hand. A wave of sensuous electricity rolled up my arm. "You can not just sit by and let Hamatsa's witches pick you off one by one," she said. "We need to go after them and drive them out of this city until such time as all the Taras are gathered for battle."

Blue Tara pulled my hand away from Red Tara's grasp. "You must find the tlogwe," she said. "That is how we will be able to defeat Hamatsa and his ghouls."

"The tlogwe? You mentioned that to me before. Just what is the tlogwe, again?" I asked her.

"The source of great power. The ultimate treasure presented by the spirits to those brave enough to enter their realm. Because we lost the crystal, we need the magic and power of the tlogwe to fight Hamatsa's magic and power."

"And just where am I supposed to find the realm of the spirits?" I asked. "Without, say, actually killing myself?"

"There is an ancient city at your very feet," Red Tara replied.

I glanced at my feet under the dining table. "There is?"

"An ancient city of the native peoples who lived here before your people arrived. A city buried under your city."

"Seattle was established on top of an old Duwamish Indian village," Michael interjected. "Is that what you mean?" Red Tara nodded. "Underneath Pioneer Square. The original part of Seattle. The part destroyed by the Great Fire of 1889. A very small part of the ruins have been opened up for all the tourists to visit. You've never been in underground Seattle?" Michael asked me.

"I'm to find the tlogwe in underground Seattle?" I replied.

"You are to find the spirit world. The spirit world that will lead you to the gift of the tlogwe," Red Tara told me.

"You know what?" Michael exclaimed. "There was something in the Boas field notes about meeting with Princess Angeline on the waterfront. Something about a tunnel."

"Princess Angeline? Another parrot?" I asked, looking at Blue Tara.

"Princess Angeline, the daughter of Chief Seattle. Boas met with her at her fishing shack on Western Avenue at the foot of Pike Place."

"You're kidding me? Western Avenue at the foot of Pike Place?" Michael nodded. "That's where Charlie's Bird Store is located. We need to pay Charlie a visit."

ΔΔΔ

Jean went back to work at her coffee shop. I drove Michael and the two Taras in their parrot form to Pike Place Market to see Charlie at his bird store, appropriately named Charlie's Bird Store. We left

Aboo, the blue and gold macaw, and Michael's black cat Margarita, Black Tara, to guard my apartment. We found Charlie's open. The sign on the door read 'Come In'. Once again Princess Tara refused to leave the truck, so I walked in with Red Tara on my shoulder. The earsplitting din of hundreds of birds chirping, screeching, and squawking knocked me back on my heels as I entered the shop.

Charlie let out a long whistle when he saw Red Tara perched on my shoulder. A tall wiry black guy with hair short cropped military style, he fancied himself to be a bird whisperer. "My god, son. That is one spectacular greenwing macaw you've got there. Did you trade in Princess Tara for another model?" he smirked. "I wouldn't blame you in the least."

"Princess Tara's out in the truck," I replied. "She refuses to come in."

"Don't blame her for that either," Charlie said. Charlie stepped to me and stared at Red Tara on my shoulder. "She's beautiful. Guessing she's a she? Looks like a girl bird."

"Charlie," I replied, "meet Red Tara." I noticed Charlie packed a forty-five on his hip.

"Red Tara?" Charlie's face brightened, like a kid turned loose in a candy shop. "My, oh my. How is it you lucked out?"

"What do you mean?"

"I've been studying up on the Taras," Charlie replied. "Red Tara is the goddess of pure sensuality and

39

desire. Whatever men desire, Red Tara provides." A grin split Charlie's face from ear to ear. "You need a place to park her son, you can park her here with me."

"Okay." I said. "Tell me, do you see a parrot or something else entirely?" I asked Charlie.

Charlie studied me quizzically. "I just see the parrot," Charlie finally said. "Have you seen her as she truly is?"

"Yep," I replied.

"Red Tara saved my butt from Kinqalatlala and her lalenox at the U Dub," Michael said.

"Lalenox? What's that?" Charlie asked.

"Living corpses. Zombies. The undead. Take your pick. They kill simply by touching their victims."

"All I see is a bright red parrot," Charlie said. "What does she look like? In her real form, that is."

"Red body. White face. Almost as tall as Blue Tara," Michael replied. "Amazon warrior. Only she's got a longbow instead of a battle axe. Oh, and she's got four arms."

"Four arms. My word, boss. You struck gold with this one. Did she wear. . . uh, any clothes?" Charlie asked hesitantly, a sly smile across his face.

"A red cape," Michael replied.

"So who's your friend here?" Charlie asked, extending his hand to Michael but looking at me.

"Oh, my bad." I put my hand on Michael's shoulder. "This is Mike, Michael Bulgakov, my old office mate at the U Dub."

Charlie shook Michael's hand. "Pleased to finally meet you, sir," Charlie said. "Heard a lot about you."

"All good, I hope," Michael quipped.

Why does Michael get 'sir', and I get 'son', I griped to myself. "We didn't come to visit just to show off Red Tara," I interjected. "Though we did want you to meet Red Tara."

"Why did you come?"

"What do you know about underground Seattle and the old Indian village buried under the city?" I asked Charlie.

"Well, there's that tour that takes tourists underneath the sidewalks. That's about all I know. Don't really pay much attention to the tourist stuff. I never go down to Pioneer Square because of all the traffic and all the bums and drunks."

"The Taras told me about something called the tlogwe, a treasure of great power that the spirits give to those brave enough to venture into their realm."

"And that's buried underneath the city?" Charlie asked.

"Apparently underground Seattle is only a small part of the realm of the spirits," I said, cracking a smile at the thought of how ridiculous I sounded.

"Who would be stupid enough. . ." Charlie chuckled, "sorry boss, brave enough to venture down into the spirit realm?"

"Well," I replied, looking at Michael.

"Don't look at me," Michael responded. "I've got classes and students to deal with. They're called responsibilities, something you wouldn't know anything about," Michael joked at my expense. And I've still got to get through those Boas field notes."

"So I guess that leaves me. And Jean."

"I wish you the best of luck son. And I sure as hell hope you know what you're getting yourself into. I'm not a particularly religious man, but I believe the spirit world is not something you should mess with lightly. There is power and mystery there beyond your wildest imagination. What can I do to help?"

"Ever hear of Princess Angeline?" Michael asked Charlie. "Chief Seattle's daughter?"

"Oh, I might have. Years ago in school maybe. What of her?"

"She lived in a fishing shack back in the 1890s right here on this very spot."

"No kidding," Charlie replied. "So?"

"Supposedly there was a smugglers' tunnel located behind her shack. A tunnel that tied into the underground passageways that led to the buried city. The old Indian village."

"What does that have to do with me?" Charlie asked.

"Her shack stood on this very spot," I interrupted. "The tunnel was around here somewhere. Very likely there's still a tunnel here."

Charlie frowned. He rubbed his eyes in contemplation. He turned to point toward the back room. "There's an old basement in the back of this shop that was sealed off years ago before I ever moved in here. The market people warned me to stay out of there. There's a trap door under my floor. They warned me never to mess with the door. Come here and see."

Charlie motioned to us to follow him into the back room of his shop where Princess Tara used to reside. He pushed a cage containing a couple of blue and gold macaws to the side. "See here." He pointed to the floor. "There's a hole here in the floor for a trap door. Been sealed tight. You can just make out the outline along the floor here." Charlie bent down and stuck his finger in the hole and tugged on the trap door. Nothing.

"Where's the poker you conked that cannibal with?" I asked Charlie. He pointed to the windows on the west wall of the building. I picked up the poker and jammed the point into the hole. I tugged. Still nothing. I stepped Red Tara up off my shoulder and set her on a parrot stand. I grabbed the poker with both hands, took a deep breath, and threw all of my one hundred and eighty pounds onto the rod. With a horrendous screech the trap door broke away from the floor and popped open. A cloud of damp and fetid black dust and cobwebs blew up into our faces. I lifted the trap door and let the door topple over with a thunderous crash. We stared into the darkness below.

Chapter Two
Part One

The old lady slowly made her way up the sidewalk along Ballard Avenue, couple blocks short of the old Ballard City Hall bell tower, a salute to the once free city of Ballard. She walked slowly, aided by a cane. One halting step after another. Short, severely bent over. She appeared so frail, a good gust of wind might blow her over. Her white bushy bouffant hair stuck out in every direction giving one to wonder how she managed to stand up at all to the weight of such a massive hairdo. White boots and white pants matched her hair and sandwiched her black coat. She held a raven's long black flight feather in her free hand.

As she approached an intersection a good Samaritan, a young woman, passing by stopped to ask if she would like her help to cross the street.

"Why thank you, young lady," the old woman said, bending up to look at the young woman. "That would be so nice of you," she said in a voice so soft the young woman could barely hear her. The young woman reached out to take the old lady's arm. The old lady touched the young woman with her black feather. Just like that, where a good Samaritan had stood reaching out to take the old lady's arm, the young woman vanished. In her place a large black crow danced a circle on the pavement in front of the old lady, cawed wildly, and took flight, flying over the adjacent building and out of sight.

"Mind your own business honey," the old lady cautioned, too late to help the young woman.

The old lady hobbled across the street only to find a huge puddle of rainwater blocking the sidewalk, thanks to a clogged storm drain. She halted and looked indecisively up and down the street. A middle-aged man walked up behind her and asked the old lady if she needed help to negotiate the puddle.

"Thank you, young man," she said.

"You flatter me," the man responded. "I'm not that young anymore." He reached out to take her arm. She touched him with her black feather. The man disappeared. A mallard duck appeared in the puddle, paddling circles in the water. A homeless man who had crouched in a nearby doorway for shelter from a rain squall screamed and ran down the sidewalk.

ΔΔΔ

Jean stopped by my apartment after she closed her coffee shop, not long after Michael and I returned from our trip to Charlie's Bird Store. She looked delectable in her tight black jeans and blue cashmere sweater. I thought to myself that Jean wore tight jeans well.

"The strangest things have been happening here in Ballard today," she blurted out soon as I opened the door.

"I'm happy to see you too," I replied with a grin as I leaned forward to kiss her. "You're just in time for dinner. Come in and have some pizza," I told her.

Jean walked into the kitchen with me. "Oh. My. God! She exclaimed. Her face froze in shock as she stared at Red Tara, sitting at the dining table with Blue Tara and Michael, feasting on pizza and beer, with Margarita at Michael's feet chewing on a slice of pizza as well. By now I had the pizza place across the street trained to have a couple of pizzas ready for me every day. Jean could not stop staring at Red Tara. Which is understandable because I mostly couldn't stop staring at Red Tara, even with a totally naked crystalline blue-skinned Amazonian warrior goddess with a battle axe sitting next to her.

"What's the problem?" I asked, my voice tinged with worry.

"I'm sorry," Jean said, her hand pressed to her face. "I was almost hoping that Red Tara had been a dream." Jean tossed a weak smile in Red Tara's direction.

"Hopefully not a nightmare," Red Tara quipped. She raised a can of Rainier toward Jean. "Join us for a libation," she said, a grin stretching from ear to ear.

I pulled a beer out of the fridge for Jean. "All this naked skin is perturbing," Jean added, a blush coloring her face.

"Consider yourself lucky," I interjected. "Only special people can see Red Tara for who she is. Michael told me that the students on campus could only see the red parrot, and not the red-skinned four-armed goddess that we are privileged to see."

Jean flashed me a grin. "What happened that caused Red Tara to need to save your butt?" Jean asked Michael.

"One word. Kinqalatlala." Michael replied. "Oh, and the lalenox. Two words, I guess."

"Lalenox?" Jean asked with a puzzled expression on her face.

"Zombies who kill people just by touching them."

"Which is why I'm here," Jean said.

"Which is why?" I asked.

"There's been the strangest goings on here in Ballard today. People are disappearing. One of my customers said some homeless guy was screaming about an old lady who turned a man into a duck just by touching him with a feather."

"Oh shit," Michael said.

"Yes?" I was almost afraid to ask.

"Sounds a lot like a hadaho," Michael replied. "A powerful witch that can transform people into birds and other animals."

"Just terrific," I said. "First Kinqalatlala. Now this. They're coming after us."

"There's more," Michael replied. "Hadahos can also transform stone and statues into animate beings as well. They can create their own zombies."

"Why are they coming after us now?" Jean asked, as she and I dropped into chairs at the dining table.

Red Tara replied, "They are not coming for you," she said. "Not yet. They are creating chaos. They want to sow fear. Keep us off balance. We need to keep our focus on our plan to defeat Hamatsa."

"Which is?" Jean asked.

"You must enter the city of the dead and find the tlogwe."

"Wait. What? I must enter the city of the dead?" Jean responded, perplexed. Her face turned even more pale than normal. "What city of the dead? And why me? And I thought nothing would surprise me anymore."

"Not you Jean," I replied. "She means me. She's talking about underground Seattle. The Taras seem to believe the source of ultimate power to defeat Hamatsa is buried below old Seattle, down in Pioneer Square."

Jean stared at Red Tara and Blue Tara for several moments, perplexity showing in her mournful eyes. "Can't we get you some clothes?" she finally asked. "All this nudity is disconcerting. Are all the Taras naked?"

"You know," I replied. "I said something along those same lines earlier. But apparently parrots have feathers to cover themselves with."

"But they're not wearing feathers now, are they?"

"Clothes just get in the way during battle," Blue Tara interjected. "You should try our way sometime," she said to Jean. Jean's face turned red as a beet.

"I'm not really interested in joining a nudist colony," she replied. "And Seattle's just too damn cold and damp to go around naked." Jean looked at me. "This must be a male wet dream," she smirked. I could feel my face flush. "Oh my god!" she exclaimed. "You guys love this."

"Not to change the subject or anything," I responded, trying exactly to change the subject, "but we need to focus on the matters at hand. Shouldn't we be out looking for this old lady that Jean's talking about? Especially since she's right here in Ballard?"

"That would be pointless," Red Tara replied. "These ghouls can change their shape at will. The hadaho most likely already has taken a new form. No. We need to keep our focus on finding the tlogwe."

"What's a tlogwe?" Jean asked.

"The source of ultimate power," I replied. "Given by the spirits to those brave enough to enter their realm."

"That sounds ominous," Jean said. "And I'm almost afraid to ask. But where is this spirit realm? And who's going to be dumb enough to take on this mission?" I coughed as I raised my hand.

Old Seattle was built on a Duwamish Indian burial ground," Michael replied. "Currently somewhere under

50

Pioneer Square. And someone who is not me needs to venture down there."

"We went to see Charlie today," I added. "There may very well be an old smugglers' tunnel under his shop that will lead us into the buried city." I took Jean's hand in mine. "You feel like doing some spelunking with me?" I asked her.

"I will go spelunking with you," Blue Tara interjected. "What exactly is spelunking?"

"Okay," Jean replied hesitantly. "I'm off tomorrow. Call me crazy but I'd love to spend the day with you looking for zombies and monsters in dark and dangerous tunnels. What could possibly go wrong?"

"I will go with you," Blue Tara stated. "To protect you," she added, with what I sensed to be an unnecessarily gratuitous tone in her voice. "Kurukulla will stay with your friend Michael to protect him."

I shrugged. "I remember reading in history books about a time long long ago when knights errant wandered the land protecting damsels in distress."

"How quaint," Blue Tara replied.

Jean stifled a yawn. "I am beat," she said. "I want to go to bed early." She took my hand in hers. "I don't suppose your bedroom door has a lock?"

Part Two

The next morning Blue Tara did her time and space bending trick to send Michael, Margarita, and Red

Tara back to Michael's office at the U Dub. Task accomplished, Blue Tara reverted to being a parrot, Princess Tara. We left Aboo, the blue and gold macaw, to guard the apartment. Then Jean and I, dressed in hiking shoes, khakis, and flannel shirts like we were heading for a hike in the Cascades, along with Princess Tara, hopped into my truck and drove down to Pike Place Market. Well, I drove anyway. We arrived early enough, well before the shops opened for the day, before Charlie's Bird Store opened, so finding a parking spot proved no trouble at all. In fact, I parked directly in front of the original Starbucks. Princess Tara became very animated when she caught a whiff of the aroma of fresh brewed coffee as we climbed out of the truck. Since I failed to brew any coffee at the apartment, Jean and I were ready for coffee too. With Princess Tara on my shoulder, we joined the line of customers.

Even though we were too early for the tourist crowd, a line snaked nearly out the door, mostly office drones on their way to work. I sensed that Princess Tara was ready to disappear half the line in front of us if she didn't get her coffee. I asked Jean to order for us while I grabbed a table out front to keep Princess Tara from an unnecessarily precipitous action.

Thankfully Jean soon appeared with three cups of coffee. She set two iced americanos in front of me. I smiled at her. Without so much as a thank you, Princess Tara ran down my arm, hopped onto my lap, and dunked her beak into the coffee. "I don't suppose the spirit world offers any lunch amenities?" I joked.

We sat in silence for a few moments drinking our coffee and watching the disparate market vendors setting up their shops for the day. The flower mongers arranged their strikingly beautiful flowers with colors so bright they almost seemed painted. T-shirt vendors arranged shirts with their Seattle scenes. Deli workers cleaned and filled their display cases. As I looked down the line of stalls, I noticed a frail old lady with a cane gingerly making her way across the cobblestone pavement near the flying fish booth, aiming toward the brass pig. She sported the whitest and wildest crop of hair I had ever seen on any woman. Or man. Then I noticed what appeared to be a long black feather in her hand. I grabbed Jean's arm and pointed. "What was that you were saying about an old lady turning people into birds just with the touch of a feather?"

Princess Tara pulled her beak out of the coffee cup. She scurried back onto my shoulder. Pinning her eye at the old lady she let out a screech right in my ear that almost burst my eardrum.

The old lady reached the brass pig. She touched the statue with her feather. The brass pig started to move. The statue's head raised slowly, almost too imperceptible to notice. The once inanimate object took a halting step forward. People rushing by halted and stared in wide-eyed amazement. The old lady turned and pointed her feather directly at me.

The gigantic pig's hoofs pawed the cobblestones. First one hoof. Then the other. Market shoppers screamed as dislodged stones pelted them. No longer frozen in brass, the animal's head raised to look directly at us. The pig started snorting. Then charged.

We sat only a short block and a half away from where the statue had stood, frozen in brass. In just moments, before we could react, the animal charged up the street directly toward us. The clanking of hooves on the cobblestones grew louder and louder. I swear I could see the animal madly snorting as the creature approached. I jumped out of my chair, knocking over the coffee cups. I upended the table hoping to create some sort of barrier. Squawking, Princess Tara fluttered down to the sidewalk.

I flinched at the sound of gunshots ringing out behind us. The front legs of the charging pig buckled. The creature's head plowed into the cobblestones only a few feet from our table. Charlie appeared next to us with his forty-five Smith and Wesson in his hand, pointed at the pig's head. Princess Tara darted onto my shoulder and screeched. I slapped my hands to my ears and pressed my eyes closed to stanch the pain of the noise.

ΔΔΔ

"You folks okay?" I heard Charlie ask. "I saw the princess from down the street so I thought I'd join you for coffee. Whatever in hell was that thing, anyway?"

I opened my eyes and looked around the market. There was no sign of the old lady. The pig once again stood frozen in brass unmoving in front of the famous flying fish booth. Three iced americanos stood unspilled on our table.

"Looks like Princess Tara reset the clock," Jean said.

I craned my head to peer up into Princess Tara's face. "Did you disappear the old lady?" I asked Princess Tara.

"She disappeared herself," Princess Tara replied. "Her magic is too strong for me."

"Disappear who?" Charlie asked. "What just happened."

"I think Michael called that a hadaho," I replied. "A witch who can turn stone and statues into living beings."

"Maybe," Charlie said. "But my friends Smith and Wesson can turn them back into stone." He patted the forty-five on his hip.

"You have a permit for that?" I asked.

"Don't need no stinking permit, son. Washington state allows open carry. At least they used to, before the new regime." Charlie pointed at our coffee cups. "I sure could use a cup of joe, though," he said.

"Don't know about joe," I replied. "Will an americano do you?" Charlie nodded. With Princess Tara on my shoulder, I dashed into the Starbucks and cut to the head of the line to purchase an americano for Charlie. I sensed the other customers were too intimidated by Princess Tara's humongous black beak to complain. I slapped a plastic lid on the cup to keep Tara's beak out of the coffee. Back outside, I handed the cup to Charlie. "I forgot to ask if you wanted cream or anything," I said apologetically.

Charlie winked at me. "I like my coffee black. Like my soul."

"Okay then." I slung the strap of my day bag over my shoulder not occupied by Princess Tara. Not having a clue what we might encounter below the streets of Seattle, I brought along a day bag with a couple of flashlights, extra batteries, some rope, a few Cliff Bars, and a couple bottles of water.

We headed toward the Pike Hill Climb leading down to Charlie's shop. I stopped momentarily at the brass pig and patted the statue's snout for good luck. And to reassure myself the statue really was a statue.

ΔΔΔ

This time Princess Tara did not resist entering Charlie's store. Once inside, Charlie said, "I want you to take my forty-five." Charlie unbuckled his gun belt. He held the belt out to me. "Better to be safe than sorry," he said. "Only thing is, you have to promise to bring the gun back to me, or don't bother coming back at all. Understand, son?"

"We've got Blue Tara with us," I replied. "What do I need a forty-five for? Been years since I've even fired a gun. This isn't the Wild West."

"You sure? What would you call that brass pig coming to life and charging you? If I hadn't shown up when I did. . ." Charlie pulled the pistol out of the holster. "It's not rocket science, as they say."

He showed me the gun. "You've got the clip release. Safety. Slide action." He demonstrated the various

56

functions. "And I'll give you a couple extra clips to put in your bag."

"I'll take the pistol," Jean said.

"You will?" I responded in shock.

"I know how to shoot. My family were big hunters when I was growing up. Spent most weekends during summers at the family cabin practice shooting with my brothers at varmints out in the woods." Jean took the holster and belt from Charlie. "Better that someone who knows how to use a weapon uses the weapon. Less chance of accidents that way." Jean winked at me.

I began to feel rather inadequate, but I knew better than to argue the point with Jean. She put on the belt and holster. *Damn*, I thought. She looked hot packing heat. "You sure you don't want to go down there with us?" I asked Charlie.

"No thanks, boss. I've still got the shop to run. And I hate dark confined spaces. And I don't mind saying, I'm scared of ghosts." I gave him a look of surprise. "Yes, even me at my age. There's powers and mysteries in this world that people are better off not messing with. I'll stay here and watch the trap door, so at least you know there's nothing sneaking up behind you. You'll just need to worry about what's in front of you. Godspeed, son."

"Don't say I didn't offer." I forced a smile.

Charlie dropped a ladder down into the basement through the trap door. Princess Tara spread her wings and jumped off my shoulder. She twirled through the air, creating a pulsating orb of blue light which coalesced into Blue Tara. "My. Oh. My!" Charlie exclaimed, staring at Blue Tara in all her naked crystalline blue-skinned Amazonian glory. "I am so sorely tempted to join you."

One by one we climbed down the ladder. Blue Tara's glowing crystalline blue skin bathed the basement in an eerily surreal light, as if we were entering another dimension. Jean and I failed to realize as we stepped toward the darkness before us, we were in fact entering another dimension.

ΔΔΔ

Charlie dropped the trap door shut over our heads with a spookily unnerving crash. I pulled the flashlights out of my pack for Jean and me. At the back of the damp and muddy basement we found a heavy wooden door sealed by a large antique steel lock, the kind that needed a skeleton key.

"This would be your department, Jean," I said.

"Cover your ears," she replied. She pulled the pistol out of the holster, aimed at the lock, and fired. The lock exploded in a cloud of metal shards. I hoped that Charlie didn't hear the gunshot over the din of the birds in his store. Encouraged by a kick, the door creaked open.

"God I hate that sound," I said. "Sounds like we're in a horror movie." I shined the flashlight into the passageway. About six feet high and three feet wide. Looked like a mining tunnel with a line of posts and beams holding up the ceiling of the tunnel. Rotting timber planks covered the walls and floor. And off we went.

ΔΔΔ

I lost any sense of distance as we made our way toward the ever-receding darkness. The tunnel grew larger the farther we walked. Timber planks gave way to rock and mud which turned into broken cement and cobblestones. We found ourselves walking on one of the old city's original sidewalks, lined with jagged stone and crumbling brick and timber plank walls. An open doorway led into what appeared to be a large basement. Jean and I shined our flashlights around the room. I stood stunned into silence. This was an historian's dream come true. Instead of being empty and desolate, furniture filled the room. Decrepit, mud stained and blanketed with dirt and cobwebs, but furnished none the less. Chairs. Tables. Even the remains of an old tattered sofa tucked in a corner.

"Nice antiques," Jean finally said.

"Damn," I replied. "Now I know where I can get furnishings for the Saint Charles Hotel. Too bad this isn't a shopping trip."

"There's another door over here," Jean called out from the back of the room. She pushed the door open.

Blue Tara and I hurried to catch up to her. We entered another room, not dark but softly lighted by a partially buried skylight in the ceiling. More furniture. Chairs. Reading tables. A couple of tattered settees. Broken hookas. We had stumbled into an opium den. Blue Tara stuck a pipe into her mouth. "Should you be doing that?" I asked.

"Just checking," she replied.

"I'm surprised you even know what that is," I said.

"There are many methods to expand the mind," she replied. "I will show them to you someday."

Another door. Another basement room. Jean screamed. I ran up behind her. She stood in the doorway shining her flashlight at a chair in an otherwise empty room. Someone sat in the chair. Dirty black hair. Pallid scalloped white skin. What appeared to be a tattered canvas bag for a shirt. "He looks dead," I observed. Blue Tara walked around the body.

"A lalenox," she said. "A warrior of the spirit world. We are on the right track."

"Is he dead?" Jean asked.

"He looks dead," I replied.

Blue Tara grabbed her battle axe. With one quick blow she lopped off the demon's head. The body remained sitting in the chair. "The demon is dead now," Blue Tara said.

"No blood," I observed. "He must already have been dead. Wonder how long he's been sitting here? And why?"

"A message to those like us who pass," Blue Tara replied. "And a warning."

I kicked the chair. The body toppled onto the floor.

"We must continue on," Blue Tara said.

Another doorway led onto a cobblestone covered street. Old sailing ships used cobblestones for ballast. When the ships docked in Seattle to pick up timber and logs, Seattle's primary export, the ships dumped the cobblestones on the beach giving Seattle free paving material for the nascent town's first streets. We looked up and down the street, lined with partly ruined timber store fronts on concrete and stone foundations, looking much like an old abandoned Hollywood movie set. I could imagine John Wayne strolling out of a saloon, saddle slung over his shoulder, Winchester rifle in his hand. I thought I could hear the sounds of a piano playing in the distance. "Listen," I said. "Do you hear that?"

"Hear what?" Jean replied.

"I thought I heard a piano playing."

"Stop that," she said. "You're freaking me out. You've watched too many John Wayne movies."

"Or Twilight Zone episodes." We walked down the street silently for about a block before the cobblestones and ruined buildings disappeared into earth and rubble. The storefronts we passed looked to be filled with derelict antiques. "This used to be street level before the Great Seattle Fire," I explained. "After the fire, this was all filled in and covered over, and what had been street level became basements for the new city built on top of this."

"Apparently not all filled in," Jean replied.

"I never in my life would have imagined how well preserved this would be," I said. "This is like walking into a time capsule. Every historian's dream come true."

"Why don't more people know about this?" Jean asked.

"Probably for safety reasons," I replied, as clouds of dust and dirt rained down on us whenever the ceiling shook from the traffic over our heads.

With the street blocked by rubble we ducked into another storefront, what appeared to have once been a saloon. The grime covered skeleton of a once elegant cherry wood bar stood along a wall below the remains of a wall length mirror. Wooden tables and chairs lay broken and scattered across the floor. A battered antique player piano stood forlorn against the back wall. I tapped a couple of dirt encrusted ivory keys. The hair on my head stood at attention as the room filled with discordant sound. "Needs tuning," I joked, trying to push back the sense of dread crowding my brain.

"I wish you wouldn't do that," Jean cringed. "That creeps me out. Not sure if we want to be announcing our presence down here."

"Sorry. Point taken," I replied.

"This way," Blue Tara interjected, pushing open a creaky old frame door behind the player piano. We peered through the doorway. Instead of another basement we found a vast cavern which stretched into the darkness beyond the reach of our flashlights.

"How is this possible?" Jean asked.

"We are at the heart of the old city," Blue Tara replied. "We are about to enter the realm of the ancients that once claimed this place. The realm of the spirit world."

"Are you talking about the old Indian village?" I asked.

"We are about to enter a place where the laws of your physics and reality no longer apply."

"Terrific," I said. "I suppose there's no turning back?"

"There is no turning back if you ever hope to find the tlogwe. There is no turning back if you ever hope to defeat Hamatsa. Our only hope is to go forward. If we turn back all will be lost."

"I was afraid you were going to say that."

"Oh come on," Jean said. "Buck up. Do you think Indiana Jones ever backed out of an adventure? How many historians ever get the chance to relive history?"

"Well, none actually," I replied.

"So you'll be the first," Jean said. "Put your name into the history books for sure." She put her arms around me and kissed me. Long and hard.

Part Three

We moved on into the cavern. At first our flashlights barely penetrated into total darkness. After a short time we seemed to be walking on forest floor. A grass and brush covered meadow between towering fir and cedar trees. I thought I could see stars flickering above the trees.

"How is this even possible?" I asked.

"Open your mind," Blue Tara replied.

I heard the sound of a large gathering of people in the distance. Shouts and cries interspersed with what sounded like chanting.

"We are coming to the village of the ancestors," Blue Tara said. "Be on your guard."

Soon we saw the lights of several large bonfires. Billowing flames tossed menacing shadows through the trees from people dancing around the fires. A magnificent Duwamish longhouse stood before us. The front decorated with a fierce double-headed serpent brilliantly painted in red and black and yellow ochre. A totem, at least twenty feet tall, stood in front of the longhouse. On the totem four frightening winged ghouls stood on top of each other. The four furies, the giant raven Qoaxqoaxual, who feasted on the eyes of Hamatsa's victims. Hoxhok, the giant crane, who cracked open the skulls of his victims with his great beak and devoured their brains, and the two condors and feathered grizzly bears Gelogudzayae and Nenstalit.

"Turn off your lights," Blue Tara ordered. "Do what I tell you. And only do what I tell you. Understand?"

"Yes ma'am," I replied.

We slowly approached the longhouse. No one seemed to take notice of us. Not the dancers. Not the audience. Not even taking notice of a tall naked glowing crystalline blue-skinned Amazonian witch with a battle axe. Blue Tara motioned us to the back of the assembly. She stood with her right foot resting on her left knee. Jean and I sat on a log lying on the ground to watch the ceremony in progress, as if we belonged there.

A cleared piece of ground between the bonfires in front of the longhouse served as a stage. Four men walked onto the clearing. They wore western clothing. Tattered, soiled, and torn. Their faces blackened with soot, eagle feathers covered their hair. Each of the four men carried a menacing lance.

Four other men entered the stage. They wore grizzly bear hides for cloaks and grizzly bear skulls on their heads. They held razor-sharp bear claws in their hands. A solitary figure walked onto the stage behind the grizzly bear dancers. A tall man with long disheveled black hair, he towered over any of the other men on the stage. Scaly pale yellowish skin under a red cedar bark cloak. The flickering light from the bonfires highlighted his gleaming red eyes. I practically swallowed my tongue in surprise. "Hamatsa!" I exclaimed. Jean grabbed my hand.

"Quiet," Blue Tara admonished, in a whisper.

I sensed Hamatsa's burning red eyes staring directly at me. The people sitting around the bonfires took up sticks and commenced beating time on planks they held in their laps. The four grizzly bear dancers lifted Hamatsa on their shoulders and paraded around the square. Once. Twice. A third time. And again. They commenced to chant to the beat of the planks:

"We follow Hamatsa to the ends of the world."

Then they paraded back the opposite way around the square, chanting:

"Hamatsa made me a warrior.
Hamatsa made me pure.
I destroy life. Hamatsa is a lifemaker."

The grizzly bear dancers and the men with the lances rushed out into the audience. They seized four people, two men and two women, who they dragged onto the stage, screaming and struggling. One of the grizzly bear dancers slashed the throat of one of the prisoners with a razor-sharp bear claw. The man fell to the ground pooled red with his blood. The other three captives immediately stopped struggling. Hamatsa walked up to each person, opened his mouth revealing glistening ivory fangs, and ripped their necks open. They fell to the ground. After a few moments writhing in pain they lay still. Dead. Standing over the bodies, Hamatsa pulled out a flask from under his cloak. He sprinkled a clear liquid over the bodies. The four people on the ground, previously dead, stirred and jumped onto their feet, their faces wild with fright. Unrestrained, they ran into the darkness.

"Water of Life," I observed.

A solitary man entered the stage and joined Hamatsa. A shaman, the man wore deerskin leggings and a chilkat blanket boldly embroidered with a double-headed serpent. He wore a crown of red cedar bark and held a rattle carved in the shape of a serpent's head. The man took handfuls of eagle feathers out of a bucket filled with eagle feathers and tossed them over Hamatsa's head. Hamatsa began to dance. First slowly. Then frenetically. He began his dance crouched down. Slowly his body rose until he danced standing straight up.

The shaman swung and shook his rattle in wide circles over his head for about ten minutes while the assembly beat time on the planks on their laps, chanting:

"Wai, hai, hai!"

The shaman signaled the assembly to stop beating their planks. Deep silence gripped the scene. Silence so deep I could hear my heart beating. Hamatsa began to chant the cannibal song:

"Ham ham amai, ham ham amai, hamai, hamaima, mamai, hamai hamamai.
Ham hamam ham am ham am amai hamei hamamai.
Ham ham amai
Ham ham amai
Ham ham amai
Ham ham amai."

The shaman stepped to the front of the stage and cried out, "Great is the fury of this great supernatural being, Hamatsa. He will carry men on his arms and torment them. He will devour skin and bones, crushing flesh and bone with his teeth."

A loud murmur broke out from the assembly as the dancers stepped to the side of the stage. Four fierce creatures stepped out of the shadows and into the light. The four furies. Qoaxqoaxual. Hoxhok. Gelogudzayae. Nenstalit. They were followed onto the stage by a striking tall svelte dark-skinned woman with piercing black eyes and long black hair flowing over her shoulders. A woman totally naked. "Oh. My. God!" I cried out inadvertently. "Kinqalatlala!"

Kinqalatlala stepped in front of the furies and signaled the grizzly bear dancers. They dragged a woman, also totally naked, onto the stage. The woman seemed drugged and unresponsive. She needed help to stay upright. Kinqalatlala stepped to the woman. She raised her hand to the woman's face. Her hand transformed into a shimmering steel blade. Kinqalatlala thrust her hand through the woman's chest, and the woman fell to the ground, dead. Bending down Kinqalatlala slashed the woman's chest open with her hand. She buried her other hand into the chest and ripped out the woman's heart. Kinqalatlala held the heart over her head. Blood dripped onto her face and outstretched tongue. Hamatsa stepped to Kinqalatlala. He took the heart out of her hand. He commenced to eat the heart. The assembly picked up their sticks and began to beat time on their planks once again while the furies fell on the dead woman's body. Qoaxgoaxual the giant raven pecked out and swallowed the woman's eyes. Hoxhok the giant crane split the woman's skull open with his giant beak and sucked out her brains. The furies ripped her flesh and devoured her body.

Jean gripped my hand. I could feel her body shaking in fear. I sat stunned into silence. Not one muscle on my body so much as twitched.

The assembly began to chant:

"Wa ha, wa ha, wa ha, wa ha, wa ha, hai ya, ye he, ya ye, yay a, wa ha, wa ha, hai ya, ye he, he ya, ye ha, ye ha, ye ha, hoip!"

Hamatsa sat on a cedar bark mat while continuing to devour the dead woman's heart, his face coated with blood. Kinqalatlala danced around Hamatsa. She took some burning cedar bark and shook the torch over Hamatsa's head, showering him with sparks. The grizzly bear dancers accompanied by the warriors with the lances returned to the stage. They picked Hamatsa up on their shoulders and carried him into the darkness. The four furies followed, dragging the remains of their victim with them. Jean and I sat looking at each other in stunned silence. "The dead live beneath the world of the living," Blue Tara remarked matter of factly.

Kinqalatlala danced back onto the stage, sweat and blood on her naked body glistening in the flickering light of the bonfires. She danced directly to where Jean and I sat. Reaching down, she grabbed my shoulders. She pulled me up on my feet and onto the stage. She commenced to chant:

"I keep down your wrath, great cannibal Hamatsa. I keep down your whistles, great cannibal Hamatsa.

I keep down your voraciousness, great cannibal Hamatsa.
You are always devouring property, great cannibal Hamatsa.
You are always devouring food, great cannibal Hamatsa.
You are always devouring heads, great cannibal Hamatsa."

Kinqalatlala put her arms around my shoulders and pulled me to her. Her breasts stuck into my chest. As I struggled to break free of her grip I could see Jean trying to get to her feet, but Blue Tara took her arm and restrained her. Kinqalatlala put her hands on my face and swiped her tongue across my lips. I could taste salty bittersweet blood. I managed to break free and stumble back off the stage as the four furies reappeared out of the darkness to surround Kinqalatlala. I fell back onto the log with Jean and put my arm across her shoulders.

"How can she know who you are?" Jean asked. "If this is the past, she hasn't met you yet."

"Time is relative," Blue Tara interjected. "The past is present. And the present is past. You must drop the constraints of your linear reality."

"Maybe we should get out of here," I said. "Quit while we're ahead."

"We can not leave without the tlogwe," Blue Tara replied. "Otherwise, all is lost."

"You keep saying that, but how and where do we find the tlogwe? And how will we recognize the tlogwe?

Will the tlogwe be gift wrapped? I don't have the slightest clue what the tlogwe is."

"Patience," Blue Tara said. "We need to get into the longhouse. We may find the answer we seek within."

"I don't think the furies are going to stand by and simply let us walk in," I replied. "So how are we going to get in?" I shouldn't have asked. Blue Tara screeched. I found myself inside a large dark timber structure, on my knees, my hands pressed over my ears. *So much for getting used to this time space bend thing*, I thought to myself. I forced my eyes open. I saw Blue Tara helping Jean to her feet. The back wall glowed with a soft tremulous light giving the nearly empty hall an eerie ethereal effect. I saw fantastical demons and serpents painted on the walls in colors so vibrant the figures seemed to come alive. Jean took my hands and helped me to my feet. We were not alone.

Hamatsa stood in the center of the room, his sickly yellow scalloped skin colored blue from Tara's glow. "What you seek is not here," he said, baring his fangs.

"How do you know what we seek?" I replied bravely.

"You seek what you can not have. The source of ultimate power. Ultimate power to destroy Dear Leader and stop the Winalagalis."

Kinqalatlala appeared at Hamatsa's side. She spoke, "Only those who have tasted death and entered the spirit world are able to seek the ultimate treasure." I could still taste the blood on my lips from Kinqalatlala's kiss, but I thought better than to tell her that. "Only those who have tasted death can achieve everlasting life," Kinqalatlala added. "Ultimate power and everlasting life rests with those who can take life and restore life."

"You're just mad we whooped your ass," I replied, probably with more bravado than warranted in this situation. "Don't think we can't whoop your ass again," I added, as I stepped to Blue Tara's side to bolster my confidence.

"There are no defeats or victories," Hamatsa said. "What matters is who prevails in the end."

Do not underestimate the power of the Taras," Blue Tara replied.

"You do not understand power," Hamatsa said. "Until you gain the power to control life and to control death you will have no power against me." Hamatsa signaled into the darkness of the longhouse. The grizzly bear dancers appeared carrying a large cedar box. Others brought in logs and sticks from outside to construct a bonfire in the center of the longhouse. Someone produced a burning feather stick from the bonfires outside to ignite the bonfire.

Kinqalatlala stepped into the cedar box and lay down. The grizzly bear dancers covered the box with a large plank. They lifted the box and placed the coffin on the fire. Kinqalatlala could be heard chanting inside the box:

"I keep down your wrath, great cannibal Hamatsa.
I keep down your whistles, great cannibal Hamatsa.

I keep down your voraciousness, great cannibal Hamatsa.
You are always devouring property, great cannibal Hamatsa.
You are always devouring food, great cannibal Hamatsa.
You are always devouring heads, great cannibal Hamatsa."

The cedar box quickly caught fire and became engulfed by the flames. After a few moments Kinqalatlala's chanting ceased. The box burned fiercely for about half an hour and everyone of us just stood and stared. Me, Hamatsa, his attendants, Jean, and Blue Tara. Not uttering a sound, we were mesmerized by the flames consuming the cedar planks of the box. I did not hear one scream or cry from Kinqalatlala trapped inside.

Eventually the box collapsed in ashes and the flames died out. The grizzly bear dancers took sticks and brushed through the ashes, kicking Kinqalatlala's charred bones to the side. Hamatsa piled the bones in a small pyramid. He placed Kinqalatlala's skull on the pyramidion. He produced his flask containing the Water of Life and poured the liquid over the pile. The shaman appeared and removed his chilkat blanket, spreading the blanket over the bones. Hamatsa began to chant:

"Ham ham amai, ham ham amai, hamai, hamaima, mamai, hamai hamamai.
Ham hamam ham am ham am amai hamei hamamai.
Ham ham amai
Ham ham amai
Ham ham amai

Ham ham amai."

I practically swallowed my tongue when the blanket began to rise off the ground and a human form took shape beneath the cloth. Hamatsa and the shaman each grasped corners of the blanket. They pulled the blanket off the body. Jean screamed. I stood dumbfounded, my knees wobbling. Kinqalatlala stood unharmed and alive before us. She stepped to me. "Until you are willing to face death you have no power over us. Are you willing to face death?" she asked me, pointing to the ashes of the cedar box.

Not really, I thought to myself. Not knowing what to say, I said nothing. I certainly did not want to go through the fire ritual I just witnessed.

Blue Tara stepped between me and Kinqalatlala, holding her battle axe in her hand. "There is more than one way to die," she said. "Are you willing to face death at my hand?" she asked, raising her battle axe. The four men holding the lances scrambled out of the darkness to surround Kinqalatlala, their lances pointed at Blue Tara.

"You may control death," Kinqalatlala said, "but you do not control life. That is your weakness. And that will be your downfall."

Out of the corner of my eye, I saw Jean pull the forty-five Smith and Wesson out of her holster.

Chapter Three
Part One

"So class," Michael said to his Introduction to U.S. History 101 class, as he fixed his eyes on the clock at the back of the room, desperately trying to push the second hand to the end of the period by willpower alone. "Did Abraham Lincoln fight the Civil War to abolish slavery? Or to preserve the Union?"

"Professor?" a female student in the front row asked, one of only two students sitting in the front row. Michael long ago discovered a direct correlation between grades and the seating chart. Well, at least he had two students actually interested in U.S. history.

Michael glanced at his seating chart. "Yes. . . Helen?"

"We covered this material last week," she said.

"We did?" Michael flipped through his lecture notes, trying to remember his last lecture to the class.

"We were supposed to read the chapter on Reconstruction for today's class," the student added.

"Oh yes. So sorry," Michael replied. "Don't know what I was thinking." Several students in the back snickered. Michael knew perfectly well what he was thinking. Red Tara sat perched on the window sill of one of the history lecture hall windows on the second floor of Denny Hall, open thanks to another gorgeous Seattle spring day. The students saw a strikingly colored red and green macaw parrot, with a pure white face scored with zebra stripes of tiny red feathers. Michael saw a stunning six foot tall red-skinned Amazonian goddess with four arms and a longbow slung over her shoulder. A red-skinned Amazonian goddess clothed only with a radiantly red cape billowing in the breeze through the window. In Michael's defense, any red-blooded male history professor in similar straits would have difficulty concentrating on his lecture notes.

"Reconstruction. Oh yes. Reconstruction. . ." Michael glanced at the clock before his eyes strayed back to Red Tara. He could feel sweat beading on his forehead. Michael became a minor celebrity at the U Dub when Red Tara started flying around the campus following Michael between his office and his classes. Some days even Margarita scampered along as well. Students began to call Michael the pied piper of the U Dub, or Doctor Dolittle behind his back. Michael did notice that women students began to smile at him more often, and even stop him for conversation as they passed on campus. Red Tara would perch on top of campus buildings like a gargoyle and wait for Michael to finish his lectures, or like on this day, sit on an open window sill.

"It's started!" a male student at the back of the hall shouted, jumping to his feet.

"Reconstruction?" Michael responded, confused. "Wait. What's started?" he asked as students scrambled to their feet.

"Deportation Police are moving into the city. In force," the student said breathlessly, holding up his tablet. Local news video on the screen showed masses of black clad Deportation Police goons surrounding Seattle Police Department headquarters downtown. "The regime nationalized the city police!" the student cried out. Anyone still sitting jumped out of their seats and surrounded the student with the tablet, trying to get a glimpse of the news broadcast on the slab.

Red Tara squawked, flapped her wings, jumped out the window and disappeared into the sky.

"Reconstruction. . ." Michael whispered, and closed his lecture book.

"They're rounding up the city police and detaining any cops that refuse to change their blue uniforms for black jumpsuits they've occupied city hall the mayor is in hiding and calling on the city to resist this federal incursion," the student continued furiously, without even pausing for a breath, attempting to explain the developing situation as students yelled questions at him.

"Class dismissed," Michael softly said, no longer waiting for the bell to ring to end the class. He was certain his students no longer cared about Abraham Lincoln or Reconstruction. He thought to say something about the next class assignment, but realized no one was listening to him. The room became a cacophony of incoherent shouts and questions yelled at the man with the tablet, while the man with the tablet tried to concentrate on following the news broadcast. Yelling and the sound of running feet in the hallway outside the classroom door competed for attention with the shouting inside the classroom. Michael gathered his lecture materials and dashed out the door. He wanted to get back to his office so he could call Charlie at the bird store to get an update on the underground Seattle expedition.

ΔΔΔ

Michael ran out of Denny Hall and smack into a line of black clad Deportation Police holding nasty looking machine guns. He almost dropped his books and lecture notes. An officer armed with a side arm and a magic harpoon stepped forward to confront Michael. Tall. Sallow face and skin. Long stringy black hair. Sunken red eyes. A laxsa. "Papers!" he ordered. Michael held out his lecture notes. With a swipe of the magic harpoon the laxsa knocked Michael's lecture notes and books out of his hands, scattering them across the lawn. "Does this look like a circus to you?" the officer asked Michael. Michael shook his head. "Then why are you treating this like a joke?"

"You asked for my papers," Michael replied. "Those were my papers from the class I teach."

The goon swung the magic harpoon and clocked Michael across the side of his head. Michael screamed in pain as his knees buckled. He fell to the ground. "Show me your campus identification!" the goon yelled at him.

Michael struggled to his feet, blood oozing from a bruise across the side of his face. He jammed his hands into his pockets, searching for his wallet. "I must have left my ID in my office," Michael tried to explain. He froze in terror as the goon lowered the magic harpoon. The harpoon slipped out of the goon's fingers and clattered to the sidewalk. Michael realized that an arrow stuck out of the goon's forehead. The goon toppled backwards, a stream of blood running down his nose.

One of the other Deportation Police goons raised his machine gun. With a thud, another arrow pierced his skull and the point stuck out the back of his head. The goon spun to the ground, firing off a burst from his machine gun as he fell. The burst of bullets cut down several Deportation Police goons standing next to him.

Michael scooped up the magic harpoon. He pointed the death stick at the remaining cops. Several collapsed to the ground, dead. The last couple of goons standing turned to run. One stumbled face first into the sidewalk, an arrow sticking out the back of his head. Michael realized that Red Tara stood next to him, bow in hand as she nocked another arrow into place. The last goon spun onto his back when a black dervish with steel claws bounded out from the corner of Denny Hall and slashed his throat, separating his head from his shoulders. The goon's head rolled down the sidewalk to stop at Michael's feet. Her back arched, fur standing on end, Margarita sidled up to Michael and rubbed her head on his leg. Students gathered around the battlefield and stared at the bodies in stunned silence.

ΔΔΔ

Michael stood frozen in shock. Holding her longbow at the ready, Red Tara grabbed Michael's arm with one of her extra hands. She shook Michael to break him out of his stupor. "Gather your wits about you!" she ordered. "Take the magic stick. This would be a good time for us to leave."

Michael mumbled something about his books and lecture notes strewn across the lawn.

"Never mind that!" Red Tara insisted. "We have more important matters at hand." Grasping Michael's arm, Red Tara dragged him along the sidewalk away from Denny Hall. Margarita bounded along warily behind them. Heading back toward Michael's office, a line of Deportation Police strung across Red Square blocked their unfettered retreat to the Suzzallo Library. Michael noticed that the espresso cart lay broken and smashed by the steps to the library and the bullet riddled body of the barista lay in a pool of blood on the red brick.

"Ah, fuck!" Michael exclaimed. Running his fingers through the blood caking the side of his head, he drew red lines of blood across his forehead and chin. Screaming his best impersonation of a war cry recalled from any number of old John Wayne movies, he lowered the magic harpoon at the goons and charged. Several goons to his left toppled to the red brick, dead. He turned to face a couple of goons to his right, but as he pointed the magic harpoon an arrow pierced one goon's head and planted itself in another's skull. They fell to the pavement dead. The black steel-clawed dervish Black Tara separated the heads from their bodies of the last couple of goons standing.

"Run!" Red Tara commanded.

Michael needed no further encouragement. He sprinted around the library building to the door leading to the subbasement and to his subterranean office.

The seconds to find the correct key to the lock seemed like an eternity. Once inside his office, Michael slammed his door shut and bolted the lock. He pushed a file cabinet against the door. "How long can we hold out?" Michael asked. "What if they decide to come after us?"

"We are safe here in this space," Red Tara replied as she peeked into Michael's mini-fridge. "No extra precautions are necessary."

"How is that?" Michael asked, perplexed, his eyes glued nervously to the door.

Red Tara pulled a can of Rainier beer out of Michael's fridge. She popped the tab and guzzled the beer. She belched. Wiping the back of one of her four hands across her lips, she explained, "I have created a different dimension here in your office. I have bent time around this space. To the ghouls outside this space no longer exists."

Michael darted to his fridge to retrieve a beer for himself. "Why can't we exist in a different dimension in the real world? A different dimension without Deportation Police and cannibals and witches?"

"A world without witches?" Red Tara chuckled. "That kind of power does not exist. This is the real world. Unfortunately the real world is more complex than you might like."

"Why didn't I take that tenure track offer at Beuhler College?" Michael blurted out, just for the sake of asking as he pressed the cold beer can against his bruised face.

"What is a Beuhler College?"

"A little Baptist College down in Southern California. They offered me a tenure track appointment for chrissakes."

"That was not meant to be," Red Tara replied.

"At least we have a magic harpoon again. That was some nifty work with that bow," Michael remarked between sips of beer. "How did you ever learn to be so good with a bow and arrow?"

Red Tara wet a towel in Michael's office sink. "There is nothing to learn." Her lips parting into a sly smile, Red Tara wiped the blood off Michael's face. "Firing a bow comes as easy to me as seducing a man. That is what I do."

"Huh?" The beer can slipped out of Michael's fingers.

With one hand Red Tara pulled the bow off her shoulder and placed the weapon next to the door. Another hand swept books and papers off Michael's desk. A third hand took hold of Michael's belt and pulled him to her. She lay back onto the top of the desk. Her fourth hand pulled Michael down on top of her. She kissed him. Her tongue slid into his mouth. Then all four hands removed Michael's clothing. Michael's hands found Red Tara's breasts. Margarita curled up on her sleeping mat next to the desk and hissed.

ΔΔΔ

Hamatsa and Kinqalatlala stood in the Department of Homeland Security's fortified control room on Level C of the basement of the Henry M. Jackson Federal Building in downtown Seattle, replaying security video from the U Dub, watching Michael and Red Tara take out a platoon of his Deportation Police on Red Square.

"Two of the Taras have answered Blue Tara's call," Kinqalatlala said.

"I have a large number of laxsa at my service," Hamatsa replied, clearly unhappy with what he watched. "But their numbers are not inexhaustible. This is not our only fight. We are stretched thin by the resistance. Our prime imperative must be to stop the Taras. Whatever the cost."

"Yes, master," Kinqalatlala replied.

"If more Taras join the resistance our position here will become precarious. We have tenuous control of the city police. With the former mayor in hiding we have tenuous control of the city government. Cells of sedition are springing up at the university like weeds. We need to secure the campus and root the Taras out of their hiding places. I am putting you in charge of this operation," Hamatsa told Kinqalatlala. "Use whatever force is necessary. Start blowing up buildings if that is what is necessary!" Hamatsa yelled at his lieutenant. "I want the man with the parrot brought to me in chains! Is that clear?"

"Yes, master."

"Why are you still standing here?"

Kinqalatlala saluted, turned, and ran out the door.

ΔΔΔ

When Michael regained consciousness he found himself sitting naked in his office chair. Red Tara stood on one leg in front of him, red silk cape draped across her shoulder. Her right foot rested against her left knee. A broad smile stretched from ear to ear. Michael stared at her brilliant red body. He jumped out of his chair and into his clothes as quickly as he could. "Shouldn't you get dressed? Or something?" he asked, his face flushed. Not moving, Red Tara continued to smile at him. Michael panicked, recalling the events of the afternoon. "What time is it?" he wondered aloud. He glanced at his watch. "Oh God! I need to call Charlie. Find out what's going on." Michael picked his desk phone up off the floor. The line was dead. He slammed the receiver down and fumbled for his cell phone in his jacket pocket. A big red ball where the signal strength bars should be. No cell phone service. He flipped on his computer. No internet service. "Well, that's just great!" he exclaimed. "What do we do now?

"We wait," Red Tara replied. "Things will happen when they are meant to happen. Our numbers are too small. We can not take on the forces of the Winalagalis just by ourselves. We need help from the other Taras."

"So we just sit here?" Michael replied.

"We are safe here. We wait for Blue Tara and your friends. We wait for the other Taras."

"I'm not good at just sitting and waiting."

"Neither am I," Red Tara said. She stepped to Michael. She put two arms over his shoulders. She pulled him to her, pressing her breasts into his chest. She licked his face and his lips. One of her other two hands undid his belt while another slid into his pants. Michael felt his body tense. "Just relax," Red Tara said. "You have nothing to fear from me."

"I'm trying to relax," Michael tried to reply, as Red Tara's tongue slipped between his lips and found his tongue. His body tingled as if from an electric shock wherever Red Tara's body touched his. He lost all sense of touch and feel. He felt his body melting into Red Tara's body. He lost consciousness, again.

Part Two

Out of the corner of my eye, I saw Jean pull the forty-five Smith and Wesson out of her holster. She pointed the pistol at Hamatsa and pulled the trigger. "Go to Hell!" Jean screamed. A huge red hole appeared in the center of his forehead before I heard the gunshot. The impact flung him backwards against the wall of the longhouse, where he crumpled to the ground.

The shaman appeared out of the darkness of the longhouse holding a magic harpoon. He pointed the death stick at Jean. I screamed, "Watch out!" I threw myself at Jean to try to knock her out of the way of the death stick. I was too late. Jean dropped her pistol as she collapsed to the ground. "Go to fucking hell!" I screamed as I scooped up the pistol and swung around to fire at the shaman. The bullet struck his

85

chest and knocked him onto the ground. The magic harpoon flew out of his hands and bounced off the wall.

Surrounded by the grizzly bear dancers and the men with the lances, Kinqalatlala walked up to me. I pointed the pistol at her chest. She put a hand on my shoulder and pulled me to her until the nozzle of the forty-five pressed against her naked skin.

"Pull the trigger," she told me calmly. I couldn't speak. Her penetrating black eyes hypnotized me. "Pull the trigger," she repeated. "Know the power of death." I felt my will succumbing to hers. My finger tightened on the trigger.

"Do not shoot her!" I had completely forgotten Blue Tara during the melee. "Do not act impulsively," she commanded. "Do as I say."

"Shoot me," Kinqalatlala said. "To gain power in the realm of the dead you must know death. Shoot me."

"No!" Blue Tara demanded. "She is not the one to die."

"Then who is?" I asked. The pistol wavered in my hand. "They killed Jean!" I screamed. Tears poured down my cheeks as I waved the pistol at Kinqalatlala's head. "What am I supposed to do?" I cried.

Blue Tara stepped to my side. "You must enter the realm of the spirits to search for the tlogwe, the ultimate treasure the spirits have to give to those brave enough to enter their realm."

"But how do I do that?" I pleaded. I stuck the nozzle of the pistol against Kinqalatlala's temple. "Do I take her life?"

"No!" Blue Tara insisted. "To enter the realm of the spirits you must know death." She placed her hand on my back. "You must die." I stared at Blue Tara, incredulous.

"Then die you shall," Kinqalatlala said. She raised her hand to her face. I watched her fingers turn into a shimmering blade of steel. I tried to pull the trigger of the pistol, but my muscles froze in fear. Kinqalatlala thrust the steel blade that was her hand into my chest. Excruciating pain overwhelmed my senses. I dropped the pistol. I could feel blood pouring down my legs. My blood. My eyes clouded. I sensed that Kinqalatlala put her arm around my neck and pulled me to her. Her lips touched my lips and her tongue touched my tongue. I had no sensation of touch or feel. My legs gave out. I blacked out before I hit the ground. Before I completely lost consciousness I thought I heard Blue Tara screech.

ΔΔΔ

Jean beat on the bottom of the trap door to Charlie's basement with a stick for several minutes before Charlie finally pulled the door open. He helped Jean and Blue Tara up the ladder. Dirt and mud coated Jean's tattered clothing and caked Blue Tara.

"What happened. Where's your friend? Where's my forty-five?" Charlie asked, staring at the empty holster on Jean's hip.

"He's dead!" Jean blurted out.

"What? Who's dead?" Charlie asked, stunned. He grasped Jean's shoulders. "My god, woman. What happened?"

"Kinqalatlala stabbed him with her hand. She killed him!"

"You're kidding? Your friend? Dead?" Jean nodded, sobbing. "With her hand? Kinq. . . who did you say?"

"The black witch," Blue Tara replied. Charlie stared at Blue Tara quizzically, his mouth gaped open.

"She stuck her hand through his chest," Jean continued. "I saw it. Her hand turned into a steel blade."

"Where is your friend. . . Where is the body?" Charlie asked hesitantly.

"We found the old Indian village. Hamatsa burned Kinqalatlala to death. Then brought her back to life. To demonstrate his powers. I shot Hamatsa," Jean rambled on frenetically, waving her arms.

"Good Lord, woman. This sounds like you were in the middle of an Indian war. So where is your friend. . . friend's body?"

"He's still in the village. His body is still in the village. I was almost killed by a magic harpoon, but he pushed me out of the way at the last moment and saved my life. I thought we were all dead."

"What village?" Charlie asked. "Where is this village you're talking about?"

"The old Indian village under the city," Jean replied.

"There's an old Indian village under the city?" Charlie looked incredulous.

"The world of the dead. Not just ruins. We were there. I couldn't stop him from getting killed." Tears poured down Jean's cheeks.

"The village of the ancients exists in a different time and space," Blue Tara said. "We traveled through time and space to get there, and I bent time and space to get us back to you."

"Why didn't you bring your friend back with you?" Charlie asked. "His body anyway?" Charlie stared at Blue Tara's naked mud caked body. "You sure you don't want a towel or robe or something to wear?"

Blue Tara shook her head. "I could not bring your friend back with us. His path lies with the spirit realm. He must search for the tlogwe, the gift of ultimate power. That is our only hope to overcome the Winalagalis."

"So he's not dead?" Jean asked, grabbing Blue Tara's arm.

"Yes, your friend is dead. He has entered the spirit world. He must complete his quest for the tlogwe."

"Why didn't you bring him back?" Charlie asked.

89

"If I had brought him back with us all would be lost. We would have no hope of defeating the forces of the Winalagalis, the forces of evil."

"You let him die!" Jean screamed, pounding her fists on Blue Tara's chest. "You could have saved him!" Charlie grabbed Jean's shoulders and pulled her back. She threw her arms around Charlie and buried her face in his chest, sobbing. "She wanted him to die," Jean blurted out.

"I had no choice," Blue Tara replied. "We had no choice. Your friend needed to die so he could commence his quest for the tlogwe."

"You could have saved him! We need to go back," Jean cried to Charlie. "We need to save him!"

"We will, young lady. We will," Charlie replied. "But first we need to get you cleaned up and we need to hook you up with that fellow who teaches at the U Dub. We need to figure out how we're going to save your friend. A whole lot of shit has come down here in town since you left on your little expedition."

"What's going on?" Jean asked.

"The Deportation Police are trying to take over the city. They've nationalized the city police and tried to arrest the mayor. He's in hiding, trying to organize a resistance."

"Oh no!" Can we call Michael at the U Dub?"

"Phones are down. No cell phone service. Even the Internet's down."

"We will return," Blue Tara told Charlie. Her head tilted back, Blue Tara screeched. When Jean opened her eyes she found herself on the floor of Michael's office with her hands protecting her ears, staring at the face of Michael's cat, Black Tara, Margarita, who sidled up to Jean and licked her face.

"Am I ever glad to see you," Michael exclaimed, his face red as Red Tara's skin as he hurriedly slipped on a polo shirt. He helped Jean to her feet. "You wouldn't believe what's happened. Say, where's your boyfriend?" Michael looked up and down Jean's tattered and soiled clothing. "Jesus Holy Christ!. You look like shit."

ΔΔΔ

This seemed an unusual way to be dead. When I opened my eyes I found myself sprawled out on a cedar bark mat outside the longhouse. The longhouse sat just below the tree line above the mud flats at the mouth of the Duwamish River, where the river empties into Elliott Bay. I could hear the surf lapping against the rocks on the beach. Wisps of fog floating off the bay rolled up to the longhouse and seemed to bring the double headed serpent painted on the front wall to life, as if smoke streamed out of the serpent's nostrils. Up the Duwamish River to the south, Mount Rainier glowed red in the light of the rising sun. In the crystal clear sky I felt like I could reach out and touch the snow-capped volcano, even though I knew the mountain stood sixty miles away. Seattleites call

Mount Rainier 'the mountain', even though any number of other mountains can be seen from the city.

Footsteps interrupted my reverie. Kinqalatlala appeared before me. The shadow of her tall, dark, svelte, naked body fell over my face. I struggled to try to get to my feet, but my muscles refused to respond to the commands of my brain. I realized if I was already dead the black witch couldn't kill me again. She reached down to grasp my hands and pull me to my feet. I was relieved to see normal hands and not steel blades. I tore my shirt open and gingerly felt my chest. I expected to see a hole where Kinqalatlala had stabbed me. I found nothing. Not even a scratch mark.

"Am I dead?" I asked her.

"Yes, you are dead," she replied.

"Then are you dead?" I asked, confused.

"Death is a relative state of existence," she replied.

I didn't have a clue what that meant. "What the hell does that mean?"

"Hell has nothing to do with this state of existence. Hell is a possible destination, if you are not careful. You have begun your journey into the spirit world. I know that Blue Tara sent you on a quest. A quest for the tlogwe."

"I don't know what you're talking about," I lied.

Kinqalatlala stepped to me. She put her arms over my shoulders. Her dark naked skin smelled pungent of cedar smoke. She ran a hand through my hair and traced the outline of my lips with the forefinger of her other hand. She pulled me to her, her breasts sticking into my chest.

"Don't spirits ever wear clothes?" I asked, more bemused than perplexed.

"I am not of the spirit world."

"What are you?"

"I am your heart's desire," she said, placing her hand on my chest. "I am your guide for your journey through the spirit world."

"You killed me," I replied. "And now you want to help me? You are a slave to Hamatsa."

"I only did what the blue witch wanted me to do, so you could begin your journey. Why do you think that witch Blue Tara failed to save you?"

"What? Blue Tara failed to save me? What do you mean?"

"She let you die. She allowed me to kill you. She wished me to kill you."

Kinqalatlala's tongue traced my lips. She forced her tongue between my lips. She pressed her tongue against my tongue. I grabbed her arms and pushed her back away from me. I ran to the longhouse to peer inside.

"Where are Jean and Blue Tara? Are they dead?"

"Your friends reside in the world outside this one. They abandoned you to me."

"No they didn't!" I exclaimed heatedly. "If they left, Blue Tara had a reason. Why are you here? If you killed me already, you can't kill me again. Can you?"

"As I said, I am your guide through the spirit world. I can help you. Or I can stop you. I can pleasure you." She took my hands in hers.

"Why do I need your help? And why would you help me? Is Hamatsa trying to trick me to confuse and mislead me?"

"You are correct that I am Hamatsa's slave in the world outside this one. But his powers are not unlimited. And I do not intend to remain his slave forever. By helping you, you can help me break free of his domination."

You killed me!" I exclaimed. "And you want me to help you?"

"Killing you was necessary," she replied. "Killing you was what Blue Tara wanted."

"What? Bullshit!" I yelled. "You're lying to me!"

"Your only hope for finding the tlogwe is here in the realm of the spirit world."

"You want the tlogwe for yourself. You and Hamatsa!"

"The tlogwe can only be bestowed on the one the tlogwala deems worthy enough to receive the magic of the tlogwe."

"The tlogwala? What is that?"

"Not what. The tlogwala is the one who holds the secrets to the tlogwe. Blue Tara knew that I could assist you to find your way to the tlogwala. That is why she did not prevent me from killing you."

"So you and Blue Tara are working together? Are you a Tara?"

"We are working to the same end."

"Which is?"

"To unleash the power of the tlogwe. To stop the Winalagalis.

"You're a double agent!"

"I do not understand those words," Kinqalatlala replied. "I am working to break the hold that Hamatsa has over me. And I am willing to help you break the hold that Hamatsa has over you."

"If I am dead, what kind of hold can he possibly have over me?"

"The Water of Life."

"Are you one of the Taras?" I asked again.

"I am not one of the Taras."

"But you are a witch."

"I have special abilities and special magic. If that makes me a witch, then I am a witch."

"I don't understand. You're not one of the Taras, but you want to help Blue Tara? By killing me. By killing Jean."

"I did not kill your friend."

"I saw her die by the magic harpoon."

"That was not my doing."

"Where is she? Where is Blue Tara?"

"I have already told you that they are not in this realm of the spirit world."

"Is Jean not dead?" I asked, begging for the answer I wanted to hear.

"I can not tell you what I do not know."

"She is alive?"

"We must begin our journey."

I felt euphoric. If Blue Tara did her time and space bend trick to get her and Jean out of harm's way, I knew that in no time at all they would came back to rescue me, with the help of the other Taras. And I knew that with Blue Tara time was relative and fluid.

"How do I know you and Hamatsa aren't setting me up? That you aren't trying to trick me?"

"You do not know. You must do what is in your best interest, which is to trust me and let me help you. I have already explained my situation. And what I can do for you. And what I expect you to do for me." Kinqalatlala put one hand on the back of my head and pulled me to her, kissing me. She ripped my shirt open with her other hand and slid her hand into my pants. My hands found her breasts. I kissed her back. I didn't know what the hell I was doing, but I couldn't help myself. I was bewitched. *Chalk this up to research*, I told myself.

Part Three

"I don't understand how we're supposed to fight ghouls like Hamatsa and Kinqalatlala that can exist in two realities at the same time," Michael said. "You saw them in the ancient village. Yet we've seen them in this world."

"I shot Hamatsa," Jean replied. "I practically blew the top of his head off with Charlie's forty-five. He must be dead."

"Hamatsa's powers are great," Blue Tara said. "With the Water of Life he can give life to the dead. With such power the boundary between life and death is fluid. He has mastered the magic to travel between the spirit world and the world of men," Blue Tara said.

"And the world of women," Jean added.

"I don't know about anyone else," Blue Tara remarked, "but I am starved." She smiled at Michael. Her head fell back. Blue Tara screeched to bend time and space.

ΔΔΔ

Jean and Michael found themselves rolling on the floor of the Ballard apartment in the Saint Charles Hotel, their hands pressed against their ears. Margarita growled at Aboo, the blue and gold macaw, Lord Garuda, who sat perched on Princess Tara's play stand. Aboo screeched a greeting, forcing Jean and Michael to protect their ears again.

"You need to buy us pizza," Blue Tara told Michael, as she walked into the kitchen with the avian Red Tara perched on her shoulder. Blue Tara opened the fridge. "Yes, beer." She reached in to grab a can of Rainier.

"While you're getting the pizza I'm going to jump in the shower and see if I can find some clean clothes to wear," Jean said.

"Maybe we shower together?" Blue Tara suggested.

"Maybe you drink your beer. I'll take a shower. You can shower after I'm done if you want. On second thought, I'll take a beer into the shower with me," Jean added. Jean took the beer can out of Blue Tara's hand as she headed for the bathroom.

ΔΔΔ

Refreshed inside and out with a hot shower and a cold beer, Jean scrounged some clothes out of the bedroom closet. A pair of Levi's and a checkered Pendleton shirt fit her reasonably well. She found Michael and Red Tara in her daemon form sitting at the dining table sharing a beer. Michael's face turned red as Red Tara's skin when Jean noticed one of Red Tara's four hands positioned on Michael's knee, although Michael made no attempt to hide the fact.

Over pizza and beer and wine Jean filled Michael and company in on the events at the longhouse. "You were standing at the original site of Seattle long before Seattle was ever established," Michael said. "How is that possible? You say you were working your way underground through the ruins of old Seattle, and suddenly found yourselves in another time?"

"Your concepts of time and space are too rigid," Blue Tara replied. "Time is not a linear construct in the real world."

"You bent time and space to get back to Charlie's, right?"

"I returned your friend and me to the ruined city. Then we retraced our footprints back to Charlie's store."

"So once we work up a rescue plan you can bend us through time and space back to the ancient village? Save us the hassle of going through all the tunnels and basements."

"Unfortunately, I can not," Blue Tara replied.

"But why not?"

"That is because time is fluid, that I can not know precisely what point in time we might arrive at. I could be a thousand of your years off, and we could be lost in time and space."

Michael glanced at Blue Tara. "Lost in space?" Michael chuckled. "I'm a big science fiction buff, you know."

Blue Tara ignored him as she gulped her beer. "We will need to go through the tunnels below the city again, as we did before, and retrace our route to the ancient village."

"But if he's dead, what can we do? Without the Water of Life I mean. Will we even be able to see him? Or will he just be a ghost?"

"I do not know the answers to your questions. We must search for the tlogwe. We may find your friend and possibly the answers to your questions. Kurukulla will come with us," Blue Tara said, nodding at Red Tara. "Aboo will remain here to await the other Taras."

"Margarita will come with us too," Michael added, peeking at his cat underneath the dining table chewing a slice of pizza. "We may need a good mouser."

ΔΔΔ

Hamatsa, his long stringy black hair tucked under a black leather fedora and his scalloped yellow skin hidden under a black leather frock coat, and Kinqalatlala, her dark-skinned svelte athletic body

100

accentuated by skin tight black leather pants and a form-fitting black leather coat, stood on the sidewalk on old Ballard Avenue across the street from the Saint Charles Hotel. They looked up at the lighted bay window in the northwest corner on the upper floor. "You explained your situation to the man with the parrot?" Hamatsa asked Kinqalatlala.

"Yes, master," she replied. "I explained how I wanted his help to break free of your hold on me."

"And he believed you?"

"I am very convincing, master. He is weak. Men are weak." She glanced up at Hamatsa's fiery red eyes burning under the black leather fedora. "Men of this world are weak," she clarified.

"Once he leads you to the tlogwe you can dispose of him once and for all. Just remember. I want to see his head mounted on the wall at Control. Is that clear?"

"Yes, master."

"Do you believe he will lead the Taras into the trap we have set for them?"

"I believe he will do whatever I want him to do," Kinqalatlala replied.

"How can you be so certain?"

"All I need to do is show him these," Kinqalatlala replied, pulling her coat open to show she wore nothing underneath.

"Then we will proceed with our plans. Once we eliminate the Taras, and once we eliminate those fools who fall under their spell, we will establish a seat of power here in Seattle. A seat of power to rival that of the Winalagalis himself."

"Yes, my master."

"Now is the time to summon Bokwus and the gagits."

"Bokwus? The Chief of the Dead?"

"Do not make me repeat myself."

"The gagits I understand. Because of Lord Garuda's power, the furies can not challenge the Taras. And although he can fly, the gagit is not a furie. But Bokwus desires to build his own empire of the dead. Do you not fear his power?"

"I will deal with Bokwus at a time and place of my choosing. But for now he is useful to me. His army of the dead can not be killed. The Taras can not fight ghosts. I will use his power to wipe out the Taras once and for all, and then I will turn his power against the Winalagalis. What happens after that will be of no concern to me."

"You are wise, my master."

Hamatsa reached under Kinqalatlala's coat and grabbed one of her breasts. "Remember who you serve," he commanded. "Fail me and I will cut these off and feed them to the furies. I will rip your chest open and feast on your heart!"

Growling, Margarita jumped to her feet underneath the dining table. She raced across the apartment floor to the bay window. Stretching herself up to her full length, she growled and pawed at the blinds. Blue Tara slammed her beer on the table. She jumped out of her chair. "Something is wrong," she said. She stepped to the window and peered through the blinds, her hand gripping her battle axe.

ΔΔΔ

As I struggled back into my clothes, I asked Kinqalatlala, "Where do we go from here? I'm guessing the tlogwe is not going to come to me, so we'll. . . I'll need to go and find the tlogwe."

"You are correct. The tlogwe will not come to you. You must seek the tlogwala, the keeper of the treasure."

"And where do I find the tlogwala? How do I even know where to look?"

"You are already on the correct path. You are in the spirit world. I can not tell you where to find the tlogwala, but know that you are closer than you realize."

"Well, that's not a lot of help. And I'm guessing the spirit world is just as big as the real world. If not bigger? Only without cars."

"The spirit world is just as real as your world. Your standing next to me talking to me should convince you of that. Do not make the mistake of denigrating that which you do not understand. That could cost you your eternal soul."

"So, if I'm dead. . ." I found myself staring into Kinqalatlala's hypnotic black eyes, like black holes into her consciousness. "If I'm a ghost, then can I just dispense with walking around this reality and searching for something I have no clue about? Can't I just levitate? Or mind meld? Or do whatever it is that Blue Tara does to bend time and space?"

"You can not change your reality and assume magic you do not possess. The spirit world is just as real as your world. And is governed by the same laws of nature. The sky is up. The world is down," Kinqalatlala said, stamping her foot on the ground. "A rock dropped will fall down, not up." She picked up a rock off the ground and dropped the rock on my foot.

"Ouch!" I cried, dancing out of the way. "No, wait. How is that possible? I'm dead. Or am I?"

"You have a narrow conception of death," she replied. "Death is simply the absence of existence. You may be dead now to your world, but you very much exist in the spirit world." Kinqalatlala poked my chest painfully with a finger. "Someday, with my help, you may be able to master the magic required to travel between these two worlds. Without my help, you may find yourself forever lost in the spirit world, or worse. Forever lost."

"Will I get hungry in the spirit world? Or thirsty?" I gazed up and down Kinqalatlala's svelte naked body. *At least I'm not dead to women*, I thought to myself.

"You waste time concerning yourself with trivial matters when you should be searching for the tlogwe."

"See, there you go again. I don't have a clue whether to go east, west, north, or south. Should I go into the forest? Or should I go out to sea? I'm not going to just charge off like a chicken without a head."

"Why would a chicken charge off without a head?"

I peered into Kinqalatlala's inscrutable eyes. "Did you just make a joke?" She looked back at me quizzically. "That's a figure of speech. Don't be so literal."

"You were a person who studied your world and your history, is that correct?" I nodded. "Then apply the same principles to this world. You face a problem. You need to solve the problem."

"But when I study the history of my world I have books and documents that give me answers. I don't see a library here," I said, as a waved my hand toward the longhouse. "Maybe I'll just sit here and wait for the Taras to rescue me."

"Then you are a fool. You would have a long wait. The Taras, as powerful as they are, have no powers in this world."

"So you say, but I'm not so sure. You might just be saying that so I don't sit here and wait for them to rescue me."

"I have no reason to lie to you. And every reason to help you."

"Then help me by telling me how to start my journey. Tell me which way to go. Tell me how far to go."

"You stand on a sacred ground, home to the ancestors who created this place. Possibly your journey is shorter than you realize."

Damn. Kinqalatlala would make a great poker player, I thought to myself. "Michael said there was an ancient Indian burial ground under the city. Is that what you mean?"

"You are in the world of the dead. This entire world is a burial ground."

I walked to the longhouse. I inspected the double-headed serpent painted on the front wall. I studied the totem standing in front of the building. The furies. Qoaxqoaxual. Hoxhok. Gelogudzayae. Nenstalit. I rubbed the polished red cedar wood with my hands.

"Of course," I said. "The tlogwala is a bird. The ancients worshiped birds. The great raven. The giant crane. The fierce condors. I'm looking for a bird."

"See. Your task is not so difficult as you might think."

"But I need a bird to find a bird. I need the Taras. I need Princess Tara and Red Tara and Garuda."

"As I have told you, the Taras can not help you here in the spirit world. They have no powers in the world of the dead."

"Then help me get back to my world. You seem to possess the magic to travel between the worlds of the living and the dead. Get me back to my world. Join with me and the Taras. We can fight Hamatsa together."

"You are dead to your world. Only Hamatsa has the power to restore life to the dead. Or possibly the tlogwala. I do not possess that magic."

"Then what good are you to me?" I asked.

"If you want to find a bird, you need to get up into the sky where birds can be found," Kinqalatlala replied.

"In case you haven't noticed, I don't have any wings."

"Neither did the furies, at first."

"Yes, but they found a cliff of crystal quartz, which turned them into birds. And then they couldn't turn themselves back into people. They had to make a bargain with the devil."

ΔΔΔ

"I saved the furies from obliteration," a voice said from the doorway into the longhouse. "The devil played no role in this matter. I saved their lives."

I recognized Hamatsa's voice. I spun around. Hamatsa stepped out of the doorway, clad in black boots, black leather pants, a long black leather frock coat, a black leather fedora, and black leather gloves. The black leather accentuated his pallid yellow face and glowing red eyes. I stumbled backwards away from him as he stepped forward.

"You enslaved the furies," I said. "You didn't save them. You gave them a fate worse than death. You turned them into cannibals, just like you."

"I gave them immortality. Eternal life. I can do the same for you. I can give you the Water of Life and send you back to your world. Or I can obliterate your very existence."

"And turn me into your slave? Just like her," I replied, pointing at Kinqalatlala. "As for turning me into a cannibal. No thanks. I'm a vegetarian."

"You found my slave pleasurable, did you not?" Hamatsa said. I stared at Kinqalatlala in surprise. Her face remained expressionless. *Did Hamatsa watch us make love*?

"You can enjoy her pleasures whenever you wish, if you help me. I can make her your slave."

I began to think my former life of celibacy didn't seem so bad. "She bewitched me," I replied, knowing that was a lame excuse. "I have no interest in helping you, and a lot of interest in stopping you. And I have no interest in a sex slave," I added, glancing at Kinqalatlala's breasts.

"Then I have no choice but to obliterate you," Hamatsa replied.

"I'm guessing you make up for your lack of intelligence with your good looks?" I told Hamatsa.

"Insolent fool!" Hamatsa yelled. He struck me across my face with his gloved fist. I fell backwards into Kinqalatlala's arms.

This being dead thing just isn't all it's cracked up to be, I thought to myself as I scrambled to my feet, trying to rub the pain out of my chin with my fingers.

Chapter Four
Part One

"I'm at a loss how to proceed," Michael said to Jean, as they sat outside Jean's coffee shop the next morning drinking coffee. Michael, Jean, three macaw parrots, Blue Tara in her Princess Tara form, Red Tara in her greenwing macaw form, Garuda in his blue and gold macaw form, the parrot Aboo, and Black Tara, Margarita in her black cat form. Red Tara perched on Jean's shoulder. Aboo perched on Michael's shoulder. Princess Tara sat on the table with her beak dunked in an iced latte. Margarita sprawled out in the sun on the edge of the sidewalk adjacent to the street. They tried to ignore the crowd of people gathered behind the coffee shop's front window drinking their coffees while staring at the menagerie outside.

"We've got to go back through the tunnel at Charlie's store and find our way back to the village of the dead," Jean replied, as she sipped her latte. Jean looked the picture of northwest chic in cargo shorts and a checked flannel shirt. Michael couldn't help admiring her long slender legs as she sat cross-legged next to him at the table.

"But is this going to be a ghost hunt? What can we do for someone who's dead?"

"I don't know that he's dead," Jean said. "And apparently dead doesn't mean what dead used to mean," she added. "Anyway, I'm going back with or without you."

"What do the Taras have to say about any of this?" Michael asked.

"More coffee," Princess Tara replied. "Please."

"That was a serious question," Michael responded. "What do the Taras think we should do?"

"Drink more coffee," Princess Tara said. "When we are ready we will return to the spirit world. We must continue the search for the tlogwe. Wherever the tlogwe is, your friend will be close by."

"Seattle is overrun with Deportation Police," Michael said. "Shouldn't we do something about that?"

"Our numbers are too small," Princess Tara replied. "Their numbers are too great. We must await the remaining Taras to join us. We need to keep our focus on Hamatsa and his slaves. Once we defeat Hamatsa then these side shows will collapse by their own dead weight."

"Classes at the U Dub have been suspended for the duration, so I'm out of a job," Michael said. "What have I got to lose? However, I need to get back to my office so I can change into some appropriate clothes and grab the magic harpoon," he added as he reached for his coffee.

Princess Tara screeched so discordantly Jean dropped her coffee cup. A red hand seemed to materialize out of thin air and catch the cup before shattering on the pavement. The hand placed the cup back on the table. Jean craned her head to look up at Red Tara's gleaming white face. She smiled. Before she could say 'thank you' Michael vanished and almost instantaneously reappeared, wearing hiking boots, blue jeans, and a flannel coat. He cradled the magic harpoon in his arms. A couple of people exiting the coffee shop tossed down their coffee cups and raced away along the sidewalk as fast as their legs could carry them.

"Wow!" Michael exclaimed. "Can I finish my coffee now? Please warn me before you do that thing."

Margarita growled. She jumped up on her hind legs, peering into the sky. Princess Tara ruffled her feathers and stood erect, head tilted to the side, her gleaming black eye searching the heavens. Michael and Jean heard the slow flapping of immense wings well before the creature appeared in the sky overhead.

"Oh. My. Lord!" Michael exclaimed.

"What is it?" Jean asked, jumping to her feet.

Michael stood, staring into the sky, mouth gaped open. "I don't believe I'm seeing this," he replied. "Ancient northwest coast legends call this creature a gagit. An immense flying monster with gigantic razor-sharp claws and teeth. A monster covered with black greasy hair instead of feathers. It's a pterodactyl. A flying eating killing machine."

"My god!" Jean exclaimed. "How big is that thing?"

"Big," Michael said. "The largest of the pterodactyls, called a Quetzalcoatlus, had a nearly forty foot wingspan, big as a fighter jet."

112

Wings spread, the gagit lazily circled overhead, slowly descending with each circle in the sky. Aboo, the blue and gold macaw, screeched. Michael and Jean bent over in pain, hands pressed to their ears. Aboo hopped onto the table next to Princess Tara. "The creature is not a bird, and not of this world," he said. "My magic has no influence over the creature's actions."

"I thought pterodactyls were extinct," Michael said. "Along with all the other dinosaurs."

"Apparently not," Jean replied. "Actually dinosaurs did not go extinct. You're looking at three of them here," she continued, waving toward the birds. "Parrots are living dinosaurs, the oldest of the avians, so I'm not at all surprised there's a pterodactyl flying overhead."

"Should I try shooting the critter down with the magic harpoon?" Michael asked.

"The gagit is just trying to scare you," Princess Tara replied.

"Damn thing's doing a good job," Jean said.

"One gagit can not harm us," Princess Tara responded.

"How do you know there's only one of them?" Michael asked. "That one might be a scout for a whole flock of those suckers."

"We will deal with whatever comes," Princess Tara replied.

Sweeping ever lower, the immense size of the creature quickly became apparent. Twenty foot wings pounded the air with each flap, sounding like a giant pile driver in the sky. The creature's menacing teeth and claws glinted in the sunlight. Dropping nearly to treetop level, the creature let out a shriek that shook the windows of the shops below. Crowds of people on the sidewalks who had stopped to stare at the pterodactyl screamed and ran for shelter. The pterodactyl dived to the ground and caught a man trying to dash across the street. Grabbing him by his head, the creature flipped the man into the air. The gagit's huge beak swallowed the man whole.

With a screech Red Tara leaped off Jean's shoulder and whirled to the ground, a four-armed red-skinned Amazonian goddess holding a longbow and a quiver of arrows in her hands. Before the gagit could leap off the pavement and take flight Red Tara nocked and released an arrow from her bow. The arrow slammed into the creature's head squarely between the creature's eyes. The gagit faltered. The creature turned and screamed. Head raised, razor-sharp teeth flashing in the sun, the monster charged at Red Tara. A blindingly brilliant blue dervish appeared at Red Tara's side. Blue Tara raised her battle axe over her head with both of her hands. She flung the axe at the monster. The axe whistled as the blade whirled through the air to strike the gagit's skull. The gagit stumbled and fell forward onto the pavement. Wings pushing against the pavement, the creature tried to climb onto its feet. Red Tara nocked and released another arrow from her bow which split the arrow in the creature's forehead. The creature collapsed to the ground, and did not move again.

"Look at the size of that thing!" Michael exclaimed, holding the magic harpoon at the ready as he slowly approached the pterodactyl. "Is the gagit dead?"

"You better hope so," Jean replied, "if you're going to stand next to the monster."

Michael backed away to a more comfortable distance. The sky filled with the deafening sound of pounding wings. Heads pivoted to search the sky. "Oh, for chrissakes!" Michael exclaimed. Two more gagits, pterodactyls, appeared overhead. Then another two. Then four more. And then another four. Soon a score or more of the hairy ferocious flying monsters filled the sky, blotting out the sun, the pounding noise from their gigantic flapping wings drowning out all conversation on the ground. Aboo, the blue and gold macaw, Lord Garuda, commenced screaming in response, with a scream of his own that threatened to burst already endangered eardrums.

ΔΔΔ

One of the pterodactyls began to circle and rapidly descend to the ground. The gagit landed on the street near the body of the dead pterodactyl. A gangly creature rode astride the long neck of the pterodactyl, a rider that literally was a skeleton. A living skeleton.

"Oh. My. God!" Jean yelled. "What is that?"

"Bokwus. Chief of the Dead!" Michael cried out. "Stay away from him. Anyone he kills becomes a ghost slave in his army of the dead." Michael pointed the magic harpoon at the ghoul, as Bokwus dismounted from the neck of the pterodactyl.

Bokwus turned and stepped toward Michael. The creature spoke, "You can not kill that which is already dead."

Michael stumbled backwards, almost dropping the harpoon while tripping over the curb. "What do you want?" Michael asked frantically.

"My master has commanded me to take the witches that you protect," Bokwus said, pointing at the Taras.

"That I protect?" Michael stammered. "Geez, are you ever misinformed. Stay back!" Michael demanded, once again pointing the magic harpoon at the skeleton stepping toward him. "Die!" Michael commanded. "The skeleton continued to step forward.

"Your weapon is useless against me."

Blue Tara stepped in front of Michael, battle axe in her hand. With one swing of the battle axe she separated Bokwus' skull from the rest of his skeleton. The skeleton crumbled to the ground as the skull rolled to a stop at Michael's feet. Michael swung the magic harpoon as hard as he could and smashed the skull to pieces. "If he wasn't dead before, he is now," Michael boasted.

"Hamatsa is not as smart as he thinks," Blue Tara replied.

Wings flapping, Bokwus' mount, the pterodactyl, galloped down the street trying to take flight. Red

Tara nocked an arrow in her longbow. She released the arrow at the creature. The arrow struck the back of the gagit's skull as the creature climbed into the sky. The pterodactyl banked sharply, wings flapping futilely, and crashed into a storefront, shattering the window. Wings pushing against the building, the gagit attempted to back out of the wreckage. Lifting her battle axe over her head with both hands, Blue Tara flung the axe at the monster. The blue steel blade split the creature's skull open. The gagit collapsed onto the sidewalk. The pterodactyls in the sky banked to the south and flew out of sight in the direction of Mount Rainier.

ΔΔΔ

"Glad I don't have to clean up that mess," Jean remarked, looking down the street at the wrecked storefront with a pterodactyl as big as a fighter jet crashed into the window. People poured out of surrounding bars and restaurants to gawk at the creature, which thankfully for Jean and Michael kept the bystanders from gawking at a couple of statuesque Amazonian warriors.

"Hamatsa is desperate," Blue Tara said. "He is throwing everything he has at us. He is coming after us. This is a sign of how much he fears us."

Michael noticed that a crowd of people had gathered around them, staring and pointing at the Taras. No doubt they had never imagined, let alone seen, a naked glowing crystalline blue-skinned Amazonian warrior with a battle axe. Certainly they had never seen a four-armed nearly naked red-skinned witch with a longbow.

"Say," Michael said. "Maybe we should get out of here. You seem to be attracting a lot of attention," he added, looking at the Taras. *Perfectly understandable attention*, he thought to himself.

"You are right," Blue Tara replied. Her head fell back, mouth open. Blue Tara screeched.

ΔΔΔ

Michael found himself on his knees in the Ballard apartment inside the Saint Charles Hotel, trying to protect his ears with his hands, along with Jean and Aboo, and the three Taras, Blue, Red, and Black. Jean grasped Michael's arms to help him to his feet. "My head just can't take much more of this," Michael complained. Hand pressed against his forehead, he stepped to the bay window to look up the street to the crowd of people gathered around the dead pterodactyls. "They're going to have some wild stories to tell their grandkids," he said. Then, looking down, he cried, "Oh, shit!"

Jean and the Taras rushed to the window. Jean looked down at the sidewalk and screamed. "I thought you killed the fucker?" Jean cried out.

Bokwus stood on the sidewalk across the street from the Saint Charles Hotel, looking up at the window. A car rear-ended a stopped car, the vehicles' occupants staring at the creature. Passersby screamed at the sight of the living skeleton, and fled in terror.

"There may be more than one," Michael said. "They all look alike."

"You crushed his skull," Jean replied.

"He did say you can't kill what's already dead."

"I need a beer," Blue Tara said, walking back to the kitchen. "As long as we stay together Hamatsa's ghouls can not harm us. He is trying to distract us and confuse us. We need to stay focused on our plan to search for the tlogwe."

"How many other kinds of monsters are out there?" Jean asked. "Are we safe here, what with a living skeleton spying on us?"

"There is safety in our numbers, as long as we stay together," Blue Tara replied, grabbing a can of Rainier out of the fridge. "You will need to get us some more beer. This is the last can."

ΔΔΔ

Once again Blue Tara screeched without warning. Michael slapped his hands over his ears and pressed his eyes closed to try to shut out the pain of the head popping screech. The din of hundreds of squawking and shrieking birds assaulted his eardrums. Someone screamed.

Hesitantly, Michael opened his eyes in time to catch a woman racing out the door, her face frozen in fright. He found himself back at Charlie's bird store, along with Jean and the Taras, all except for Aboo, the blue and gold macaw. Blue Tara stood drinking her can of beer. She handed Michael the magic harpoon. "Do not lose this," she commanded. "This weapon may save your life."

"Lordy! Lordy!" Charlie stepped up to the group, hands on his hips, admiring the two naked and almost naked Amazonian witches. "Did you folks see those giant birds that flew overhead? They even scared my birds. You could hear a pin fall in here when they flew over."

"They're not birds," Michael replied. "They are gagits. Flying monsters. Pterodactyls. Living dinosaurs."

"What were they doing?" Charlie asked.

"They were coming for the Taras," Michael replied. "We killed two of them."

"The Taras killed two of them," Jean interjected.

"Right," Michael added.

"We need to return to the city of the dead," Blue Tara told Charlie, polishing off her beer.

Part Two

Hamatsa stood before me with his gloved hand on my neck. His body reeked of the stench of death. I wanted to gag, but his hand squeezed my throat so hard I almost passed out. "Master," Kinqalatlala entreated him." "He is our best chance to capture Blue Tara. If you destroy him we lose that chance."

Hamatsa released his grip on my neck. I collapsed to the ground. Hamatsa reached down and grabbed my shoulders to pull me to my feet. "This pathetic excuse of a man does not deserve another chance," Hamatsa said. "However, I give him to you as a play thing to do with as you wish. On the condition you complete my instructions."

"Yes, master," Kinqalatlala replied, her head bowed submissively.

Hamatsa pushed me into Kinqalatlala's arms. He turned and disappeared into the longhouse. For a moment a flash of light illuminated grotesque monsters and demons painted with black and red and yellow ochre that I could see through the doorway on the inside walls. Kinqalatlala put her arms over my shoulders and pulled me to her. She licked my lips and stuck her tongue into my mouth. "Kiss me," she commanded. I failed to respond. "You heard the master. You are my slave now." I stood unmoving. "Kiss me, or you'll be damned to Hell!" She pressed her breasts against my chest, her lips against my lips, and her tongue against my tongue. I squirmed out of her grasp and pushed her away from me.

"Shouldn't we be looking for the tlogwe?" I asked. I peered through the doorway into the darkened longhouse looking for Hamatsa.

"We have all of eternity to search for the tlogwe. You are dead. Or have you forgotten?"

With her tongue sticking in my mouth I almost had forgotten I was dead. This certainly was not anything like what I ever imagined death might be like. *Thankfully Jean was not here with me to witness Kinqalatlala's tongue in my mouth*, I thought to myself.

121

"Assuming you find the tlogwe," Kinqalatlala said, "what do you intend to do with the magic the tlogwe will bring you, if the tlogwe is granted to you?"

"Are you kidding? That should be obvious. Destroy Hamatsa. Destroy the Winalagalis. Bring down Dear Leader. Destroy you."

"Why would you do that, even if you could?" Kinqalatlala asked me, putting her hands on my shoulders. "Hamatsa wants to save your world. Dear Leader only wants peace and prosperity for his people. I wish you no harm," she added as she quickly kissed me.

"Would you stop that," I responded. "Hamatsa is trying to subjugate my world. Dear Leader is a self-absorbed narcissistic megalomaniac who has substituted a cult of personality for government."

"We could be friends. And allies," Kinqalatlala said, kissing me again.

"Oh, for chrissakes!" I grabbed her arms and pulled Kinqalatlala to me. I pressed my lips against hers, kissing her as hard as I could. "Is that what you want?" I asked, pushing her away from me.

"That is a start," she smiled.

"We could never be allies, let alone friends, as long as you serve Hamatsa. Hamatsa wants to destroy the Taras. I can't have that."

"The Taras are witches. They have bewitched you. You need to beware the Taras. You do not understand the kind of forces you are allied with. As far as Hamatsa is concerned, I have already explained to you my relationship with Hamatsa. And how we can help each other."

"I will help you search for the tlogwe, only because I don't think I have any choice in the matter. But one way or another, I will destroy Hamatsa. And you!" I turned and walked into the longhouse.

"Where are you going?" Kinqalatlala asked.

"I want to see where Hamatsa disappeared to." I looked inside. As far as I could see, the longhouse sat dark and empty. "There must be some kind of portal in here that allows Hamatsa to travel between the world of the living and the world of the dead. Can we use the portal to do the same?"

"Hamatsa's magic is beyond your comprehension," Kinqalatlala replied. "You are only avoiding the task at hand to search for the tlogwe. I know you are stalling in the hope that the Taras rescue you. But that is a lost hope."

Well, I could hope, I thought to myself. "Fine," I said. I stepped out of the longhouse and started walking into the forest behind the structure.

Kinqalatlala raced after me. "Where are you going?" she asked, grabbing my shoulder to stop me.

"What do you think? Searching for the tlogwe." I struggled to break free from her grasp.

"But where are you going?" she repeated, as she restrained me.

"Searching for the tlogwe," I repeated. I stopped and faced her. "I told you that already. I don't have a clue which way to go or even what I'm looking for. So I'm just going to go and hope for the best. Unless you can point me in the right direction. This way looks as good as any," I added, pointing into the trees.

Kinqalatlala took my arm in her hand. "Brash actions can have undesirable consequences," she said. "You should not just charge off into the unknown without a clear idea of what you are doing and where you are going."

I got the distinct impression that Kinqalatlala was the one stalling now. "You know something," I said. "You should just tell me. Everything would be so much easier if you'd just tell me where I should go and what I should do."

"Nothing is ever that simple," Kinqalatlala replied with a faint smile. "You need to prove yourself first."

Now I knew that Kinqalatlala knew something she wasn't telling me. "You're talking in riddles now," I said. "I'm not very good with riddles."

"Life is a riddle. And death is a riddle. To find life requires solving the riddle of death." Kinqalatlala took my hands in hers. "The future is a riddle. You do not wish you could see your future? See if you have a future? If you help me I can show you magic that will not only let you see your future but shape your future as well."

"I seriously doubt such magic exists," I replied. "Or you would already know where to find the tlogwe."

"You do not know that I may already know where the tlogwe is."

"There's an old riddle about the future," I replied. "I never was, am always to be. No one ever saw me, nor ever will. And yet I am the confidence of all, to live and breath on this terrestrial ball."

"There is another old riddle," Kinqalatlala responded. "What begins and has no end? What is the ending of all that begins?"

"That's easy. Why, death of course."

"But all I have shown you should convince you that is not true. Death can have an end just as life can have an end. I can give you the magic to allow you to travel between life and death."

"Yes. But at what cost? To be your slave for the rest of eternity?"

"There are worse fates."

"Not many. And why would you want me for your sex slave? I'm just a retired history professor. There must be all kinds of studs and jocks in the world you could corral into your stable."

"But none as special as you," Kinqalatlala replied, a wry smile across her face. "Of all the studs and jocks as you call them in your city, Blue Tara picked you. That is the riddle I want most to solve. Why did she pick a goofy retired history professor?"

"Goofy? What does that mean?" If I wasn't already dead I would be insulted.

Kinqalatlala put her arms over my shoulders. "I am just teasing you. You are a very special man. And I want to discover what makes you so special."

"Right now I sure as hell don't feel so special, what with being dead and all."

"Yes, but you are special even in the manner of your death. Blue Tara chose you for a specific reason. She knew you must die. And she knew you must die at my hand." Kinqalatlala raised her hand to her face. As she looked at her fingers her hand transformed into a shimmering steel blade. She ran the tip of the blade across my cheek. I felt a sharp pain as the blade cut my skin. I could feel blood trickling down my neck. The blade reverted to her hand. Kinqalatlala rubbed my blood across my cheek with her fingers. She licked the blood with her tongue.

How could I be dead, and still bleed? I wondered as I looked at my blood on her fingers. "Well, I guess I had to be dead to search for the tlogwe." I sighed. "The tlogwala will only give the treasure of the tlogwe to one brave enough to enter the realm of the dead. But you never gave me a choice. No one asked me if I wanted to be dead or not."

126

"Only someone who can prove themselves worthy of that magic can receive the gift of the tlogwe. And of all the people that blue witch Blue Tara could choose in your world, she chose you. She thinks you are worthy."

"When the Taras show up to kick your butt I will ask her why she chose me. Why did Hamatsa choose you to be his slave. And not turn you into a zombie?"

"My master chose me because I am special as well."

"How so?"

"I am Dluwulaxa, one of those who descend from the heavens. My people reside in a city in the sky. The sky is my world, and the sun is my father. All the heavens serve as our playground where we can fly and soar among the sun and stars."

"So how did you fall in with Hamatsa?"

"Our weakness is curiosity. My people are safe as long as we stay in our world above the clouds. But on occasion someone of us is enticed to explore the wonders of the world below the clouds. Once that someone was me. And Hamatsa captured me. Once we are forced to descend to your world we take on the form of your people, or your creatures."

"How does Hamatsa prevent you from simply flying back into the sky?"

"Once we cease being Dluwulaxa, we are no longer able to return to our original form."

"What makes you so special to Hamatsa? Special enough to make you his slave? Are you his sex slave?"

"Hamatsa has no use for sex. He eats people. He does not sleep with them."

"So what makes you special to Hamatsa?" I asked again.

"I am what you call a shapeshifter. I can take many forms. People. Animals. Objects. I do Hamatsa's bidding. I procure the bodies he needs to feed on. I root out his enemies and destroy them." She raised her hand again and watched her fingers transform back into a steel blade.

A revelation struck me as if a light bulb turned on in my head. "You were a bird!" I exclaimed. "You're a Tara."

"Bird, yes. Tara, no."

"Maybe you're not a Tara. But I bet you know where the tlogwe is. I'm guessing you might even know who the tlogwala is. What I don't understand is, why you need me if you already know where the tlogwe is?"

"You do not understand. I need you to find the tlogwe. Only those deemed worthy by the tlogwala are able to receive the gift of the tlogwe."

"You're talking in riddles again. I'm guessing Hamatsa is preventing you from revealing the location of the tlogwe. . . Or. . ." Kinqalatlala's piercing black eyes drilled into my brain. "Hamatsa is the tlogwala."

ΔΔΔ

You're going to need more than that stick to take on the demons," Charlie told Michael, "if you're going back underground into the spirit world."

"This is a magic harpoon," Michael replied. "This death stick kills anything I point the weapon at. Anything smaller than a pterodactyl anyway."

"Just in case, I brought in some hardware from home. I was a Boy Scout a hundred years ago, and I still believe in the Boy Scout motto, 'Be Prepared'." Charlie walked into his storeroom and returned with another forty-five Smith and Wesson, and a double-barreled pump action shotgun. Charlie gave the weapons to Jean. She buckled the gun belt around her waist, and slung the shotgun over her shoulder. Charlie handed a bag to Michael. "And here's an electric torch and a bag of extra clips and shotgun shells." Charlie pointed at the shotgun. "That's a twelve gauge. A double barrel of that will stop Sasquatch. But be careful when you fire the shotgun. The sucker kicks like a bucking brahma bull."

"I've fired many a shotgun in my life," Jean replied. "I know my way around shotguns."

"You do?" Michael responded.

Charlie looked over the Taras. "I'm guessing you ladies do just fine with the weapons you have. Anything else I can get you before you go?"

"Got any beer?" Blue Tara asked.

"Beer? Why no. But tell you what, honey. You bring your friend back in one piece and I'll buy you a case of Stella Artois."

"Is that a beer?" Blue Tara asked.

"Best there is." Charlie pried open the trap door to the secret basement and dropped the ladder into the darkness. With the light from her glowing crystalline blue skin to illuminate the way, Blue Tara climbed down the ladder first, followed by Jean and Michael, with Margarita riding on his shoulder. Red Tara brought up the rear. "Godspeed," Charlie said as he dropped the trap door closed.

ΔΔΔ

Following the trail of the original expedition proved easier than expected, because the argonauts could simply follow their own footprints in the dirt and mud. Then they discovered extra sets of footprints converging on their original prints. Large footprints.

"Everyone be alert," Blue Tara commanded. "We had company we were not aware of," she added.

The group retraced their steps without incident into the basement where the dead laxsa had been found, sitting in a chair. They found the body of another laxsa. Sitting in the chair. Head attached to the body. "Another warning," Blue Tara said. Blue Tara grabbed her battle axe and with one swipe removed the head once again.

Michael abruptly stopped. He nervously glanced around the room. He dashed back out onto the streetscape, magic harpoon at the ready. Michael slowly scanned the storefronts along the street. The remainder of the party joined him. "What?" Jean asked, a worried look across her face.

"Do you hear that?" Michael replied.

"Hear what?"

"The piano playing."

"Oh god. Not you too?"

"Not me too, what?"

"Too many John Wayne movies. Next thing you know you'll be in the middle of a shootout at the OK Corral."

"That was Burt Lancaster. Not John Wayne. And what do you call that?" Michael responded, pointing down the street."

Half a dozen enormous creatures stood at the end of the street, shoulder to shoulder, clubs the size of logs in their hands. When Michael pointed in their direction the monsters growled and began to pound their clubs against the cobblestones. Margarita commenced howling in Michael's ear. "I don't believe what I'm seeing," Jean said, fear coloring her voice.

"Dzonoqwa," Michael responded. "In northwest coast mythology, supernatural beings of immense physical power."

Gigantic, the creatures stood easily seven feet tall. Skin hidden under thick mats of greasy black hair that shined like fur. Menacing razor-sharp claws could be seen on the hands holding the clubs. "Sasquatch," Jean replied, pulling the shotgun off her shoulder. "My brothers and I saw one once years ago when I was a kid. We were hunting varmints in the wilderness east of Rainier. We never told anyone."

Part Three

The six dzonoqwa raised their clubs over their heads and charged, screaming wildly. Jean bent down on one knee. She aimed and fired both barrels of her shotgun. The recoil knocked her onto her butt. The head of one of the creatures in the middle of the pack disappeared in a cloud of blood red pulp. The creature's body tumbled backwards. Red Tara nocked an arrow in her bow and aimed. The arrow pierced the skull of one of the dzonoqwa squarely between the creature's eyes. The creature stumbled forward and sprawled dead on the cobblestones. Michael aimed his magic harpoon first at one charging dzonoqwa. Then another. The creatures collapsed. Another dzonoqwa stumbled and fell face first into the cobblestones, an arrow protruding from the back of the monster's skull. Blue Tara stepped forward with her battle axe raised over her head as the last dzonoqwa halted about ten feet away from her. The creature's club waved wildly overhead while the monster's head twisted and turned to search for his companions. When the dzonoqwa realized his companions were dead the creature dropped the tip of the club to the cobblestones. Studying Blue Tara warily, the dzonoqwa grunted incomprehensibly.

"We mean you no harm," Michael said, holding his magic harpoon at the ready.

"The fuck we don't," Jean retorted, pointing her shotgun at the dzonoqwa's head.

"Do you understand anything we say?" Michael asked. "Who sent you?"

Looking back at his fallen companions sprawled across the cobblestones, the dzonoqwa screamed as he raised his club. Before the monster could take a step forward, Blue Tara swung her battle axe and separated the dzonoqwa's head from his body. The body fell to Blue Tara's feet. Blood gushing from the severed neck turned the cobblestones red with blood.

"That was impressive," Michael remarked. "Wonder what that was all about?"

"Hamatsa's slaves are legion," Blue Tara replied. "He knows we are coming and he is going to do everything he can to stop us."

"Oh my!" Jean exclaimed. "Look!" she cried, pointing along the street. A skeleton stepped onto the street.

A living skeleton appeared out of a storefront and slowly walked toward Jean and Michael and the Taras. "Oh shit," Michael said. "Bokwus again. Chief of the Dead." Bokwus cautiously stepped to within a few feet of the group and stopped. "What do you want?" Michael asked, holding the magic harpoon in front of him.

"I come for Blue Tara," Bokwus replied. "My master has commanded me to take Blue Tara to him."

"Fuck that," Jean said as she raised her shotgun to Bokwus' skull. She pulled the trigger.

Another living skeleton appeared out of a basement door and stepped forward, but not quite so far as the first. "I come for Blue Tara," the daemon repeated.

"How many of them are there?" Jean asked in frustration.

"More than one, apparently," Michael replied. "I don't understand what Hamatsa is doing. They don't seem to be armed. Or dangerous."

"Their intent is simply to harass us," Blue Tara replied. She stepped to the living skeleton. With one swing of her battle axe Blue Tara lopped off the skeleton's skull. "We must continue forward," she said.

Yet another living skeleton appeared in a basement doorway. Michael pointed the magic harpoon at the creature, but the skeleton kept walking forward. "You can't kill what's already dead with that thing, remember?" Jean said as she aimed her shotgun and pulled the trigger. Jean charged into the basement, kicking the bones out of the way. With her shotgun at her shoulder, she scanned the room, ready to fire. Michael and the Taras followed behind her. The room appeared to be completely empty.

Growling fiercely, Margarita leaped off Michael's shoulder onto the floor. She spun into the air as another living skeleton burst into the room behind them. The black dervish flashed her claws of steel and separated the skeleton's skull from the body. The bones collapsed to the floor. "Bokwus is persistent, if nothing else," Michael remarked.

"We are almost there," Jean called out from the back of the room. Michael found Jean looking through another doorway. The Taras stepped through the doorway as Michael and Jean followed behind.

ΔΔΔ

"Oh my god!" Michael exclaimed, looking out onto a forested landscape, the realm of the dead. "How is this even possible?" He looked back through the doorway into the empty basement. "It's like we just stepped into another dimension," he said.

"You are correct," Blue Tara replied. "We have entered another time and space. Hopefully the same time and space your friend is lost in."

"Now you're starting to scare me," Michael responded.

"You're scared?" Jean replied. "You should have witnessed what we witnessed the first time here. Then you'd have reason to be scared."

"We need to stay together," Red Tara remarked.

"Kurukulla is correct," Blue Tara replied. "We can protect each other. If you get separated," she added, looking directly at Michael, "there is nothing we can do for you. You would be at Hamatsa's mercy."

"Hamatsa has no mercy," Red Tara responded.

"Where do we go from here?" Michael asked.

"Looks like we just keep following the trail," Jean replied, as she pointed at footprints disappearing into the trees.

"Oh shit!" Michael exclaimed. Another living skeleton stepped out of the forest. This one was not alone. An army of white phantoms appeared out of the trees behind the living skeleton, stretching as far as could be seen in either direction. "The army of the dead," Michael explained. "We're fucked."

The living skeleton, Bokwus, Chief of the Dead, stepped forward. He pointed a bony finger at Blue Tara. "I come to take Blue Tara," he commanded.

"What do you intend to do with Blue Tara?" Michael replied.

"My master has commanded me to bring Blue Tara to him."

"What do we do now?" Jean asked.

"The army of the dead can't be killed," Michael replied.

"Well, we're not giving up Blue Tara," Jean responded, as she aimed her shotgun at Bokwus' skull and pulled the trigger.

Another living skeleton emerged from the forest and stepped through the line of phantoms. "I come to take Blue Tara," the living skeleton repeated.

"Anybody have any ideas?" Michael pleaded. "This could go on for an eternity. Eventually we're going to run out of ammo."

"We ignore them," Blue Tara replied.

"What?" Michael and Jean responded simultaneously.

"We ignore them," Blue Tara repeated. "The army of the dead can not be defeated. But we are not dead. The army of the dead has no influence among the living. As long as we stay alive the army of the dead can not harm us."

"Are you sure?" Michael asked dubiously.

"We continue forward," Blue Tara replied. "We will find out soon enough if I am right."

"If you are right? I'm not reassured," Michael complained. "What if you're wrong?"

"We will know soon enough." The Taras commenced walking forward. Blue Tara held her battle axe ready, and Red Tara her longbow. Michael and Jean quickly ran to catch up, with Margarita following at Michael's heels. They walked past Bokwus, who turned to watch them as they passed. They walked through the line of phantoms. Michael swept his hand through one of the apparitions. He felt a slight tingling, but figured that could just as well be a case of nerves as anything else. As they stepped into the forest they heard Bokwus repeat his refrain, "I come to take Blue Tara."

ΔΔΔ

Kinqalatlala took my hand in hers. "We must leave," she told me.

"I must be going crazy. That's what I planned to do," I replied, "Until you stopped me. I wish you'd just tell me where the tlogwe is. Where Hamatsa is. Just tell me. Is Hamatsa the tlogwala?"

"You do not understand. We must leave before they find us."

"Before who finds us?"

"Your friends are on their way to rescue you. We must not allow that to happen."

"What?" I exclaimed. "Hel. . . lo!" I screamed as loud as my lungs could muster.

"We must leave," Kinqalatlala insisted.

"Bull! Shit! I'm going to stay right here until they get here. I was right!" I cried out. "I knew Jean and Blue Tara would come back for me." I stood, ears alert, and listened intently. I took a deep breath. "Jean!" I yelled, as loudly as possible. "Jean!" I yelled again. "Michael!"

"You do not understand," Kinqalatlala repeated. "They can not hear you. They can not help you. They do not possess the Water of Life. If they take your body back to their world, all hope is lost."

"You mean if they take me back to my world. And how do you know they are coming. You haven't left my sight. Are you telepathic or something?"

"This is your world now," Kinqalatlala replied. "Their world is no longer your world. You are dead to them. You are dead to your world. You are dead. You must continue the search for the tlogwe. If they find you they will only find your dead body."

"Tell me where to go, for god sakes," I replied, exasperated.

"I'll do better than that. I'll show you." Kinqalatlala whistled. She gazed up into the sky. I could hear the flapping of enormous wings. Wings pounding the air like pile drivers. Two great winged creatures appeared overhead. Gagits. The pterodactyls. They circled over the trees and glided to a landing in the clearing below the longhouse.

ΔΔΔ

With their huge scale-covered feet and giant claws the gagits awkwardly stepped to me and Kinqalatlala. The winged creatures dropped their heads to the ground submissively. Their breath, the putrid stench of death and decay, caused me to take a couple of steps back. "Mount their necks," Kinqalatlala commanded. "We will ride them into the sky." She straddled the neck of one of the gagits, taking clumps of long greasy hair in her hands for reins. "Do as I do," she added. Holding my breath, I gingerly climbed onto the neck of the second gagit. "Hold onto their hair," she called out.

Turning and taking several halting steps, the creatures stretched out their wings and leaped into the sky. Climbing rapidly with each powerful flap of gigantic wings, the gagits banked to the south. I could see Mount Rainier towering on the horizon before me. "Where are we going?" I yelled at Kinqalatlala over the noise of the flapping wings.

"We are going to the city of the Dluwulaxa. To my world above the clouds. You have much to learn about me."

"I think I know just about everything I want to know about you," I retorted.

"You need to understand why we should be allies and not enemies," she said. *Like that would ever happen*, I thought to myself. I peered over the gagit's neck and watched the landscape pass rapidly below me. The pterodactyl proved to be much better at flying than I expected. The slow steady flapping of the immense wings made for a smooth ride on the gagit's neck. Furthermore, the heat radiating from the creature's body kept me pleasantly warm even at altitude. We were flying well above tree top level, and climbing steadily. Mount Rainier loomed ever larger before us in the mountain's glacier capped glory. A massive lenticular cloud obscured Rainier's peak. The gagits flew directly for the cloud.

ΔΔΔ

The gagits flew a lazy circle around the summit and to my utter amazement landed on top of the lenticular cloud shrouding Rainier's peak. What appeared at first glance to be transparent and ethereal proved to be tangible and solid. A translucent sheet of pure crystal at our feet extended in every direction as far as I could see in the cloud. Wisps of cloud drifted over us, giving the scene an eerily surreal aspect. Kinqalatlala jumped off her gagit and took my hand, helping me dismount. "Come with me," she said, as the pterodactyls flapped their wings and took flight, disappearing into the clouds.

Seemingly appearing out of thin air, a building loomed before us. I realized the building was in fact a massive wall. A translucent crystal wall shimmered all the colors of the rainbow in the blazing sunlight above the clouds. Kinqalatlala waved her hand and a doorway appeared at the base of the wall. She led me to the doorway. I stood mystified in front of the structure. I ran my hand over the cool crystal surface. "The furies," I said. "Crystal made the furies fly."

"Come with me," Kinqalatlala replied. We passed through the doorway. Stepping inside I stopped. I stared in awe at an incomprehensible vista. As far as I could see. Nothing but crystal structure after crystal structure, walls towering into the sky and clouds. Hundreds if not thousands of crystal structures. Innumerable birds cavorted through the sky around and above the structures. Birds landed on clouds to rest. Large birds. Small birds. Black birds. Red birds. Blue birds. Green birds. Brown birds. Brightly rainbow colored birds. Flying. Circling. Soaring. Gliding with the wind. Birds stood on the translucent floor preening themselves. "Dluwulaxa," Kinqalatlala said, waving her hand toward the scene. "Welcome to my world."

"This is incredible," I replied, stunned. "This is your home?"

"This was my home. These are Dluwulaxa. These are my people."

"Can they see us? Talk to us""

"Unfortunately, no. Remember, you are not of the living. They do not see us."

"And there is no way for you to revert back to your original form?"

"There may be one way," she replied.

"What is that?"

"The one with the tlogwe may possess the magic to make that possible."

"So that's why you want me to find the tlogwe. To help you become Dluwulaxa again."

"And I can help you," Kinqalatlala replied. I gave her a blank stare. "I can give you the freedom of the sky. If you find the tlogwe and restore me to my world, you would possess the magic to join me in my world."

"By becoming a bird?"

"By becoming anything you wanted to be. You would possess that magic. You could make a home here in the world of the Dluwulaxa with me. A home free from strife. Free from conflict. Free from want. Free from jealousy. Free from pain. Free from Hamatsa."

"Shangri-La," I responded. "But at what cost? By becoming your slave?"

"By becoming my partner." She placed her arms over my shoulders and pulled me to her. She pressed her breasts against my chest. She kissed me. "Every dream. Every fantasy you have could be realized. I could show you a life of perfect freedom."

"And give up my world to be ground down by Hamatsa and the Winalagalis?" I pushed Kinqalatlala away from me. "Lady, I have a life. I want to get back to it." I turned and walked through the doorway back onto the cloud.

Chapter Five
Part One

"Listen!" Jean exclaimed, as she, Michael, and the Taras walked through the forest. Everyone halted. They could hear the flapping of enormous wings, flapping that moved away from them and faded into the distance.

"Gagits," Michael said. "The pterodactyls. They seem to be flying away."

"We are there," Blue Tara said, pointing into the forest. They could see the longhouse through the trees, with the double-headed serpent painted on the front wall, guarded by the totem of the four furies. Jean broke into a run. "Hey! Wait up," Michael yelled after her.

They found the longhouse deserted. Innumerable tracks and footprints in the clearing in front of the longhouse obscured any particular set of prints. Michael pointed to a muddy patch of ground. "Looks like blood," he said.

"There was no lack of blood," Jean replied uneasily.

"What do we do now?" Michael asked, to no one in particular.

"We wait," Blue Tara replied. "Be watchful."

"Wait for what?" Michael responded.

"For whatever comes," Blue Tara replied.

They didn't need to wait long. A flash of white light lit up the interior of the longhouse, like a strobe light. Bokwus, the Chief of the Dead, appeared at the door to the longhouse. "I come for Blue Tara," he stated.

"Of course you have," Michael replied, pointing the magic harpoon at the creature to no avail.

Jean pulled the shotgun off her shoulder, but Blue Tara grabbed the barrels to stop her. Blue Tara stepped to the Bokwus, battle axe in her hand. "What do you want with me?"

"My master has commanded me to take you," the living skeleton replied.

Blue Tara swung her battle axe and smashed the creature's skull. Another flash of light, and another living skeleton appeared in the longhouse's doorway. "I come for Blue Tara," the creature repeated.

"This is getting old," Michael replied.

Blue Tara stepped to the Bokwus. "If your master wants me, let him show himself." She swung her battle axe and lopped off the creature's skull. Margarita growled as a tall pale yellow-skinned figure with gleaming sunken red eyes hiding under the brim of a black leather fedora, his body clad in matching black leather, stepped out of the longhouse.

"Hamatsa!" Michael exclaimed. Before Michael could level the magic harpoon at Hamatsa a club flew out of the trees and struck Michael on the side of his head, knocking him to the ground unconscious. Jean dropped to her knees at Michael's side, relieved to find him bloodied but still breathing. Half a dozen giants covered with matted black hair, swinging huge clubs in their hands, appeared out of the forest surrounding the longhouse.

"Sasquatch!" Jean yelled.

"Dzonoqwa," Blue Tara replied.

Behind them appeared an equal number of deathly pale phantoms with wild black hair and sunken red eyes, clad in tattered western clothing, carrying lances. "Beware the laxsa," Red Tara cautioned. "Warriors of the spirit world. Zombies."

Hamatsa strode directly to Blue Tara. "You were pitifully easy to capture," he chortled.

"I could say the same," Blue Tara replied, holding her battle axe in her hand. Red Tara pulled her longbow off her shoulder.

"If you resist me, your friend is lost," Hamatsa said.

"What have you done with him?" Jean yelled, scrambling to her feet, shotgun in hand. Blue Tara grabbed the barrels to restrain Jean.

"You would make a tasty meal," Hamatsa said, extending a gloved hand toward Jean's throat. Red Tara nocked an arrow in her bow and aimed the point at Hamatsa's head. "I can not be killed by you," Hamatsa said. "But I can destroy your friend."

"What do you want?" Jean cried.

"What do I want?" Hamatsa replied. "Is that not painfully clear? I want this witch," he replied haughtily, pointing at Blue Tara.

"There are twenty other Taras," Blue Tara said. "Destroy me, but you will still have to deal with them."

"There is only one Blue Tara. The mother of all the Taras.

"And what do you offer in return?" Blue Tara asked, pointing her battle axe at Hamatsa.

"You are in no position to bargain. I could destroy you all."

"If that was the case you would have done so already."

"Do not test my patience."

"Restore our friend and I will surrender to you," Blue Tara said.

"What? No you won't!" Jean exclaimed. "I won't let you."

"Do not interfere," Blue Tara replied. "This is something I must do."

Jean pointed the shotgun at Hamatsa. Red Tara grabbed the barrels and yanked the weapon out of Jean's hands before she could pull the trigger. "This is all part of the plan," Red Tara whispered.

"Plan? What plan?" Jean replied.

"I am sorry sweetie, but we must go our separate ways," Blue Tara said, turning to face Jean. "Do not fear for me. I have foreseen this. Understand that this is the only way to get your friend back to you alive."

"You can't do this," Jean cried, dashing to Blue Tara. Several of the laxsa rushed between the two, pushing Jean back with their lances.

Hamatsa stepped to Blue Tara. He put a gloved hand on her breast. "You will be served up to me as a special feast," he gloated. "Take her!" he commanded the dzonoqwa. One of the giants snatched the battle axe out of Blue Tara's hand. The weapon nearly slipped out of his fingers before he managed to secure his grip on the handle. Another dzonoqwa snapped a steel collar around her neck, attached to a long chain held in his hand. Smirking, Hamatsa entered the longhouse. Blue Tara and the ghouls surrounding her quickly followed. Another flash of brilliant white light briefly illuminated the inside of the structure, revealing fantastical demons painted on the walls with black and red and yellow ochre.

"Stop!" Jean yelled. She ran after Blue Tara, but halted at the doorway. "They're gone!" she cried out. Jean found the building dark and empty.

"Let them go," Red Tara replied, handing the shotgun back to Jean. "This is all part of the plan."

"What plan?" Michael asked, pushing himself up, struggling to get to his feet. Jean dropped to his side. "Whoa! What the hell happened? My head feels like it's going to explode." Margarita rubbed her body against Michael's ankles and purred.

"You were knocked out by one of the Sasquatch," Jean replied.

"Knocked out? Feels like my head got knocked off. Oh, that hurts," he said, feeling the side of his head with his fingers.

"Just a bruise," Jean said, lying. "Thankfully the bleeding has stopped. Can you stand up?" she asked. She helped Michael climb to his feet. He stood unsteady, one hand against the totem of the furies, his knees wobbling as he stared at his blood-stained fingers.

Red Tara picked up the magic harpoon with one of her four hands and handed the death stick to Michael. "Maybe this will work better as a crutch than as a weapon," she quipped.

Michael glared at her. "So, what plan are you talking about?" Michael pressed Red Tara. "Why don't I know anything about a plan?"

"First I've heard anything about a plan," Jean added. Jean asked Red Tara, "Why haven't you shared this plan with us? You're just leading us around blindly."

"This was necessary to get your friend back," Red Tara replied. "Our ultimate goal is to find the tlogwe. The only way to defeat Hamatsa is by finding the tlogwe. With the magic of the tlogwe we can rescue my sister and destroy Hamatsa."

"Why didn't you tell us?" Jean asked, perturbed.

"We could not take the chance, as long as your friend is in Hamatsa's hands. My sister Blue Tara knew this was a sacrifice she would need to make to keep Hamatsa from destroying your friend."

"Where is he?" Jean asked plaintively. "Why isn't he here?"

"Listen," Michael responded, putting his hand on Jean's shoulder. In the distance they could hear the flapping of enormous wings, flying toward them.

ΔΔΔ

Leaning over the neck of the pterodactyl I rode I could discern the longhouse in the clearing below us, the brightly painted double-headed serpent clearly visible on the front wall. The two gagits banked into a tight circle and descended toward the ground. I could make out several people huddled in the clearing in front of the longhouse. I recognized Red Tara first. Hard to miss a four-armed red-skinned Amazonian goddess with a longbow slung over her shoulder. Then I recognized Jean and Michael and Margarita. I began to yell and wave one hand while holding onto the pterodactyl with the other. I could see Jean waving her arms below.

The creature's wings still flapping, I jumped off the gagit's neck to run to Jean. I threw my arms around her and kissed her. Jean put her hands to my face and kissed me back. Jean tore my shirt open and rubbed her fingers across my chest. "You're alive!" she cried. "I watched you die. That witch stabbed you with her hand." Jean's fingers caressed my chest. I felt Margarita's head rubbing against my ankle. I glanced down to see Margarita purring up at me.

The second pterodactyl landed. Kinqalatlala slipped off the creature's neck. Jean pushed away from me. She pulled the shotgun off her shoulder. "It was her!" she screamed. "She killed you." Jean pointed the shotgun at Kinqalatlala.

"Wait!" I cried. "Don't shoot!" I jumped between Jean and Kinqalatlala. "She saved my life!" I exclaimed. I put my hands out to try to keep the two women apart.

"She killed you," Jean repeated.

"She saved my life," I replied. "Blue Tara made her kill me."

Michael hesitantly stepped to me. "What are you talking about? Jean said she saw you die." Michael stared at me in wide-eyed confusion. "Blue Tara made who kill you?"

"Blue Tara could have saved me, but didn't," I replied. "She let Kinqalatlala kill me so I could enter the spirit realm to search for the tlogwe."

Michael warily put his hand on my arm. "So are you alive? Or dead?"

"Your friend is alive," Kinqalatlala said, stepping to my side. Jean held her shotgun ready. "Hamatsa fulfilled his part of the bargain."

"Bargain? What bargain?" I asked, confused, glancing between Michael and Kinqalatlala. "Where is Blue Tara?" A sense of panic threatened to overwhelm me.

"Hamatsa took Blue Tara," Jean replied. "She gave herself up to Hamatsa to save your life."

"Oh no!" I cried. "What have you done?" I asked Kinqalatlala, grabbing her shoulders.

"I have shown you the possibilities," she replied. "The blue witch chose to trade her life for yours."

I shook Kinqalatlala. "Is Blue Tara dead? What did Hamatsa do to her?"

"The witch you call Blue Tara is not dead. That is not my master's plan for her."

"We have to save her," I said. I turned to Jean. "I thought I lost you. I watched you get killed by that magic harpoon," I said as I noticed Michael holding a magic harpoon in his hand.

"I didn't die," Jean replied. "You saved me. You pushed me out of the way at the last moment. That's when I saw that witch stab you with her hand," she said, pointing the shotgun at Kinqalatlala.

"Well, apparently I was dead," I replied. "She did kill me. But she also saved me from Hamatsa. I guess killing me was part of the plan. . ." I looked at Kinqalatlala and then back at Jean, ". . . part of Blue Tara's plan for me to find the tlogwe. Somehow she," I pointed at Kinqalatlala, "and Blue Tara are connected in the plan to find the tlogwe."

"I don't trust this witch," Jean said. "I've seen what she's capable of. She's Hamatsa's slave. I should shoot her where she stands."

"She showed me another world that's beyond our comprehension," I told Jean. "She's not what she appears to be."

"Nothing is what anything appears to be anymore," Jean replied with some exasperation. "What is she supposed to be?"

"She is Dluwulaxa. She comes from a world above the clouds."

Jean stared at me, her mournful brown eyes clouded with confusion. "What is Dluwulaxa?" she asked, perplexity coloring her voice.

"People who descend from the sky," Michael replied. "Ancient northwest coast legends talk about a world of bird people above the clouds who occasionally fly down to the ground. They're shapeshifters. They can take on human or animal form."

"But once they do so," I said, "they can never go back to their world. She's one of them."

"And you believe her?" Jean asked.

"Not only do I believe her. She took me to the city of Dluwulaxa above the clouds. Her world in the sky. I saw her world with my own eyes. She wants to help me find the tlogwe so I can use the magic of the tlogwe to restore her to her world."

"I don't believe her for a minute," Jean replied. "I saw her hand sticking through your chest. I saw you standing in a pool of your own blood."

"I only want to return to my world," Kinqalatlala stated. "In return I will help you find the tlogwe and help you rescue that witch you call Blue Tara. I only ask that you consider my offer to join me in my world."

"What?" Jean said. "What is she talking about?"

"She wants me to become Dluwulaxa. To join her world above the clouds."

"No fucking way!" Jean exclaimed. She jumped at Kinqalatlala. Before I could react Jean slammed the butt of her shotgun against Kinqalatlala's head, knocking her onto her back, unconscious. "She's playing you for a fool!" Jean yelled at me. "You need to focus on your world! And your friends!"

"I did," I replied. "I turned her down cold. All I wanted was to get back to you. I love you Jean."

Kinqalatlala groaned and struggled to get up. I took hold of her hands and helped her to her feet. "You're bleeding," I said. Red blood oozed out of her black hair. She took my hand and pressed my fingers against the side of her head. She drew lines of blood across her breasts with my fingers.

"We should kill her and then figure out how we're going to rescue Blue Tara," Jean said.

"We can't kill her," I replied.

"And why not?"

"She knows where the tlogwe is. And she knows where Blue Tara is." I saw Jean staring at Kinqalatlala's hand holding mine. I pulled my hand out of Kinqalatlala's grasp.

Part Two

I noticed the bloody gash on the side of Michael's head. "Jesus Holy Christ!" I exclaimed. "What in the hell happened to you?"

"Dzonoqwa," Michael replied. "Or Sasquatch, as Jean calls them. More of Hamatsa's ghouls. They took Blue Tara away in chains." Michael pointed toward the longhouse.

"Oh my god. We've got to rescue her!" I cried out. I dashed to the longhouse to peer into the darkened interior.

"We will rescue Blue Tara. In time," Red Tara replied. She had been standing on one foot so quietly, right foot resting against her left knee, I forgot she was there. "Your plan to rescue her is already underway as she has foreseen."

"My plan?" I replied, confused. "I don't have a plan."

"Your plan is to find the tlogwe," Red Tara said.

"We need to kill this witch," Jean said, pointing her shotgun at Kinqalatlala. "I don't trust her. You're making a big mistake if you let her join us."

155

"We need her help," I replied. "I need her help to find Blue Tara."

"Then make her tell us where Hamatsa and Blue Tara are. And then we kill her."

I returned to Jean. I grasped her shoulders. "I don't know how to make her tell us, or I would. I don't trust her either. Completely. But we need her. We need to find the tlogwe and rescue Blue Tara. She can help us with that. And then we can deal with her."

"Or better yet," Michael offered, "We can let Hamatsa deal with her."

"I like that plan even better," I replied.

"You need to trust me," Kinqalatlala said. "I am the only weapon you have to use against Hamatsa."

"I'd prefer to blow your head off, and deal with the consequences," Jean said.

"You do not understand," Kinqalatlala replied. "Your weapons are useless against me. Go ahead and shoot me, if you do not believe me. I possess the magic to travel between the worlds of the living and the dead. Otherwise your friend would not be standing here with you."

"Don't tempt me," Jean replied.

"You are in my debt," Kinqalatlala insisted. "I could easily send your friend back to the world below this one, if I so chose." Kinqalatlala raised her hand to her

156

face and watched her hand transform into a steel blade. Jean pulled her shotgun off her shoulder and swung the barrels toward Kinqalatlala. I grabbed the barrels and pointed them at the ground.

"Everybody relax!" I yelled, my heart racing, far from relaxed. "We need her, Jean. I promise you, if she double-crosses us, I'll tie her to a post and let you blow her head off. Until then, we need her to lead us to Hamatsa and Blue Tara."

"I promise you," Kinqalatlala said, as the steel blade reverted back to her hand, "I will help you rescue that witch you call Blue Tara. I will help you destroy Hamatsa. I will do whatever I need to do to earn my freedom to return to my world of Dluwulaxa."

"As long as you understand you're going alone. He is my friend," Jean said, pointing to me. "Not your friend."

Kinqalatlala stepped to Jean. "You owe this to me. Allow me the chance to earn your trust. If I fail you, then I will submit to whatever punishment you choose."

"Can you at least put on some clothes," Jean replied, her naturally pale face flushed red with embarrassment.

"Hold on," Michael said. He pulled his shirt over his head. He handed the shirt to Kinqalatlala. "This should help. And please take care of my Ralph Lauren." I stared at Michael. "What? I got the shirt at Value Village. And I believe in layering. I've still got two T-shirts on," he said, pulling up his T-shirt to show another tee underneath.

"Nothing like being prepared," I quipped.

"I have to say," Michael continued. "I'm with Jean on this one. I have a really bad feeling about taking her along," he said, pointing at Kinqalatlala.

"What do the Taras have to say about all this?" I asked, turning to Red Tara and Margarita. Margarita growled and rubbed her body against Michael's ankles.

"We take her at her word," Red Tara replied. "If she fails us, I still have recourse to this," she said, tapping her longbow.

Growling softly, Margarita stretched up on her hind legs. She spoke, "It is time for this witch to lead us to Hamatsa."

"Okay," I said, turning to Kinqalatlala. "This is your show now. How do we find Hamatsa and Blue Tara?"

"Follow me," Kinqalatlala replied. She stepped into the longhouse. We followed her inside the darkened space. "Take a seat along the wall," she continued. We sat on a polished cedar log placed against the wall.

"Now what?" I asked.

"We wait for the ceremony."

"What ceremony?" I asked, perplexed.

"Wait," she replied.

ΔΔΔ

Brilliant light illuminated the longhouse, light so bright I reflexively shielded my eyes with my hand. The wall at the far end of the longhouse appeared to turn into a sheet of pure light. The sound of sticks beating cedar planks filled the room. Half a dozen dark-skinned men and women dressed in deerskin cloaks and cedar bark blankets marched out of the light to sit in a circle in the center of the hall, beating time on cedar planks. My skin crawled like a tarantula fell into my lap when I realized the light revealed a swarm of serpents and dragons and demons painted on the cedar plank wall behind me with black and red and yellow ochre so realistically I thought they might come to life and spring at me. The demons disappeared into the darkness that replaced the light.

Several men dressed similarly to the drummers carried logs and sticks into the longhouse through the doorway. They constructed a bonfire at the center of the circle. Men with deathly pale skin and sunken blood red eyes appeared out of the darkness at the back of the longhouse carrying lances. They formed a circle around the drummers. "Laxsa," Michael observed.

Grizzly bear dancers danced out of the darkness in time with the drumming. Fierce men wearing bearskin cloaks with bear skulls tied to their heads like crowns, they held menacing razor-sharp bear claws in their hands. Each dancer stopped and stood in front of each of us.

159

A tall gaunt man clad in black leather from boots to fedora and gloves stepped out of the darkness following the grizzly bear dancers. The flickering light of the bonfire illuminated his pallid scalloped yellow face and burning red eyes. "Hamatsa!" I exclaimed. Jean took my hand. He stopped near the bonfire and fixed his gleaming red eyes directly on me.

"You have witnessed the power I hold over life and death," he said. "And yet you choose to challenge me."

"Do I have a speaking part?" I whispered to Kinqalatlala.

"Be patient," she replied.

"Now is the time for me to demonstrate my power once and for all," Hamatsa continued. "My power to stamp out any resistance to my dominion. My power to stamp out the scourge of those that oppose me." Out of the corner of my eye I could see Red Tara slip her longbow off her shoulder.

Hamatsa waved a gloved hand toward the darkness at the back of the hall. Four giants covered head to foot with matted black hair so greasy the hair appeared to be fur, bearskin capes draped across their shoulders, emerged into the light of the bonfire carrying a large cedar box. "Sasquatch," Jean observed.

"Dzonoqwa," Michael replied.

The dzonoqwa placed the cedar box next to the fire. Two more of the giant creatures emerged out of the darkness. "Oh my god!" I cried out. I tried to jump to my feet, but Red Tara grabbed my arm to restrain me.

The dzonoqwa led Blue Tara into the center of the hall by a long chain attached to a steel collar around her neck. The beating of the cedar planks stopped. "I intend to stamp out the scourge of the resistance once and for all," Hamatsa continued. "Bring that witch to me." The two dzonoqwa holding Blue Tara's chain pushed her to Hamatsa. "Get down on your knees before your master!" Hamatsa ordered. One of the dzonoqwa kicked Blue Tara behind her knees. She buckled to the ground. "Are you ready to submit to your master?" Hamatsa demanded. Blue Tara tilted her head and defiantly stared up at Hamatsa with her one gleaming yellow eye. Hamatsa slapped her across her face with a gloved hand. "Submit or be destroyed," he demanded. Blue Tara said nothing. "Take her," he ordered the dzonoqwa. "Place her in the box." The dzonoqwa lifted Blue Tara by her arms.

"No!" I yelled as I leaped to my feet. Michael jumped to his feet. He pointed the magic harpoon at one dzonoqwa, who crumpled to the ground. Red Tara stood at my side. She nocked and released an arrow at the other dzonoqwa. The arrow pierced the creature's skull between his eyes and the creature tumbled over backwards, and did not get up. The laxsa spun around. They pointed their lances at our heads.

"Your heroics are useless here," Hamatsa insisted. "My army is vast. You can change nothing."

161

"Don't bet on that," I replied. I pushed aside a couple of the laxsa and stepped to Hamatsa. "Take me," I said. "Release Blue Tara." That was the adrenaline talking. I'm not usually that brave or selfless.

"What are you doing?" Jean screamed. She tried to push her way to my side but the laxsa blocked her with their lances. "You don't need to do that!" Jean yelled.

"Why would I trade the life of that witch for yours?" Hamatsa asked.

"Because I am the key to finding the tlogwe. Without the tlogwe the Taras are powerless against you."

His long red tongue licking his lips, baring his fangs, Hamatsa chortled. "Take him," he ordered. Two of the dzonoqwa grabbed me. "Release the witch." A dzonoqwa took hold of the steel collar and snapped the collar in two, leaving bloody gashes on Blue Tara's neck from his razor-sharp claws. "Put him in the box," Hamatsa commanded. The dzonoqwa lifted me off my feet and carried me to the cedar box. Their putrid breath nearly caused me to gag.

"Wait!" someone yelled. I struggled in the grip of the dzonoqwa to see who spoke. Kinqalatlala pushed her way through the ring of laxsa.

"You dare interfere?" Hamatsa exclaimed furiously.

Kinqalatlala fell to her knees. She dropped her head to the ground to kiss Hamatsa's boots. "My master," she said. "I offer myself as a sacrifice in his place. Take me instead."

Hamatsa grasped Kinqalatlala's hair with a gloved hand and pulled her to her feet. "Why would I do that?" he asked.

"Because I know where the tlogwe is. Destroy me. Then the Taras, and the man with the parrot, will be powerless to stop you."

"You dare to oppose me?" Hamatsa said, seizing Kinqalatlala's throat in his gloved hand, lifting her off her feet.

Kinqalatlala struggled to speak as Hamatsa choked her. "I had thought to trade the tlogwe for my freedom."

"You fool." Hamatsa dropped her onto the ground. He ripped Michael's shirt off her.

"Not my Ralph Lauren!" Michael exclaimed.

Hamatsa nodded at the dzonoqwa. They lifted me out of the cedar box. They seized Kinqalatlala, dropping her into the box in my place. They quickly hammered a large plank lid onto the box and set the box directly into the bonfire. A deathly stillness engulfed the longhouse as the bonfire slowly consumed the crate. I could hear Kinqalatlala plaintively chanting from inside the box as sticks commenced beating time on cedar planks:

"I keep down your wrath, great cannibal Hamatsa.
I keep down your whistles, great cannibal Hamatsa.
I keep down your voraciousness, great cannibal Hamatsa.

163

You are always devouring property, great cannibal Hamatsa.
You are always devouring food, great cannibal Hamatsa.
You are always devouring heads, great cannibal Hamatsa."

After what seemed like an eternity the last vestiges of the cedar coffin collapsed in ashes into the fire. "Destroy them all!" Hamatsa ordered, sweeping his gloved hand across the wall where Jean and Michael and Red Tara stood.

I heard Jean yell "Fuck You!" She pumped her shotgun and fired both barrels at Hamatsa's head. His fedora and his head underneath the hat disappeared in a cloud of blood red pulp. I fell to the ground in agony with my hands slapped over my ears as Blue Tara screeched, my eyes squeezed shut trying to close out the pain from my head. When I dared to open my eyes I saw Blue Tara and Red Tara helping Jean and Michael to their feet while Margarita lay curled up on the ground licking her fur. I realized the longhouse was otherwise empty. No dzonoqwa. No laxsa. No grizzly bear dancers. No Hamatsa. No Kinqalatlala. I pushed myself up on my knees.

"What. . . what the hell happened?" I stammered.

A gleaming smile bright enough to light the longhouse broke across Blue Tara's face. She grasped my arms to lift me up on my feet. She threw her arms over my shoulders and pulled me to her, pressing her breast into my chest. "I made them go away," she told me. And then she kissed me. And I let her.

I felt Jean's hand on my shoulder pulling me back from Blue Tara. "Is Blue Tara okay?" Jean asked, worry etched across her face.

I saw blood oozing down Blue Tara's neck from the gashes made by the dzonoqwa's claws. "You're hurt," I said.

"Nothing to worry about," she replied.

"What did they do to you?" Jean asked.

"Hamatsa could do nothing to me," Blue Tara said. "In spite of what Hamatsa believes, he has no power over me. His magic can not hurt me."

I turned to Jean and kissed her. "Jean killed Hamatsa," I said. "Blew his head off. That means he's dead. Right?"

"Life and death are meaningless in this world of the dead," Blue Tara replied. "You have destroyed his body, but you have not destroyed Hamatsa. Only the magic of the tlogwe can do that. I fear that we will face Hamatsa and his army of the dead again soon enough."

"I have no idea where to find the tlogwe," I said. "Kinqalatlala knows. . . knew," I corrected myself, "where the tlogwe is. I think she was about to tell me. But the tlogwe is lost to us now without her."

"Do not give up hope," Blue Tara replied. "You are closer to finding the tlogwe than you realize."

ΔΔΔ

Hamatsa and Kinqalatlala stood together in a void. Blackness illuminated only by Hamatsa's gleaming red eyes. "Does the one with the parrot believe you?" Hamatsa asked Kinqalatlala.

"Yes, my master."

"He believes you will help him find the tlogwe in exchange for your freedom?"

"Yes, my master."

"He will help restore you to the Dluwulaxa?"

"I believe he will, master."

"Do you believe he will succumb to your entreaties to join him in the world of the Dluwulaxa?"

"The men of his world are weak, my master. He will succumb to these," she said, taking Hamatsa's gloved hands and placing them on her breasts.

"With you as my queen I will command the worlds of the earth and the sky," Hamatsa gloated.

Part Three

I sat down on a log outside the longhouse and flipped a couple of pebbles toward the mudflats extending down into Elliott Bay. "I'm open to suggestions," I muttered, to no one in particular. "If anyone has any good ideas about what we should do next, now's the time to share." I turned toward Blue Tara. "What did you mean when you said I was closer to the tlogwe than I realized? Why does everyone keep talking in riddles? I wish someone would just tell me what to do."

"Jean sat down on the log next to me and put her arm around my shoulder. "What would be the fun of that?" she joked. "Life should be a struggle. Nothing should come easy." I stuck my tongue out at her. "Is that an invitation?" she asked.

"I wish," I replied. I rested my head on her shoulder.

"You said that Kinqalatlala was about to tell you where the tlogwe is," Michael said. I nodded. "With her dead that puts us in a bind," he added. "You have no clue where it is?"

"Oh, big clue alrighty," I replied. Michael gave me a perplexed look. "Dluwulaxa. The city above the clouds. That has something to do with it. And I'm pretty sure the tlogwala is a bird." I turned and pointed to the totem of the four furies guarding the doorway to the longhouse. "And I'm also pretty sure Kinqalatlala knew who the tlogwala is."

"I think we can safely say who the tlogwala isn't," Michael replied.

"Hamatsa," I said.

"Precisely."

"Dluwulaxa holds the key to this riddle. The city above the clouds. The world of the bird people."

"And you saw Dluwulaxa?" Michael asked.

"Not only did I see Dluwulaxa, Kinqalatlala gave me a personal tour. Get this. The city is constructed entirely of crystal."

"The four furies!" Michael exclaimed, glancing at the totem.

"And the connection to Hamatsa," I replied. "If the tlogwe is located in the world of the bird people, then the Dluwulaxa are not safe from Hamatsa."

"Imagine if Hamatsa gained control of the skies," Michael said. "Those of us on the ground would be in a world of hurt."

"Which is why we needed Kinqalatlala," I added.

"As I told you," Blue Tara interjected, "you are closer to the tlogwe than you think." I stared in awe to see both Blue Tara and Red Tara resting quietly on one foot, their right feet pressed against their left knees. My jaw dropped as a small parrot with white feathers highlighted in pink darted out of the sky and landed on Blue Tara's shoulder. Red Tara screeched with joy. She jumped to Blue Tara's side. Margarita howled. She jumped up on her hind legs, stretching her front paws above her head.

"Oh my," Jean said. "A Goffin's cockatoo."

Blue Tara put her hand up to her shoulder. The white parrot hopped onto her hand. "Greetings to you, my sister," Blue Tara said. "I had wondered when you would make your appearance."

"Always my pleasure to answer your call, my sister Ekajati," the white parrot replied.

Red Tara bowed before the newcomer. "I am so happy to be in your company once again, my sister White Tara."

"White Tara!" I exclaimed. "Are all the Taras parrots?"

Standing on her hind legs, Margarita growled. "Of course not!" she blurted out.

"My apologies," I replied, nodding to Margarita.

"No apologies required," White Tara said. She bolted off Blue Tara's hand and landed on my knee as I sat on the log.

"My sister White Tara is the Tara of healing," Margarita added.

"So this is the one that Blue Tara chose to be our savior?" White Tara remarked, her head cocked with one pink eye pinned to my face.

"Savior?" I replied. "Not hardly. Not sure who's saving whom anymore."

White Tara turned her head to fix her other pink eye on me. "He seems somewhat unprepossessing," she said. "Whatever caused you to pick this one?"

"That's me," I replied, laughing. "I'm the epitome of unprepossessing." I put my hand out to White Tara. Without warning she nipped my finger with her beak. "Ouch!" I exclaimed, pulling my hand back. Blood appeared on my finger from a small tear caused by her beak. I stuck my finger in my mouth to lick off the blood.

"Assumptions can be your downfall," White Tara scolded me. "You assumed you could safely stick your finger in my beak just because I am a Tara. Let that be a lesson."

"Goffin's cockatoos are the juvenile delinquents of the parrot world," Jean interjected. "They should come with warning labels. Always smart to be on your guard."

"Wise words from a lovely lady," White Tara commented. "Give me your finger," she added. I didn't respond. "Put your finger out to me," White Tara commanded sternly. I hesitantly offered White Tara the bleeding finger. She tapped the finger with her beak. The blood and gash disappeared.

"My word!" Jean exclaimed.

"The timing of my arrival seems to be propitious," White Tara said.

"There is one you need to restore to us," Blue Tara said. "One that holds the key to the tlogwe."

"Most certainly," White Tara replied.

"Kinqalatlala!" I blurted out. "You can bring Kinqalatlala back to life?"

"Apparently my sister Taras have been deficient in your education," White Tara responded. "You know nothing of the magic of the witches. Witches like Kinqalatlala exist in a reality where there are not boundaries between life and death. A reality where existence is defined by being or not being. A reality where existence has no beginning and no end."

"I'm sorry," I replied, "but this is getting way too deep for me."

"That is because your reality is too linear and inflexible," Blue Tara said. "My sister, White Tara, the Tara of healing, possesses the magic to restore Kinqalatlala to existence."

"Now you're talking language I can understand," I said as I jumped to my feet. White Tara flew off my knee and twirled into the air. The white parrot melted into a translucent white mirage of a magnificent woman with pink hair and seven pink eyes, one in the middle of her forehead as well as one on each hand and foot. The mirage solidified into a goddess of pure white skin clad in a multitude of brilliantly colored gauzy silken skirts, with a filmy pink silken scarf wrapped around her neck accenting her sculpted breasts.

"My god!" Jean exclaimed. "Don't any of the Taras believe in proper clothes?" I could feel my face flush as Jean stared at me.

"Take me to the one you wish me to restore," White Tara said.

"This way," Blue Tara replied, leading the way into the longhouse. We circled the ashes of the bonfire. I could see what appeared to be charred bones in the ashes.

White Tara removed one of her skirts and flung the skirt over the ashes. "This is where a lesser witch would spout some nonsense chant to impress the gullible," she remarked, looking directly at me. "I will just raise my hand over the victim's remains." She lifted her hand over the skirt spread across the remains of the bonfire. As she lifted her hand the skirt came off the floor and the figure of a woman took shape and rose underneath the skirt. Once the skirt stopped rising, White Tara grasped the fabric and yanked the skirt away from the body.

Kinqalatlala stood before us, naked, but seemingly unhurt. And very much alive. Kinqalatlala blinked her eyes and smiled. Seeing me, she dashed to me and threw her arms over my shoulders. She kissed me. "You saved me!" Kinqalatlala exclaimed.

"Hold on a minute!" Jean cried out.

White Tara raised her right foot, pressed the foot against her left knee, extended her arms and twirled, dissolving into a white Goffin's cockatoo parrot. The parrot flapped her wings and flew onto Kinqalatlala's shoulder. She bit Kinqalatlala's ear. "Ouch!" Kinqalatlala exclaimed, brushing the bird off her shoulder.

White Tara darted onto my shoulder. "Just checking," White Tara said. "That is to remind you who just saved your sorry ass."

"No reminder necessary," Kinqalatlala replied, bowing to the white parrot. "I am in your debt."

"And you are expected to repay that debt." White Tara brushed her beak against my chin. "I still do not understand what these witches see in you," she whispered in my ear. "Yet this black witch jumped into your arms, without so much as a thank you."

"Maybe because of your sparkling personality," I replied, only partly in jest.

White Tara tried to nip my ear but I brushed her off and she hopped onto Red Tara's longbow. "Chew that bow," Red Tara stated, "and I will use you for target practice."

"Enough," Blue Tara interjected. "Now that we have Kinqalatlala restored to us we can resume our search for the tlogwe."

"I am at your service," Kinqalatlala replied, bowing to Blue Tara.

"I'm guessing the tlogwe is hidden somewhere in the city of the Dluwulaxa," I said. "I think you were just about to tell me where before Hamatsa interrupted us."

Kinqalatlala took my hand in hers. "You are very astute. The Dluwulaxa are in fact guarding the tlogwe."

"Hamatsa is as much a threat to your world as he is to mine," I said. "Can you take us to the tlogwe? To the tlogwala?"

"The tlogwe is a gift of magic. The ultimate treasure. The tlogwe is not something I can show you."

"Here we go with the riddles again," I replied with a note of exasperation.

"I can not show you the tlogwe. But I can take you to the tlogwala. The tlogwala will determine if you are worthy enough to receive the tlogwe."

"Well," Michael interjected. "Let's get this show on the road. Please lead us to the tlogwala." White Tara jumped off Blue Tara's shoulder and alighted on Michael's shoulder. And screeched. "Not in my ear! Please," Michael exclaimed as he slapped the palm of his hand to his ear.

"I like you," White Tara replied. "A man who knows what he wants. You are not so unprepossessing," White Tara added.

"I'll take that as a compliment," Michael replied with a grin. Margarita jumped up on her hind legs and growled at the parrot. Margarita crouched and sprang up onto Michael's shoulder, pushing White Tara off and back to Blue Tara's shoulder.

"So, Dluwulaxa," I said. "How do we get back up there?" I pointed toward Mount Rainier looming to the south, a cap of lenticular clouds anchored to the mountain's peak, the world of the Dluwulaxa.

Kinqalatlala turned to face the mountain and whistled. Within moments we could hear the slow flapping of enormous wings. Soon half a dozen gagits, the pterodactyls, appeared in the sky bearing down toward us. Flying overhead they spread their twenty

174

foot wings and banked into a tight circle, gliding to a landing on the mudflats below us.

"Let's mount up boys and girls!" I called out.

Kinqalatlala reached for my hand but Jean jumped between us and took my hand in hers. "Never flown a pterodactyl before," she joked.

"Interestingly enough, I have," I smirked. "Quite the ride. Grab some hair in each hand and hold on."

"Oh, I've ridden horses bareback since I was a kid," Jean replied. "Shouldn't be much different." My estimation of Jean kept climbing.

We mounted the gagits. Margarita rode Michael's shoulder. White Tara perched on Blue Tara's shoulder. Kinqalatlala whistled again and the gagits spread their wings, took several halting steps, and leapt into the air. The creatures rapidly climbed into the sky with each powerful flap of their wings. Airborne, the gagits banked to the south and flew up the Duwamish River directly toward the mountain looming on the horizon before us. My eyes fixed on the lenticular clouds capping the summit of the volcano. I tried to imagine a world lost above those clouds, like Shangri-La.

ΔΔΔ

Jean shouted to me from an adjacent gagit. "Why doesn't Blue Tara just time and space bend us up there with her magic?"

"Probably because she's never been there. She may be a parrot, but she's not of the world of the Dluwulaxa. Come to think of it, I didn't see any parrots up there when I was there. Dluwulaxa is a bird world, but not a parrot world." I shrugged. "Actually, I don't have a clue."

"Dluwulaxa is not of this world," Blue Tara shouted from the gagit she rode flying slightly above us. "I do not know what power my magic will have in that world."

ΔΔΔ

The gagits flew directly for the lenticular clouds shrouding the mountain's peak and we soon found ourselves flying into fog. The gagits broke through the clouds into brilliant sunshine and alighted on the crystalline plain that supported the city of the Dluwulaxa. The crystal palace that was the city of the Dluwulaxa towered before us, the city's wall extending as far as we could see across the horizon. The crystal wall climbed straight up into the sky seemingly without limit. Sunlight streaming through the crystal wall bathed the plain in every color imaginable. The gagits lay their heads down on the crystal plain and we dismounted. "We're standing in a rainbow!" Jean exclaimed with delight.

The pterodactyls turned, spread their wings, and leaped back into the sky. The winged creatures quickly disappeared into the clouds below us. We stood on the crystal plain and marveled at the gleaming structure before us. "This is incredible!" Michael exclaimed.

Margarita growled and jumped off Michael's shoulder, landing on her hind legs. "I don't like this for one minute," Margarita complained. "This is a mistake."

Kinqalatlala walked ahead of us toward the crystal wall. She waved her hand. A doorway appeared at the base of the wall. "You are perfectly safe here in my world," she replied. "You have my word."

"Will your people be able to see us? Talk to us?" I asked.

"Yes. We are in the world of the living."

We stepped through the doorway. Kinqalatlala paused at the doorway and waited for us to enter the city. Once inside, she waved her hand again. The doorway morphed into crystal wall and disappeared. I stopped, stunned. The hundreds if not thousands of massive crystal buildings spread out before me all gleamed every imaginable color of the rainbow in the brilliant sunlight. My jaw dropped to my shoes. Instead of the myriad variety of birds I had seen before, now I saw a multitude of people. The people, each and every one of them, all of the thousands of people we saw standing before us, they all appeared identical. Not only did they all appear identical, each and every one of them looked exactly like Kinqalatlala. Tall. Dark skinned. Black haired. Svelt. Athletic. And naked. We all turned and stared at Kinqalatlala.

Chapter Six
Part One

The thousands of Kinqalatlalas in the crystal city before us all stopped and turned to stare at us. "Someone want to tell me what's going on here?" I asked, perplexed.

"I think this is where the black witch explains why everyone in her world looks like her," White Tara replied.

"To make you comfortable. For you see my people in a form that is familiar to you," Kinqalatlala responded.

"Seeing everyone looking exactly like you makes me distinctly uncomfortable," I stated. "If your people are shapeshifters, why can't they take different shapes? Like birds. That was much less unsettling to look at."

"I am sorry you find me unpleasant to look at."

"What? No. That is not at all what I mean. You should know that."

"I only know what you tell me."

"Seeing all these people looking exactly like you makes me a bit confused. And a tad uncomfortable."

One of the Kinqalatlalas of the thousands standing before us walked out of the crowd and stopped in front of us. "Welcome to Dluwulaxa," she said. "Know that I speak for all of Dluwulaxa when I tell you I am pleased to see you again, Kinqalatlala," she added, bowing to the original. "We had feared you were lost to us."

"I am happy to be home again," Kinqalatlala replied. "I hope the time comes soon that I can return to my world."

"Is this the one?" the duplicate asked, looking at me.

"The one what?" I responded.

Kinqalatlala put her hand on my shoulder. "This is the one who is searching for the tlogwe."

Michael stepped to my side. "We have been assured that the tlogwe is located here in your city. How about you just show us where the tlogwe is?"

"I have explained to my friends that the tlogwe is not an artifact that can be displayed for anyone to see," Kinqalatlala replied.

"Then take us to the tlogwala," I insisted. "Please help us. Take us to your leader," I quipped, trying to ease the anxiety I felt.

"Hey," Michael responded, elbowing me. "How come you get that line?"

"Dluwulaxa have no leader," the duplicate replied. "We are all equal."

"That must be why you look all the same," I commented.

"When the time is right, the tlogwala will find you," Kinqalatlala replied. "If you are deemed worthy."

"Then why are we here?"

"To find the tlogwe."

"You're giving me a headache," I replied.

"Everything will be explained in due time," Kinqalatlala retorted. "To find the tlogwe one must first prove themselves worthy of receiving the gift of the tlogwe."

"In the meantime we wish you to enjoy the hospitality of the city," the duplicate said, sweeping her hand back toward the crystal pavilions. "Please follow me."

Before I could take a step, Kinqalatlala grabbed my hand. She whispered in my ear, "Beware. Do not believe everything you see is real." She released my arm and walked away.

I put my arm around Jean's shoulder. "Be alert. Something is wrong." Jean gave me a quizzical look but didn't respond.

We followed the duplicate Kinqalatlala to the nearest crystal structure. The building towered above us. The duplicate waved her hand and a doorway appeared at the base of the wall. She entered and we followed her inside. Michael and I both halted and whistled in stunned surprise. While the outside of the building appeared to have limits, the inside of the building seemed limitless. Here I saw the wide expanse of sky and clouds that I witnessed on my first trip to this world. And here we were greeted with the chirps, calls, and birdsong from the myriad assortment of birds I previously witnessed. I turned to look back out the doorway, but the doorway had vanished. "These are Dluwulaxa?" I asked.

"Here you see my people as they really are," Kinqalatlala replied. "A life of perfect peace and perfect freedom."

"Yeah, I know. Shangri-La. You can forget the sales pitch. I'm not interested."

"You may not be, but maybe your friends are."

"We are here to see the tlogwala. Nothing else."

"Please follow me," Kinqalatlala's duplicate said. She waved into the void and another crystal structure appeared where previously we saw only clouds and sky. A doorway opened at the base of the wall and we followed the duplicate inside. This crystal pavilion stood completely empty.

"Just one massive empty fishbowl," I observed.

"You will wait here," the duplicate said. She stood silent, looking at her feet. She dissolved into a small black bird. Wings flapping, the bird flew away into the ether.

"I need coffee," Blue Tara blurted out.

"Don't get me started on how hungry I am," Michael replied.

"What do your people do for food?" I asked Kinqalatlala.

"The sun is our food," she replied.

"But of course. In the meantime we're getting hungry."

"Please be patient. You will be provided with everything that you need."

"What did you mean when you said not to believe everything we see?"

"This is not the place," Kinqalatlala replied testily. "Do not speak of that again."

The doorway appeared in the wall behind us and the duplicate Kinqalatlala reappeared. She walked to us. "Please accept our hospitality," she said, pointing across my shoulder. We turned to see a table where only void had existed before. The table literally sagged under a cornucopia of breads, fruits, and vegetables.

"Pizza?" Blue Tara asked.

"I'd settle for a cold beer," I replied.

White Tara darted off Blue Tara's shoulder and alighted on the table. She took a bite out of one of the fruits and violently shook her head, spitting the fruit out of her beak. "This food is poisonous!" she exclaimed, disappointedly shaking her head.

"What the fuck," I said, looking at Kinqalatlala. I grabbed her arm and pulled her to me. "This is your idea of hospitality?"

"This is my idea of hospitality," the duplicate replied. Her voice had changed. We turned to look at her. In the place of Kinqalatlala's duplicate stood a tall dark man clad in black leather. His black fedora only partially hid his long stringy black hair and pale scalloped yellow skin. The brim of the fedora shielded his gleaming sunken red eyes.

"Hamatsa!" I cried out.

Jean swung the shotgun off her shoulder. "I blew your fucking head off!"

Hamatsa pointed a gloved hand at Jean. "By now you should know how useless your weapons are against me."

Kinqalatlala grabbed Jean's arm. "If you spill blood you will doom the world of the Dluwulaxa to destruction."

"What if Hamatsa spills blood?" I replied.

"Hamatsa's lust for the tlogwe is the only thing saving Dluwulaxa from destruction," Kinqalatlala said. "Once Hamatsa secures the magic of the tlogwe, Dluwulaxa's destruction is assured. I beg you. Do not give Hamatsa the opportunity to spill blood."

"And what? We just let him poison us?"

"Run away while you have the chance," Kinqalatlala replied, pointing to the doorway behind Hamatsa. "The gagits await. Save yourselves."

"Remember your place!" Hamatsa exclaimed. His gloved fist struck Kinqalatlala's chin, knocking her down.

I took a step toward the doorway. Blue Tara stepped in front of me, hand on her battle axe. "We came to find the tlogwe. If we leave empty handed we are doomed."

"Damned if we do. Damned if we don't." Michael responded.

White Tara flitted off Blue Tara and onto Hamatsa's shoulder. She took hold of the brim of Hamatsa's fedora with her beak and flung the hat off his head. Hamatsa craned his head to look at the parrot riding his shoulder. He batted at her with his hand. She jumped off but not before taking a bite out of his ear. "You stupid witch!" he exclaimed. "You will pay for your insolence."

"Oh fuck all," I said in exasperation. I turned to Jean. "Blow his head off." Before Jean could unsling her shotgun, Hamatsa dropped his chin to his chest, looked at his feet, and dissolved into a small black bird. Wings flapping, the bird took flight and disappeared into the sky. "What in the hell was that?" I blurted out.

"A test of your forbearance," Kinqalatlala replied. She extended her hand up to me. "Help me up," she asked me. I pulled her to her feet.

"A test? You're testing me? That wasn't the real Hamatsa?"

"In whatever form Hamatsa appears, he is a very real threat to you and your world, as he is to mine."

Before I could respond Hamatsa stepped through the doorway into the crystal pavilion and stopped in front of us. Then a second creature looking exactly like Hamatsa walked through the doorway, stopping behind the first Hamatsa. Then a third. And a fourth. A steady stream of duplicate Hamatsas walked into the crystal pavilion, quickly filling the visible space. "This is getting silly," I said. "None of them are real."

"How can you be sure?" Kinqalatlala replied. "You do not understand the extent of my master's powers."

"For one thing, there haven't been any snarky comments from any of these impostors." I walked up to the first Hamatsa and stared into his gleaming sunken red eyes. "Eyes are the windows into the soul," I said. "I sense no soul behind these eyes." I stepped back. Every Hamatsa dropped his chin to his chest, looked at his feet, and dissolved into a small black bird. The birds flapped their wings, took flight, and disappeared into the sky.

"Come with me," Kinqalatlala said, taking my hand in hers. We walked a short distance into the pavilion. I turned to look back at Jean and Michael and the Taras, but a crystal wall materialized between us, blocking any view.

"Hey, wait!" I exclaimed.

"Do not fear. They are safe."

"What are you doing?" I asked.

"I want you," she replied. She took my hands and placed them on her breasts. She put her arms across my shoulders and pulled me to her. Her tongue licked my lips, and slid between my lips to meet my tongue. She slowly pulled me to the floor and on top of her.

ΔΔΔ

"Wait!" Jean yelled, as a crystal wall materialized in front of her.

"What the hell!" Michael exclaimed. He dashed to the wall. Michael ran his hands over the crystal surface. "There doesn't seem to be any kind of doorway here," he observed.

"Oh no!" Jean exclaimed. "The outside doorway is gone too." An unblemished blank crystal wall obscured the doorway that previously opened to the clouds. "We're trapped."

"This is getting weirder by the minute," Michael said.

"Wonder if I could blow a hole through the wall with the shotgun?"

"I wouldn't try. You might hit them on the other side. You might bring the whole wall down on us. Or the buckshot might blow back right in our faces. Let's not try that. Maybe Blue Tara can bend time and space through the wall?" Blue Tara's head fell back, her mouth gaped open. A screech rolled out of her mouth before Jean and Michael thought to cover their ears. Michael and Jean peered at the wall. Nothing. The crystal wall still blocked them. They still stood on the wrong side of the wall. "Or not," Michael said with a sigh. "We could just stand here and wait," he added, as the crystal wall disappeared. "Or not."

ΔΔΔ

As Kinqalatlala pulled me down on top of her she whispered in my ear, "I want to feel you inside of me." She kissed me again.

"Enough!" I cried out. I pushed myself up and off Kinqalatlala and struggled to my feet. "What are you trying to do?"

"I want you."

"I'm already spoken for."

"What can your friend offer you? I can offer you immortality."

"A damn fine cup of coffee."

Kinqalatlala climbed to her feet. She stared at me in stunned silence. She waved her hand. The crystal wall disappeared. Jean and Michael and the Taras ran to us.

"What did she do?" Jean blurted out.

Nothing," I lied, as I put my arms around Jean and hugged her.

187

"You're a piss poor liar," Jean replied, kissing me. She smacked her lips and pushed me away from her. "Someone else has been kissing you."

"She tried," I pleaded. "But I stopped her."

The doorway reappeared at the base of the crystal wall. Hamatsa walked into the pavilion once again. "Oh fuck," I sighed. I pulled the shotgun off Jean's shoulder, pumped two rounds into the chambers and pointed the barrels at Hamatsa's head. I pulled the trigger. Hamatsa's head exploded in a cloud of blood red pulp.

"No!" Kinqalatlala screamed.

I pointed the shotgun at Kinqalatlala's head and pulled the trigger again. The firing pins clicked harmlessly on empty chambers. "I guess I failed your test."

"Do not believe everything you see," Kinqalatlala replied cryptically.

Hamatsa's headless body dissolved into a small black bird which cantered out the doorway in the crystal wall just as another Hamatsa entered. Blue Tara pulled her battle axe off her belt. With a single swing Blue Tara separated Hamatsa's head from his body. The head rolled back out the doorway as the body collapsed to the floor. The body dissolved into another small black bird. Wings spread, the bird jumped off the floor and flew out the doorway. "How long is this game going to go on?" I asked Kinqalatlala. "What are you testing us on now?"

Before Kinqalatlala could respond, yet another Hamatsa entered through the doorway. I froze. I sensed a malevolence I hadn't sensed before. "Oh shit," I said.

"What?" Jean asked.

"Hamatsa!" Blue Tara exclaimed. About a dozen gangly lance bearing pale-skinned sunken-eyed laxsa warriors followed Hamatsa through the doorway.

"This is the real deal," I said.

"How foolish of you to fall into my trap," Hamatsa gloated.

"Yep. Snarky comment and all."

Part Two

"This sucks big time," Michael said, rubbing his hand along the shaft of his magic harpoon. The laxsa surrounded us and stuck the points of their lances in our necks. They seized our weapons.

Kinqalatlala leaned over to me and whispered in my ear, "Remember, do not believe everything you see."

Hamatsa grabbed Kinqalatlala's shoulder. "Let us all hear, slave. My slaves do not keep secrets from their master."

"I warned him that resistance is futile," Kinqalatlala replied, bowing to Hamatsa.

189

"And so I intend to prove that this very day."

Hamatsa leaned over to me so closely his nose almost touched mine. I staggered back from the stench of his putrid breath, breath that smelled of death. "I wish I'd brought some breath mints to share," I said.

Hamatsa gripped my throat with a gloved hand. "I should break your neck. But if I spill your blood the destruction of Dluxulaxa is assured. And I still have use for this world." I coughed violently as I felt his hand squeeze my throat. "I will mount your head on the wall of Control before I am done with you," he added. "After I feast on the heart I cut out of your chest."

"I know who the tlogwala is," I stammered. Hamatsa released his grip on my neck. "Kill me and you will lose that knowledge."

"That is not possible," Hamatsa insisted.

"Can you afford to take that chance?"

Hamatsa snarled and bared his fangs. He grabbed Kinqalatlala and dragged her out the doorway. "What did you tell him," I could hear him say as they disappeared from view. The laxsa followed Hamatsa out and the doorway vanished. Jean, Michael, the Taras, and I stood alone and unarmed.

"Something's weird," I remarked.

"Kinqalatlala told you who the tlogwala is?" Michael asked.

"I wish. I lied," I replied. "Hamatsa's not very bright. But Kinqalatlala warned me not to believe everything we see."

The second crystal wall reappeared inside the pavilion and a doorway opened at the base. Kinqalatlala, or a creature that looked exactly like Kinqalatlala, emerged.

"I am me," she said.

"Who are you?" I replied dubiously.

"I am Kinqalatlala."

"No. You are not. Hamatsa just dragged Kinqalatlala out of here."

"That was not me. I am me."

"What? I'm confused. I. . ." I glanced at Jean. "She. . . kissed me. She proposed to me. I know that was her. The other one. Not you." Jean glared at me quizzically.

"The other was not me. That was a copy of me. Testing you."

"Then Hamatsa doesn't know he dragged a copy of you out of here?"

"Hamatsa is a fool."

"Just like most men." White Tara chortled.

"Hamatsa has our weapons."

Kinqalatlala whistled. The laxsa warriors entered through the doorway in the second wall, carrying our weapons. Blue Tara grabbed her battle axe out of a laxsa's hand and raised the blade, preparing to strike. Kinqalatlala raised her hand. "Wait!" she demanded.

We took possession of our weapons. The laxsa stood still, dropped their chins to their chests, and looked at their feet. They dissolved into big white birds that looked like seagulls. Flapping their wings, they leaped into the air and flew out the doorway they came in. The second crystal wall vanished. "So explain something to me," I said.

"Yes. I will try."

"Hamatsa didn't harm us because he believes drawing blood will result in the destruction of Dluwulaxa."

"That is correct."

"Yet we blew the heads off several fake Hamatsas, and we're still here."

"As you say, they were fakes. Apparitions. You wanted to believe they were real, so to you they became real."

"I don't know what's real anymore."

"I am real. The people around you are real."

"We need to get out of here," Michael suggested. "Hamatsa's going to figure out that's not the real you with him out there."

"You are correct," Kinqalatlala replied. "We can not maintain this deception for long. However, you can not leave."

"What?" I stammered. "Are we your prisoners?"

"Not at all," she replied. "You need to continue your search for the tlogwala. You are closer than you realize."

"God, I'm getting tired of hearing that. Why can't someone just introduce me to the fucker?"

"The fate of Dluwulaxa rests on your finding the tlogwala. Hamatsa will soon realize his error and unleash his vengeance on my people. We can fight him with deception only so long. We can not match the numbers and power of his armies and his magic."

"If we try to fight Hamatsa, somebody or something is going to get killed. Blood will be spilled. Won't that result in the destruction of Dluwulaxa?" I asked.

"Ultimately only the magic of the tlogwe can save Dluwulaxa from Hamatsa and his army of the dead. I fear however, we may have to risk the destruction of Dluwulaxa to impede Hamatsa's plans by use of your weapons. If Hamatsa seizes this world, all hope is lost. For my people. And for your people."

"Where is Hamatsa now?" I asked.

"He is on the crystal plain gathering his army. His gagits are ferrying his forces to the city as we speak."

Blue Tara spoke up. "White Tara will fly out and spy on Hamatsa and his army of the dead and warn us when he is ready to march on the city." Kinqalatlala waved her hand and the doorway appeared at the base of the crystal wall. White Tara leaped off Blue Tara's shoulder and darted out the doorway. "What kind of defenses do you possess?" Blue Tara asked.

"Only the defense of deception."

"You have no weapons?" Red Tara asked as she flexed her longbow.

"My world is a world of peace. My people have no need for weapons."

"Until they do," Jean smirked, pumping shells into the chambers of her shotgun.

"What can we do against Hamatsa's army of the dead?" Michael asked. "We've got two guns and a magic harpoon, which doesn't necessarily work against things that are already dead."

"And a Swiss Army knife," I added, pulling a red folding knife out of my pocket.

"Well, that changes everything," Michael replied sarcastically.

"Don't forget Blue Tara's battle axe and Red Tara's longbow," Jean added.

"And Black Tara's claws," Michael said, as Margarita purred and rubbed her body against his ankles.

"Alrighty then," I replied. "We're in business."

"I sure would like pizza and beer right now," Blue Tara said.

"When I get home I'm going to fill the bathtub with beer and drown myself," I replied, wistfully.

"I will join you," Blue Tara replied, "and help you drown yourself." We all turned and stared at Blue Tara.

ΔΔΔ

White Tara flew out the doorway, executed an inverted loop, and shot straight up into the sky. From her vantage point she could see the gagits resting on the edge of the crystal plain outside the city. Waves of fog rolling up from the lenticular clouds anchored to the mountain below washed over the winged beasts. White Tara banked and glided silently toward one of the unwary creatures. Several towering dzonoqwa stood guard off to the side, leaning on their clubs.

White Tara alighted on a gagit almost hidden by the fog. The gagit rested standing on one foot, eyes closed, beak nestled behind the creature's wing. White Tara scurried up the long neck and planted her beak into one of the creature's ears. The gagit's neck whipped out. Beak spread wide, the creature screamed. The beast wheeled around and clamped huge razor-sharp teeth on the neck of a gagit resting nearby.

White Tara darted onto another nearby gagit. She planted her beak into a patch of bare skin on the creature's shoulder. The creature jumped with a howl. The creature's tail whipped around, taking out the feet of an adjacent gagit, which tumbled to the surface. Jumping back up with a roar, the offended creature sunk equally razor-sharp teeth into the neck of the offending gagit. Both rolled to the surface. Several other gagits, spooked out of their sleep by the uproar, extended their wings, leaped into the air, and took flight, escaping into the clouds. Awakened out of their slumber, the dzonoqwa rushed about. They waved their clubs and growled, attempting to corral the escaping pterodactyls. An injured gagit, reeling from a bloody gash across the creature's neck, spun around and clamped jaws of death on the neck of a dzonoqwa. The pterodactyl lifted the giant off his feet and shook him violently in the air, snapping the dzonoqwa's neck. The gagit flung the lifeless body into the fog. The remaining dzonoqwa charged the pterodactyl, raining blows on the creature's head with their clubs, beating the gagit senseless. The hapless creature collapsed dead.

White Tara darted onto the shoulder of the closest dzonoqwa and bit the demon's ear. Howling in pain, the monster spun around and smashed his club into the head of the dzonoqwa behind him, knocking his victim down. The remaining dzonoqwa attacked the offending giant, knocking him off his feet and smashing his skull with their clubs. White Tara flew into the air, banked into a lazy loop, and noted the gagits disappearing into the clouds. She turned and flew back to the crystal city.

ΔΔΔ

White Tara flew through the doorway of the crystal pavilion to find everyone feasting at a table laden with fruits and vegetables of every conceivable kind. Goblets of wine filled to the brim covered every space on the table not filled with food. Looping around the table she alighted on Blue Tara's shoulder and screeched. "What are you doing?" she cried out. "The food is poison."

"The food is perfectly safe," Kinqalatlala replied, standing with a goblet of wine in her hand. She sipped wine from the goblet. "Please join us." Blue Tara craned her head and nodded in agreement. White Tara scurried down Blue Tara's arm and dived into a platter of fruit.

"What did you discover?" Blue Tara asked. White Tara continued eating in silence. "Whenever you are ready," Blue Tara added as she drained a goblet of wine.

After several minutes of eating, White Tara stood erect, her white beak dripping red with cherry juice. She furiously shook her head to fling the juice off her beak. She stretched both her wings. First her right wing. Then her left wing. She fluffed her feathers. Cocking her head to peer one pink eye at Blue Tara, she commenced to speak. "I scattered the gagits and drove them off the crystal plain. And I seem to have created some confusion with the dzonoqwa. Enough so they were attacking each other. A temporary setback for Hamatsa, but far from a fatal one."

White Tara seemed to me to be grinning. "Good girl," I said. Everyone turned and looked at me. "Sorry. Isn't that what you're supposed to tell a parrot? Positive reinforcement?" Dead silence. "Right. She's not a parrot. Good work!"

"If nothing else," Michael noted, "she no doubt pissed Hamatsa off. Maybe that'll cause Hamatsa to react and do something stupid."

"Or more stupid than usual," Jean added.

"We should take advantage of this opportunity," I added, "and strike while they're confused and disoriented. Take the battle to them instead of sitting here drinking wine and waiting for them to attack us." I chugged the remaining wine in my goblet.

"A very good plan," Blue Tara replied. "As soon as we finish this wine." She chugged the remaining wine in her goblet.

"Is there anything like a bathroom around here?" Jean asked sheepishly, looking around the crystal pavilion. "What do your people do for bathrooms?" she asked Kinqalatlala. We all turned and looked at Jean. Before Kinqalatlala could respond, from outside the pavilion, off in the distance across the crystal plain, we heard a terrible scream.

ΔΔΔ

Hamatsa dragged Kinqalatlala out of the pavilion and across the crystal plain to the edge of the clouds where his gagits landed his minions to prepare for the coming assault on the city of Dluwulaxa. "Tell me

198

what you whispered to your new friend," he demanded.

"As I told you, my master, I said to him that resistance is futile."

"Do not lie to me you witch. You are not an accomplished liar. Tell me what you told him."

"I promise, my master. I told him resistance is futile."

"If you refuse to tell me what you told him I will cut off your breasts and feed them to the furies. And then I will tear open your chest with my hands and feast on your heart." Hamatsa seized Kinqalatlala's throat with his gloved hands and lifted her off her feet.

"I told him resistance is not futile," she gasped as Hamatsa squeezed her throat. She struggled to break his grip. Hamatsa squeezed Kinqalatlala's throat until her neck snapped. Her arms and legs fell limp. Hamatsa released his grip on her neck and the body collapsed to the surface. As Hamatsa pulled a dagger out from under his coat the body dissolved into a small black bird. Wings flapping furiously, the bird darted into the clouds.

Hamatsa heard his gagits scream and howl, followed by the beating pulse of enormous wings flapping and disappearing into the distance. He scurried to where the gagits had been left to rest on the edge of the crystal plain. He found the gagits gone, except for a couple of torn and lifeless bodies crumpled on the surface. His dzonoqwa stood stupidly around a dead pterodactyl with a crushed skull sprawled next to a dead dzonoqwa. Out of the corner of his sunken red eyes Hamatsa caught the flight of a white parrot back toward the crystal pavilion. He shut his eyes closed to concentrate his anger, extended his arms over his head, took a deep breath, and let out a scream so discordant the dzonoqwa dropped their clubs and fell to their knees, hands pressed to their ears.

"Get up you fools!" Hamatsa screamed at the dzonoqwa. "Gather the laxsa. Enter the city and bring those witches to me in chains. And bring the heads of Kinqalatlala and her new friend to me on silver platters. Get up. Go!" he yelled, pointing to the city of Dluwulaxa shimmering in the sunlight across the crystal plain.

ΔΔΔ

"That can't be good," I said as the scream faded.

"Apparently my efforts to impede his plans do not please Hamatsa," White Tara smirked.

Blue Tara slammed her wine goblet on the table and stood up, battle axe in her hand. "Now is the time to act," she stated. "Hamatsa's feeling of omnipotence has been tarnished. He will be prone to rash judgments and mistakes. Now is the time to strike."

Jean looked at me. "Any chance we could take a bathroom break first?"

Part Three

"We need the element of surprise," Kinqalatlala said, "if our plan to harass Hamatsa's cohort is to have any chance of success. If we try to walk across the crystal plain we will be discovered long before we reach our objective."

"The Taras can turn themselves into parrots and fly," I replied. Margarita growled at me. "Almost all the Taras," I clarified. "You are a shapeshifter, so you can turn yourself into anything you want. But where does that leave Jean and Michael and me? We're certainly not going to sit this battle out."

"There is a way," Kinqalatlala noted. "Come with me." A crystal wall appeared inside the pavilion, and a doorway appeared at the base of the wall. We followed Kinqalatlala through the doorway. Inside we found a massive reflecting pool with a fountain shooting a geyser into the heavens, so high we couldn't see the peak.

"How beautiful!" Jean exclaimed.

The fountain made the reflecting pool bubble and roil, throwing a dense mist into the air. The brilliant rays of sunlight streaming through the wall of the crystal pavilion, scattered by the mist, reflected every color of the rainbow. "How can you have this gigantic pool of water up here?" I asked.

"This is not water," Kinqalatlala replied. I looked at her quizzically. "This is a pool of liquid crystal."

"Oh no!" Michael exclaimed. "You're not thinking what I'm thinking you're thinking?" he asked Kinqalatlala.

"What are you thinking?" I asked Michael.

"The four furies. She wants us to bath in the crystal and turn us into birds."

"No way!" Jean cried out.

"The crystal is perfectly harmless," Kinqalatlala insisted.

"If the crystal is so harmless, why were the four furies never able to turn themselves back into people?" Michael replied.

"The furies did not possess the magic to reverse the effect of the crystal. And once they were enslaved by Hamatsa they were trapped."

"I refuse to become a furie," Michael insisted.

"I wish to assure you," Kinqalatlala stated, "that I possess the magic to reverse the effect of the crystal on you. The effect would only be temporary."

"This is part of her plan to enslave you into her world," Jean remarked. "That's what she's wanted all along. To make you hers."

I stared into Jean's mournful brown eyes. I turned to Kinqalatlala. "What do we do?" I asked her, stepping toward the fountain.

"No!" Jean yelled out.

I took Jean's hands in mine. "I take her at her word."

"Take off your clothes," Kinqalatlala said.

"What?" Jean exclaimed.

"You must take your clothes off for the crystal to work on your bodies," Kinqalatlala explained.

Jean yanked her hand out of mine. "No fucking way!" she insisted.

"What the hell," I sighed. I kicked off my shoes and commenced to strip off my clothes.

"No!" Jean exclaimed.

Naked, I held my hand out to Jean. "Come on babe. What the hell." Jean pouted, shaking her head. I stepped to her and started to remove her clothes.

"Damn it all!" Jean blurted out. She relented and stripped. I took her hand in mine as I admired her naturally athletic body.

"You need to step into the pool and submerge yourself. Completely," Kinqalatlala explained.

"Come with me," I said to Jean. "Let's do this. Haven't you always wanted to fly?"

"Oh, what the hell," Jean responded.

We stepped into the pool. I took a deep breath. Jean too. We dunked ourselves in the liquid crystal. I wasn't sure what to expect. But what I didn't expect was feeling nothing. Unlike water, the crystal offered no resistance to my body. No pressure. No warmth. No coolness. No taste. No smell. The liquid crystal acted like water but didn't feel like water. I seemed to be bathing in pure color.

"Come out now," I heard Kinqalatlala say. We stood up and stepped out of the pool.

"You completely disappeared in the crystal!" Michael exclaimed. "Are you okay?" He touched my arm. "You're not wet, or anything," he remarked.

"That's not water," I replied. "That's not like anything that I can describe." I turned to Jean. "Are you okay babe?"

Jean nodded. "I guess so," she said as she stood with her arms stretched out, examining herself.

"How about you Mike?" I asked. "Want to dip your toe in the pool?"

"Naw. I'll stay myself and keep Margarita company." Margarita sidled up to Michael and rubbed her head on his ankles, purring. "We'll guard the rear," Michael added, bending down to rub the cat's head, "and keep you from being surprised."

I turned to Kinqalatlala. "So did anything happen? I don't feel or look any different."

"Close your eyes. Stretch out your arms and imagine yourself flying," Kinqalatlala replied.

I stretched out my arms and imagined I was a bird. I moved my arms up and down. I felt my feet leave the surface of the crystal pavilion. I felt weightless. I opened my eyes to find myself airborne. I dropped onto my heels with a painful thud. "Good God!" Michael cried out. "You're a bird!"

"I am?" I looked at myself. "I look like myself. To me."

"You look like a big black bird," Michael said. "A raven."

"You're kidding?"

"And Jean looks like a raven too."

I looked to Jean, except Jean looked to me to be a big black bird. A raven, hovering in the air. "Oh shit! Jean looks like a bird!" I exclaimed.

Jean's wings stopped flapping and she too dropped to the surface. "Ouch!" she cried out. "That hurt."

"Keep imagining yourselves to be birds," Kinqalatlala said as she extended her arms and dissolved into a big black raven as well. "You must continue to flap your arms or you will fall to the surface." Her wings flapping, Kinqalatlala, the bird, rose into the air. "Do as I do, and follow me." Kinqalatlala circled the crystal pavilion, banked, and flew out the doorway.

Screeches reverberating through the crystal palace told me that Blue Tara and Red Tara had transformed themselves into macaws and took flight after Kinqalatlala, with the cockatoo parrot White Tara trailing the macaws. I looked at the raven that was Jean, circling above me. "Let's go!" She yelled at me. I commenced to move my arms and rose into the air. Adjusting the motion of my arms I found I could propel myself forward. Jean flew out the doorway and to the best of my ability I flew out after her.

"Good luck!" I heard Michael yell as we flew out of the city and into the open air.

We followed the black raven that was Kinqalatlala and the brightly colored parrots that were the Taras to the clouds roiling up over the edge of the crystal plain. I seemed to be able to fly as long as I kept my arms extended and moving. Anytime I dropped my arms to my sides I lost altitude. Quickly. I circled Jean a couple of times as she experimented with a barrel roll and a few lazy loops. We alighted in a fog bank where we saw the others land, where we would be safe from discovery by Hamatsa's ghouls.

Kinqalatlala, Blue Tara, and Red Tara greeted us in their naked Amazonian goddess glory. Only White Tara retained her parrot form, perched on Blue Tara's shoulder.

"How do you see us?" I asked. "Are Jean and I still birds?"

"What form do you wish?" Kinqalatlala asked.

"To be people again," I replied.

"You are people again," Kinqalatlala said, a wry smile cracking across her face. I could feel my face flush as Kinqalatlala's eyes swept up and down my body.

"You are your handsome self once again," Blue Tara said, a grin stretching across her face. I couldn't tell if she was being sarcastic. "I am most pleased to see

206

you without clothes," she added as she stepped to me and kissed me. I could feel my face burn red. I hoped that the fog shielded my embarrassment. Blue Tara put her arm over Jean's shoulder and kissed her as well.

"How strange," I said. "I didn't feel any different. But you say we looked like birds?"

"Yes you did," Blue Tara replied. "That is not so strange at all."

"Maybe not to you," I said. "Because that's your nature. That's certainly not my nature. To be a bird and fly."

"Did you not enjoy flying?" White Tara asked as she flitted onto my shoulder.

"Certainly," I replied, as I craned my head to look at her. "Flying has always been a fantasy of mine. Ever since I was a little kid."

"So enjoy the magic of flying while you have the ability," White Tara said, nipping my ear before darting back to Blue Tara.

"Watch out!" I blurted out. "I'll turn myself into a raptor and take a bite out of you."

"Now is the time for us to take a bite out of Hamatsa," Kinqalatlala said. "I did not see any gagits as we flew here."

"Nor I," Blue Tara added.

"For now Hamatsa has no means of escape nor means to reinforce his position. We need to drive his ghouls off the crystal plain to their destruction," Red Tara said.

"At the least we need to show Hamatsa we are not afraid of taking the fight to him," Blue Tara replied as she took hold of her battle axe.

ΔΔΔ

We stepped softly through the fog bank until we came to Hamatsa's encampment on the edge of the crystal plain. 'Encampment' probably is an overly generous word. We encountered a field of gigantic mushrooms that thrived on the edge of the crystal plain, perpetually bathed in cool and moist fog. Hamatsa's ghouls rested against the mushroom stalks, sheltered by the caps of the gigantic fungi. *The geoducks of the fungi world*, I smirked to myself.

The laxsa, Hamatsa's zombie warriors, leaned against the stalks of the giant fungi and polished their lances, or just sat and stared into space. The dzonoqwa stood off to the edge of the fungi forest and lazily leaned on their clubs, drowsy from the brilliant sunlight beating down on their heavy fur. A pack of monstrous dogs wandered among the dzonoqwa, the size of grizzly bears, with long black fur and gleaming ivory teeth, and claws as deadly as any grizzly. As they stopped to rest, one or another of the monstrous dogs opened their jaws and a tongue of yellow flame shot out of their mouths. Even the dzonoqwa seemed wary of these creatures and kept moving out of their way. "Beware the fire breathers," Blue Tara cautioned. "They are the nontsistalal. Their fire consumes anything unlucky enough to fall into the flame."

"I think we used those in Vietnam," I joked. "So what's the plan?" I felt awkward having no clothes and no weapons. My eyes futilely searched the mushroom forest for potential weapons.

Red Tara flexed her longbow with two of her hands while pulling several arrows out of her quiver with her two other hands. Blue Tara stood on one leg, her right foot resting on her left knee, tossing her battle axe from hand to hand. "Simple," Blue Tara replied. "We will surprise the enemy and sow confusion in their ranks. Try to stampede them off the crystal plain to their destruction."

"I will launch the first strike," White Tara offered. "My size and color will protect me from detection by Hamatsa's ghouls." White Tara leaped off Blue Tara's shoulder and disappeared into the fog.

ΔΔΔ

The small white parrot flitted through the fog undetected by Hamatsa's ghouls. White Tara chose the nontsistalal as her target. As she did with the gagits, she alighted on the neck of the first monster she encountered and sunk her beak into the demon's ear.

The creature roared in anguish, rearing back, forelegs pawing the sky. A tongue of yellow flame rolled from the demon's mouth to light the fog overhead. As the monster spun around to confront White Tara the flame struck the legs of one of the dzonoqwa. The dzonoqwa tumbled to the surface screaming in terror as he burst into flame. Several other dzonoqwa seized their clubs and smashed the head of the nontsistalal, dropping the demon dead. Infuriated, the other nontsistalal lunged at the dzonoqwa, turning several of the creatures into howling fireballs. Consumed with flame, the dzonoqwa stampeded into the dense rolling fog, their screams fading into the distance as they stumbled off the crystal plain and plummeted toward the earth like fireballs.

The surviving dzonoqwa panicked and ran for the safety of the fungi forest, clubbing any laxsa that fell into their path. Some of the laxsa rallied and speared the dzonoqwa as the creatures stumbled by, chased by the nontsistalal. The laxsa quickly retreated into the fog bank when the nontsistalal turned several of them into burning cinders.

Blue Tara and Red Tara struck. Masked by the fog, Blue Tara lopped off the heads of any laxsa she encountered with her battle axe as they stumbled by, seeing her too late to defend themselves with their lances. Red Tara dropped dzonoqwa after dzonoqwa, arrows piercing their skulls. One of the dzonoqwa, an arrow sticking through his head, screamed and charged Red Tara. He knocked Red Tara off her feet with a glancing blow to her head from his huge club. As the creature lunged at Red Tara to finish her off, Kinqalatlala leaped in front of him. She thrust the steel blade that was her hand through the creature's chest. A nontsistalal jumped out of the fog behind the dzonoqwa. Rearing back on hind legs, maw gaped open, the demon illuminated the fog over Kinqalatlala's head with a tongue of burning flame. The monster turned to fall on Kinqalatlala with her hand embedded in the dzonoqwa's chest. I scooped up a lance laying next to a dead laxsa and thrust the spear through the demon's skull. The fire breather collapsed at Kinqalatlala's feet, smoke streaming out from between clenched teeth. "Don't say I never did anything for you," I told Kinqalatlala with a laugh. She smiled at me as she yanked her arm out of the dzonoqwa's chest.

Dazed and bleeding badly from a gash across the side of her head, Red Tara struggled to regain her feet. White Tara darted onto her shoulder and rubbed her beak across Red Tara's forehead. The gash and blood disappeared. Blue Tara grabbed two of Red Tara's hands and pulled her to her feet. "I thank you for your assistance," Red Tara said, nodding her head to White Tara.

Boots pounding on the crystal surface in the fog caught our attention. Everyone spun around, weapons ready. "Don't shoot," a familiar voice called out from the fog. Michael appeared, the magic harpoon cradled in his arms, Jean's shotgun slung across his shoulder. Margarita trotted out of the fog behind him.

"Always late to the party," I joked, stepping forward to shake his hand.

"We were worried," Michael said. "I heard a lot of screaming in the fog, but I couldn't tell who was doing the screaming. I feared the worst."

Jean grabbed her shotgun off Michael's shoulder. "Am I glad to see that. Don't suppose you brought my clothes?" Michael's face flushed. He tried not to stare at Jean's body while he glumly shook his head.

"So far so good," I replied. "We've got them on the run. In fact, thanks to White Tara, we ran some of them clear off the plain into the sky."

White Tara darted onto my shoulder. "Why, thank you for the compliment. Maybe you are not so unprepossessing as I thought." She rubbed her beak against my chin.

"These are incredible," Michael said, poking the giant mushrooms with the magic harpoon. "Think of the feast you could have with just one of these."

"Careful where you point that stick," I said. "Did you see anything of Hamatsa when you came up upon us?"

"Not a thing," Michael replied. "The crystal plain is deserted."

"That's good news," I said. And immediately regretted saying that when a horrendous screech assaulted our eardrums, a sonic wave buffeting our bodies like a spring rain squall off Elliott Bay. Michael, Jean, and I fell to our knees with our hands pressed against our ears, trying to stop the pain. I could see that even Blue Tara and Red Tara winced. The screech seemed to have no point of origin, but appeared to fall out of the sky like a summer monsoon, enveloping everything in creation.

Kinqalatlala spoke first as the screech faded away. "We need to fall back to the city of Dluwulaxa as quickly as possible. If we stay exposed on this rim we are certain to meet our destruction."

"What is happening?" I asked, fearing the worst.

"The Yagis," Kinqalatlala replied, her voice shaking.

"That is not possible!" Blue Tara exclaimed. "The Yagis is locked in a cage in the sky by Lord Garuda himself."

"Someone please tell me what in hell is a Yagis?" I pleaded.

"You are correct," Blue Tara replied. "The Yagis is a creature of Hell. A monstrous bird of enormous size and power that devours everything the creature encounters. Of such size and power to even challenge Lord Garuda."

"How is that possible?" Red Tara asked. "Lord Garuda captured the Yagis and confined the monster to an unbreakable cage in the sky, from which the demon hurls tornadoes and storms at the earth in his fury."

"Somehow Hamatsa has freed the creature," Kinqalatlala said. "Even the furies fear the Yagis. We must run back to the city with haste before the Yagis finds us."

"Why don't we just fly back?" I asked. "Since we're all birds now. Well, almost all," I added, glancing at Michael and Margarita.

"We can not risk flight," Kinqalatlala replied. "If the Yagis spotted us he would strike us down and consume us. Our chances are best if we stay together on the crystal plain and protect each other. But we must run. We can not tarry."

"Let's go then," I said, as we stumbled out of the fog and faced the towering crystal city of Dluwulaxa shimmering across the crystal plain.

"Let us hope Lord Garuda heard the scream of the Yagis," Blue Tara added.

Chapter Seven
Part One

We jogged back toward the crystal city of Dluwulaxa single file. Kinqalatlala took point and Red Tara brought up the rear, longbow at the ready. Jogging behind Kinqalatlala, I asked, "We just spilled blood. What's going to happen to Dluwulaxa?"

"I do not know the answer. This has never happened before to my world. Legends of long ago tell of a time when Dluwulaxa was shaken by explosions from the mountain below and almost destroyed."

"Volcanic eruptions?" That can't be good," I said. "Eruptions big enough to destroy this world would devastate the Seattle area."

"Unfortunately, we will know soon enough," Kinqalatlala replied.

"We have more immediate problems," Red Tara cried out. We stopped jogging and turned to discern the bad news. A line of nontsistalal approached, rapidly loping across the crystal plain toward us. Tongues flopped out of their open jaws. Their huge canines glistened in the brilliant sunlight. Occasional bolts of yellow fire scorched the crystal plain. Laxsa, the zombie warriors, mounted each monster. One hand held a lance while the other hand grasped clumps of fur. Their legs bounced out to the sides almost like balance bars.

"We'll never outrun them!" I yelled. "We need to make a stand."

"As long as you're not talking Custer's Last Stand," Michael replied, dropping to one knee with his magic harpoon stretched forward. Red Tara nocked an arrow in her longbow, two of her other hands holding arrows at the ready. Jean dropped to one knee next to Michael, her shotgun cocked and aimed.

"Don't fire until you see the whites of their eyes," I joked.

"That would not be very useful," Blue Tara replied. "I can already see the whites of their eyes."

"That was a joke," I replied. "Just trying to bolster everyone's spirits."

"The spirits ride the nontsistalal," Blue Tara said. "We need to kill them. Not bolster them."

"I give up," I responded with a shrug.

"Way too early to give up," Blue Tara replied. "The battle has not yet begun."

Before I could think up a witty response, White Tara leaped off Blue Tara's shoulder and flitted into the sky. "We have help from the city," she called out.

We turned to see a flock of enormous golden eagles flying in our direction from the crystal city. The eagles sped over our heads directly toward the charging demons. Dropping their gleaming talons they dived toward the nontsistalal. The giant eagles seized the laxsa and yanked them off their mounts. Furiously flapping their great wings the eagles pulled back up

216

into the sky and flew out beyond the edge of the crystal plain. Once clear of the plain the eagles released their prey and the laxsa tumbled toward the earth and oblivion. The eagles circled back to the city of Dluwulaxa and disappeared.

Losing their riders, the nontsistalal faltered. Their pace slowed considerably. Several of the monsters drew to a walk and fell behind the others. Jean aimed and fired both barrels of her shotgun. Two of the creatures running side by side plowed face down into the crystal plain, turning the surface red with blood where they fell. Clouds of red crystal spray billowed into the air before them.

Red Tara aimed her longbow and methodically began to release her arrows. One by one the nontsistalal tumbled head over hoofs to the surface of the plain, their skulls pierced with arrows.

Michael aimed his magic harpoon at the last couple of fire breathing demons charging us. One collapsed dead. The other spun around to flee in the opposite direction. Red Tara nocked one more arrow into her bow and the creature tumbled to the surface. Dead.

"We should go now," I said, pointing toward the city of Dluwulaxa. The terrible screech of the Yagis hit me like a cyclone and knocked me off my feet. Once again I found myself on my knees with my hands pressed to my ears trying to block out the crushing sound. Jean and Michael both fell to the surface, hands pressed to their ears. Screeching, White Tara dropped to the crystal plain. Hard. I could see Blue Tara's and Red Tara's faces squirm with pain.

"We must go!" Kinqalatlala cried out. Blue Tara helped me to my feet. She scooped White Tara off the crystal plain. Red Tara yanked Jean and Michael onto their feet with her four arms. "The Yagis is getting closer," Kinqalatlala said. "We do not have much time. Make haste!"

I jogged a couple of paces and stopped. "The Yagis is the least of our problems right now!" I yelled.

"What's the matter?" Michael asked, stopping next to me.

"Look," I replied, pointing toward the city.

"Shit!" Michael exclaimed.

I counted at least a dozen dzonoqwa standing in a pack between us and the city. Behind us, toward the rim of the crystal plain I could distinctly hear the baying and howling of the nontsistalal. "Hamatsa is going to try to hit us from both sides," I observed.

"We charge!" Blue Tara called out as she raised her battle axe. White Tara darted into the sky. Blue Tara dashed toward the dzonoqwa. Red Tara rushed to catch up.

"Crap," I responded, waving the lance in my hand. "Charge!"

We scrambled toward the dzonoqwa, surprising them even more than ourselves. As we approached the dzonoqwa fanned out in a line facing us. Club waving wildly over his head, one of the dzonoqwa jumped forward and commenced to scream. Without slowing,

Blue Tara raised her battle axe over her head with both hands and flung the blade at the monster. I could hear the blade whistle as the axe whirled through the air, striking the creature squarely between his eyes with a heavy thud. The dzonoqwa flew backwards as if yanked by a rope. Blue Tara leaped on the dead creature's body and gripped the handle of her battle axe to pull the weapon out of his skull. A couple of dzonoqwa raised their clubs to fall on Blue Tara. One club went flying as the dzonoqwa tumbled backwards with an arrow sticking out of one of his eyes. Jean aimed and fired both barrels of her shotgun. The other club fell harmlessly to the surface when the creature's head disappeared in a cloud of blood red pulp. Another dzonoqwa leaped, screaming, at Jean as she reloaded. I thrust the lance in my hands over Jean's head into the dzonoqwa's throat. Jean jumped out of the way as the body crashed down on her. Jean blew me a kiss.

Michael brought down one of the demons with his magic harpoon. Another dzonoqwa leaped at Michael. Margarita jumped onto her hind legs and whirled. The whirling black dervish Black Tara knocked the creature back, slashing his throat with her gleaming steel claws. Wobbling on unsteady legs, screaming in pain with bright red blood coating the long black fur of his chest, the dzonoqwa attempted to raise his club. Blue Tara swung her battle axe and deftly severed the creature's head. The body collapsed at her feet. The head and club fell harmlessly to the surface next to the lifeless body. The remaining dzonoqwa dropped their clubs to flee. I tried to pick up one of the clubs. First with one hand. Then with both hands. I could barely budge the weapon.

"Look!" Jean yelled, pointing toward the rim of the crystal plain. "They're coming back." We spotted another line of nontsistalal loping across the plain toward us, once again with laxsa riders mounted on their backs.

"If at first you fail. . ." I muttered.

"We're never going to get back to the safety of the city!" Michael cried out frantically.

"Then the city will have to come to us," Kinqalatlala replied.

We turned to stare at her. "What do you mean by that?" I asked, more than a little bewildered, and plenty skeptical.

Kinqalatalal clapped her hands. A crystal wall appeared about a hundred yards outside the city. She clapped her hands again. A second crystal wall appeared another hundred yards beyond the first. Standing about a half mile short of the city, I quickly did the math in my head. The equation required Kinqalatlala clapping about fifteen more times for the wall to reach us. Meanwhile the laxsa commenced to fling their lances at us. I could hear the spears whistle through the air and thud harmlessly into the crystal plain. But as the nontsistalal got closer to us so did the lances. I was never particularly good at math, but in this instance the math seemed problematic whether the wall or the lances would reach us first.

White Tara landed on Blue Tara's shoulder. "Allow me," she said surprisingly cheerfully. She jumped off Blue Tara's shoulder and flew toward the charging ghouls. White Tara darted over the heads of the laxsa and their lances. Swinging wide of their charging line she twirled to the ground in the form of the white-skinned silken skirted Amazonian goddess. She waved and whistled at the creatures galloping by. The nearest nontsistalal glanced at her and veered away from the others, the creature's pace dropping to a slow trot in spite of the entreaties of the laxsa rider.

The nontsistalal came to a stop facing White Tara, claws pawing the crystal surface, like nails dragging across tin siding. Tongues of yellow fire flicked out to scorch the crystal surface at White Tara's feet as the demon panted, jaws opening and closing like a bellows. The creature growled and hissed at White Tara. Heels jabbing the creature's haunches, the laxsa warrior mounted on the demon's back yanked the creature's fur, attempting to turn his mount back to the charge.

Seeing the first nontsistalal swing to a stop in front of the white goddess, the next monster swung around and followed suit. And the next. And the next one after that. The entire line of charging monsters swung around and loped to a stop to face White Tara. The laxsa riders tried to spur the creatures around to resume the charge. Several of the laxsa commenced beating their mounts with their lances. One of the nontsistalal bucked onto hind legs, flinging the laxsa rider backwards onto the surface. The laxsa fell into the tongue of fire from a nearby nontsistalal and burst into flames. Several laxsa speared the nontsistalal, only to get flung off their mounts. Frenzied bucking and roaring by the nontsistalal unseated the remaining laxsa. The laxsa that avoided becoming torches ran back toward the rim of the crystal plain.

Their maws smoking, the nontsistalal crouched to pounce. White Tara raised her right foot, placed her foot against her left knee, and extended her arms. She began to twirl. Faster and faster. She became a white dervish. The white dervish coalesced into a white parrot. The nontsistalal leaped at the bird. Wings furiously flapping, the parrot darted into the sky and banked away from the nontsistalal to fly back to Blue Tara's shoulder.

Kinqalatlala clapped one more time and a crystal wall appeared directly before us, towering into the sky. "Wow!" I exclaimed. "I don't know which one of you is more impressive."

"No time for accolades," Kinqalatlala replied. "We must go while we still can." She waved her hand and a doorway appeared at the base of the crystal wall.

"You can always shower me with accolades," White Tara responded, darting onto my shoulder and rubbing her beak against my chin.

ΔΔΔ

The terrible screech of the Yagis hit us like a sonic tsunami that seemed to obliterate everything that stood unprotected. I tumbled to my knees. White Tara fluttered to the surface. We stumbled through the doorway as the screech faded. I collapsed onto my hands and knees. As we fell through the doorway Kinqalatlala waved her hand and the doorway disappeared. I raised my throbbing head to see the city of the Dluxulaxa spread out before me. We were no longer a half mile outside the city but within the city itself. "The crystal wall should protect us from the Yagis, at least for a while," Kinqalatlala said.

"For some reason, I'm not reassured," I replied as I struggled to my feet. I saw Blue Tara and Red Tara pulling Michael and Jean up off the floor.

"How did we get from out there to here?" I asked Kinqalatlala.

"The city expanded through space to meet us and contracted to the city's original space once we passed through the wall."

"I like that. Think how much gas we could save if every city did that."

"The oil companies would ban that," Michael quipped.

Another terrible screech of the Yagis shook the crystal pavilion. This time the crystal walls of the city muffled the sonic blast of the screech. "The Yagis is getting closer," Blue Tara observed. "These walls will be breached eventually."

"How can we defend ourselves?" Michael asked. "There's nowhere else for us to run."

"And I'm running out of shotgun shells," Jean added.

"Just great," I said, putting my arm around Jean's shoulder. "We'll just have to throw crystals at them."

"How many laxsa and dzonoqwa do you suppose Hamatsa has at his service?" Michael asked.

"As many as I need," a deep guttural voice replied.

We spun around in shock, our illusion of safety behind the crystal walls shattered like a falling crystal chandelier. Hamatsa stood in an open doorway, his black leather garb silhouetted by the gleaming white crystal plain behind him.

"You have little time to gloat before my army of the dead overruns this city and smothers any resistance from these witches."

"That's because they've been doing such a great job so far," I retorted, with some smug satisfaction. "No wait. I got that wrong. That's us been doing such a great job. We're the ones who've been kicking your ass. Easy to get confused."

"I will ignore your feeble boast," Hamatsa replied, "because before this day is over my slave will serve up your head to me on a silver platter."

I grasped Kinqalatlala's shoulder. "If you're talking about Kinqalatlala, she seems to be helping us just fine."

"Your gullibility will be your demise," Hamatsa said. "Kinqalatlala serves me. Everything that has happened has happened according to my plan. According to my plan to seize the worlds of the sky and the earth."

"Ambitious much?" I replied.

"Go on. Your boasts and your swagger belie your precarious position within this city. Do you really think you can withstand the onslaught of the Yagis?"

"We seem to have done just fine so far," I retorted with as much bravado as I could muster.

"At my command the Yagis will blow down these flimsy walls that surround you. I offer you this last chance to surrender and bow down to your master." As Hamatsa spoke laxsa after laxsa entered the doorway and lined up against the crystal wall behind Hamatsa, lances pointed at us. Several dzonoqwa followed the laxsa into the pavilion, their clubs resting across their shoulders.

"What do we do now?" I asked, turning to Kinqalatlala. "Whose side are you on? Really?"

Kinqalatlala raised her hand above her head. Hundreds of black birds flew out of the crystal buildings throughout the city and landed on the crystal floor before us. She clapped her hands and the hundreds of black birds transformed into exact duplicates of Kinqalatlala. Kinqalatlala put her hand in front of her face. Her fingers morphed into a shimmering steel blade. The hundreds of duplicates raised their hands and their fingers too became steel blades.

Part Two

Jean pointed her shotgun first at Hamatsa. Then at Kinqalatlala. "What do I do?" she cried out.

"My, my," Hamatsa replied, a lecherous grin breaking across his face. His long red tongue caressed his glinting fangs. He stepped to Jean. "What have we here?" he said, his sunken red eyes sweeping up and down her sweaty naked body. "You would make a fine addition to my harem."

I turned and faced Kinqalatlala. "Help us," I said.

"That is my intention," she replied.

One of Hamatsa's gloved hands grasped Jean's breast. "Bow down to your master!" Hamatsa ordered.

Kinqalatlala jumped between Hamatsa and Jean. Without saying a word she stabbed her hand through Hamatsa's chest. His eyes bulged out of his face in surprise as he toppled backwards. The hundreds of duplicate Kinqalatlalas charged the laxsa and dzonoqwa.

The laxsa fought and died silently. Many of the duplicate Kinqalatlalas fell to dzonoqwa clubs and laxsa lances. The dzonoqwa died with blood-curdling cries on their lips. Those not killed by the army of Kinqalatlalas fled out the doorway in the crystal wall back onto the crystal plain. An eerie quiet fell over the crystal pavilion. The duplicate Kinqalatlalas halted, dropped their chins to their chests, looked at their feet and transformed into black birds. The birds quickly and noisily disappeared into the crystal city.

I don't think I twitched a muscle during the short-pitched battle. I noticed the crystal floor turning red with the blood of the fallen warriors. I recalled Kinqalatlala's warning, '*An ancient prophecy foretold the destruction of the city once the crystal walls became stained red with blood.'* The crystal walls commenced to rattle. I looked up to try to find the source of the unusual noise. I felt the walls shaking. Then the floor below my feet. "Earthquake!" I cried out.

"Hardly," Michael replied. "We're not exactly on Earth."

"Don't be so damn literal," I griped.

"Is that the Yagis?" Jean asked.

"The prophecy is coming true!" Kinqalatlala exclaimed.

"What? How do you know?" I asked, confused, my voice tinged with panic.

"The destruction of Dluwulaxa," she replied. "Blood has been spilled. The prophecy has been realized." I glanced down at my feet. The red stain from the blood of Hamatsa's ghouls and Kinqalatlala's Dluwulaxa spread across the crystal floor.

"Mount Rainier," Michael said.

"What about Mount Rainier?" I asked, trying to shake off the panic engulfing me.

"The mountain must be erupting. The volcano is affecting Dluwulaxa."

"Do you know what that means for Seattle?" I cried out. "We need to get off this island."

"We have unfinished business," Blue Tara interjected. "And no means to return. I am not able to bend time and space from this world to your world."

"I don't know," I replied, my emotions bouncing between dread and exasperation. "So we dive into the crystal pool and fly down."

"Do so," Blue Tara replied, "and you may suffer the fate of the furies."

"We've defeated Hamatsa," I insisted. "What more is there to do?"

"Do not be so cocky," Kinqalatlala responded. "Hamatsa is far from defeated. He is most certainly not destroyed. We will face him again, and he will throw even greater forces against us than he has before."

"Our track record has been pretty good so far," I responded.

"Hamatsa has yet to unleash the Yagis against us," Blue Tara added. "Once he does so, this city is doomed. There is not magic in this world powerful enough to stop such a formidable creature. Our only hope is with Lord Garuda."

"We have Kinqalatlala's people to help us," I said. "They showed Hamatsa what they're capable of."

"My people are few in number," Kinqalatlala replied. "We suffered great losses this day. Our losses are devastating to us and can not be replaced. Hamatsa's forces are virtually unlimited. He can afford tremendous losses without affecting the forces he wields against us."

The crystal walls of the city shook again. This time not from any volcanic eruption below, but from the terrible screech of the Yagis. The great bird approached. The hair on the back of my head bristled as the presence of the creature became palpable.

"Well, fuck," I said. "So what do we do?"

"A hot bath with a cold glass of wine would feel so good, right about now," Jean interrupted me. I realized she stood before me fully clothed again. She thrust a pile of my clothes into my arms. "You might want to get dressed," she smirked. "Or not." She winked at me.

"Pizza and beer," Blue Tara said.

"At least we're inside the crystal city," I suggested as I jumped into my clothes. "No one's hurt. We've got White Tara to thank for that," I added. I smiled as White Tara darted onto my shoulder and rubbed her beak against my chin.

"We've still got our weapons," Michael said. "The magic harpoon seems to still be functioning."

I asked Jean, "How many shells you have left in the shotgun?"

"Probably enough for a very short fire fight. But I've still got the forty-five," she added, patting the Smith and Wesson strapped to her hip. "I haven't fired a single round of that yet."

I glanced over Red Tara's shoulder. Her quiver seemed well stocked with arrows. "How come you never seem to run out of arrows?" I asked her.

"Magic," she replied.

"Of course. I should have known."

"Can we count on the people of Dluwulaxa when Hamatsa unleashes his next assault against us?" Blue Tara asked Kinqalatlala.

"Of course," she replied. "My people will do what we can to protect our world."

"Being stuck in here we have no idea what's going on out there," I observed. "Can we send White Tara out to reconnoiter?"

"Not with the Yagis approaching," Blue Tara replied. "That would not be safe for people or birds."

"That's the problem," I noted. "We have no idea what Hamatsa is up to. And we have no way of finding out."

"That may not be entirely true," Kinqalatlala replied

"Is there a way to send a spy out?" I asked.

Without responding, Kinqalatlala began to melt onto the floor of the crystal pavilion.

"Of course," Michael said. "She's a shapeshifter."

First Kinqalatlala's feet turned to liquid. Then her ankles. Then her knees and hips dissolved into a pool of quivering black liquid. As her body dissolved she waved her hand and a doorway opened at the base of the crystal wall. The quivering black pool elongated into the form of a scaly python which snaked hissing out the doorway onto the crystal plain, rapidly disappearing from view. "Well, that is definitely different," I remarked.

"Now we've got a doorway that won't close," Michael observed. I waved my hands. First my right hand. Then my left hand. The doorway remained open. I clapped my hands. The doorway remained open. "You must need an ancient gene or something to get the door to work," Michael commented.

"Ancient gene?" I replied. "What are you talking about?"

"Don't you watch Stargate?" Michael quipped. I glared at Michael. "With Kinqalatlala gone, how do we call her people to help us, if Hamatsa attacks?" Michael asked.

"Oh, I think they'll probably notice." I turned to Blue Tara. "What do the Taras think we should do?"

"Nothing," Blue Tara replied.

"Nothing?"

"We wait," Blue Tara added. "We wait for Hamatsa. We wait for the Yagis. We wait for Kinqalatlala. We are not in a position to act. We wait for Garuda. By now Garuda most likely has heard the cry of the Yagis and will be on his way to assist us."

∆∆∆

"You will get no help from Garuda. Or from Kinqalatlala. Or from the Dluwulaxa," a menacing voice responded from the open doorway. We spun around to find Hamatsa standing in the doorway, his black leather garb silhouetted by the brilliant white crystal plain behind him. Only his gleaming red eyes kept him from looking like a cardboard cutout. "Where is my slave?" Hamatsa demanded. His booming voice echoed around the interior walls of the crystal pavilion. ". . . my slave. . . my slave. . . my slave?" His sunken red eyes searched the pavilion. "Bring Kingalatlala to me," he demanded.

"We don't know where she's at," I replied. Which was true to a point. We really didn't know where Kinqalatlala was at, specifically.

"You lie!" Hamatsa exclaimed. "You will pay for your insolence with your lives."

"They do not lie, my master."

"What the. . ." I spun around.

A crystal wall stood before me inside the pavilion, a doorway open at the base of the wall. Kinqalatlala stood in the doorway. "They had no knowledge of my activities," she added.

"Where did you come from?" I asked, confused.

"That does not matter," Kinqalatlala replied. "What matters is that you bow down to your master, Hamatsa." She dropped to her knees and bent her head down to kiss Hamatsa's boots. Hamatsa grabbed her hair to pull Kinqalatlala to her feet.

"You are not Kinqalatlala," I insisted. "She's helping us fight Hamatsa. She's out scouting Hamatsa's forces on the crystal plain right this very minute."

"I can not be doing that when I am standing right here talking to you."

"You're a duplicate. You're not the real one."

"You do not think so? Let me show you." Kinqalatlala stepped to me. She put her arms over my shoulders and pulled me to her. She pressed her lips to my lips and slid her tongue into my mouth. "Does that remind you of anything?" she asked me.

"That's enough. Stop it!" Jean demanded, leveling her shotgun at Kinqalatlala's head for emphasis.

Kinqalatlala stepped back and bowed her head to Jean. "This is all part of my master's plan to crush the resistance," Kinqalatlala said. She stepped to Hamatsa's side. She bowed to Hamatsa. I noticed she held her hand in front of her face. Her fingers transformed into a shimmering steel blade. Before her hand could move Hamatsa grabbed her throat and squeezed. I heard her neck snap. Her body fell limp and dangled in his hand. Hamatsa released his grasp on her neck. As the body fell to the surface, the body dissolved into a large black bird. Wings spread, the bird flew out the doorway.

"So you can't tell which is real and which is Memorex," I said to Hamatsa in a taunting tone.

"You fool," Hamatsa replied. "None of what you see is real. This world of Dluwulaxa is an illusion. This world only exists in my mind to send you on a fool's errand. I have manipulated every experience of yours. Every action you take. Every reaction to every action. You and your witches have fallen into a trap that I have constructed in my mind. A trap that will result in your destruction."

"Dluwulaxa is very much a real place," Kinqalatlala said, stepping through the doorway in the interior wall. Or a duplicate of Kinqalatlala. I gave up trying to discern a difference. Maybe in this world the people of Dluwulaxa could exist in several forms at once. "I am Kinqalatlala," the new Kinqalatlala said. "Dluwulaxa exists. My world is not a figment of anyone's imagination. Dluwulaxa is as real as you are. As real as I am." *That might not be the best argument in her support*, I thought to myself.

"Then bow down to your master!" Hamatsa demanded. Kinqalatlala stepped to Hamatsa and bowed. Hamatsa grabbed her throat and lifted her off her feet. I heard her neck snap as he squeezed her throat. He released her neck and her limp body fell to the surface. The body dissolved into another black bird. Hamatsa tried to kick the bird, but the bird jumped out of the way, wings flapping, and flew out the doorway to the crystal plain.

"I grow weary of this game," Hamatsa sighed.

"You and me both buddy," I replied. "But that puts a lie to your claim that this world is a figment of your imagination. You don't have any more of a clue who the real players are than I do." The way Hamatsa glared at me suggested I struck a nerve.

"I am a real player," said Kinqalatlala, standing in the doorway to the crystal city. We all turned to stare as Kinqalatlala entered the pavilion. She stepped rapidly to Hamatsa. Before he could command her to bow to him, she transformed her hand into a shimmering steel blade and thrust the blade through Hamatsa's chest. Hamatsa collapsed to the floor. His body dissolved into thin air.

I watched the steel blade that was Kinqalatlala's hand transform back to her hand. "So he was right about being a figment of our imagination," I said. "That wasn't the real Hamatsa. Are you the real Kinqalatlala? Not that the difference matters anymore."

"That Hamatsa was an illusion created by Hamatsa," Kinqalatlala replied. "A projection of his mind. But beware. As long as the illusion existed, the illusion was just as real and just as dangerous as Hamatsa."

"Just like Anubis," Michael interjected.

"Anubis? Oh, stop with the Stargate references already," I snapped back. "Are you real?" I asked Kinqalatlala again.

"I am the real one."

"Prove it." Kinqalatlala stepped to me. She took my hands in hers and placed my hands on her breasts. She leaned to me to kiss me. I pushed her away. "Unfortunately, that doesn't prove a thing," I said. I heard Jean chamber a couple of rounds into the barrels of her shotgun.

"But I am the real Kinqalatlala. I just came back from my survey of the rim to assess Hamatsa's forces."

"What did you find?" Michael asked.

"The gagits have returned. They are ferrying more of Hamatsa's soldiers up to the rim to attack this world. The laxsa and dzonoqwa are massing for an assault on the city."

"If the gagits are back," I noted, "that means we have a way off this world."

"We would not stand a chance against the Yagis," Blue Tara replied.

"What about the Yagis?" I asked.

"There is a monumental enclosure on the rim of the crystal plain, encased in crystal. That must be where Hamatsa has the Yagis confined."

"That's great!" I responded.

"How so?" Michael asked, perplexed.

"If the Yagis is confined to an enclosure, then maybe we can still effect our escape."

"We would doom Dluwulaxa to destruction," Blue Tara replied. "And lose the tlogwe. We must hold our position until Lord Garuda arrives with the magic necessary to guarantee our safety."

"Just a thought," I continued. "But maybe, if the Yagis is confined to a crystal cage, we could try another preemptive strike? Keep Hamatsa off balance."

"Or we could use the time we have to search for the tlogwala," Blue Tara said. "We must not lose sight of our original mission to this world."

"If you know who the tlogwala is," I said to Kinqalatlala, "now would be a great time to tell us."

"That is not that simple," she replied, throwing me a weak smile.

"Yes. That is that simple!" I cried out in exasperation. "By your own admission, the tlogwala is someone of this world. That's a finite number of possibilities. You said your numbers are small. I'm willing to go out on a limb and bet that you know who the tlogwala is."

"There are no limbs here to go out on," Blue Tara replied. "That would be unwise and unsafe."

"What? No, never mind," I replied, shaking my head. "I'll bet a case of beer Kinqalatlala knows who the tlogwala is."

"I will take that bet," Blue Tara said.

"You would win that bet," Kinqalatlala replied.

Part Three

"I was right!" I exclaimed, stamping my foot on the crystal surface of the pavilion for added emphasis. Then I found myself on my butt. A sonic wave created by another terrible screech of the Yagis literally bowed in the crystal wall of the pavilion. Me, Jean, Michael, Kinqalatlala, and the Taras found ourselves rolling across the floor.

White Tara jumped off Blue Tara's shoulder, took flight, and screeching, flew frenzied circles over us. "We must get away!" Kinqalatlala cried out. A shower of crystal dust rained down upon us as extensive cracks spider-webbed across the crystal wall of the pavilion. Kinqalatlala scrambled to her feet. "Hurry!" she prodded us. "The wall is coming down. We need to get away." She clapped her hands and another crystal wall appeared behind us. A wave of her hand and a doorway opened at the base of the wall. "Come!" she yelled. Kinqalatlala pulled Jean to her feet while Blue Tara pulled me off the floor. I saw Red Tara push Michael through the new doorway as Margarita scampered between his feet.

We scrambled into the new space. Kinqalatlala waved the doorway closed just as the original crystal wall collapsed. An avalanche of crystal shards pounded the new wall like hailstones beating a windshield. A huge crack ripped across the crystal. A sound like sheet metal tearing accompanied the rip across the wall. Smaller cracks branched off from the primary crack and spider-webbed across the crystal wall. "Run!" Kinqalatlala yelled. She clapped her hands and another crystal wall appeared behind us. A wave of her hand opened a doorway for us to scramble

238

through as the previous crystal wall crumbled. Before Kinqalatlala could wave the doorway closed, I saw laxsa charging through the crystal cloud outside the wall, magic harpoons and lances in their hands.

"They're coming!" I cried out. "Give me the forty-five!" I yelled to Jean. She handed me the pistol and pulled several extra clips out of the pockets of her cargo shorts. "How do I use this?" I asked her frantically.

"Pull the slide," she pantomimed with her hands. "Make sure the safety's off. Point and squeeze."

"You rock girl!" I replied as I attempted to pull the slide. *Damn.* That was tougher that I thought. I braced the pistol between my knees and finally managed to pull back the slide.

"You only have to do that with each new clip," she clarified. I winked at her.

Kinqalatlala clapped her hands again and another crystal wall appeared behind us. As soon as she waved the doorway open I grabbed Jean's hand and pulled her through without waiting for someone to tell us to run through. Everyone else quickly followed and Kinqalatlala waved the doorway closed. We found we had company within this new space.

Hundreds of duplicate Kinqalatlalas stood in several rough lines facing us, holding out steel blades where their hands should be. They stared at us stone faced as we ran into the space. Then they stared up as a sound like tearing sheet metal accompanied cracks ripping through the crystal wall. "Get back!" Blue Tara commanded as crystal shards rained down from the wall. We ran through the lines of duplicate Kinqalatlalas. The wall collapsed in a thunderous storm of crystal shards. A great wave of crystal dust billowed out and rolled across the surface of the pavilion, lapping up at the feet of the duplicate Kinqalatlalas. Brilliant sunlight reflected every color of the rainbow through the crystal dust.

The laxsa horde emerged out of the cloud of crystal dust. They stumbled clear of the dust and haze and halted upon seeing the lines of Kinqalatlalas arrayed against them. The laxsa formed a line and beat the butts of their magic harpoons and lances on the crystal floor. The dzonoqwa, carrying their clubs over their shoulders, emerged through the cloud of crystal dust and formed a second line behind the laxsa. "This is not good," I cautiously observed.

"Do not fire until you see the whites of their eyes," Blue Tara quipped. I sheepishly grinned back at her.

An arrow whistled past my ear and struck the head of a laxsa in the first line squarely between his eyes, sending him tumbling backwards. I glanced behind me to see Red Tara nock another arrow into position. She looked back at me, bemused. "What? I can see the whites of their eyes," she explained.

White Tara darted off Blue Tara's shoulder and raced across the space between the opposing lines. She landed on the head of a laxsa, let out an ear-popping screech, sunk her beak into the demon's nose, and jumped away. A dzonoqwa swung his club at White Tara, but smashed the head of the laxsa instead. Other laxsa screamed in anger. They aimed their magic harpoons at the dzonoqwa, who collapsed dead. Another dzonoqwa attacked the laxsa, only to be impaled by a laxsa with a lance through his heart.

Without any audible order to commence, the Kinqalatlalas screamed and charged. All the hair I had left on my body bristled at the sound of the screams, like a hundred cats fighting outside your bedroom window in the middle of the night. I raised the Smith and Wesson and held my breath as I prepared to fire. The laxsa and dzonoqwa turned to face the charging Kinqalatlalas. The laxsa dropped to their knees and pointed their magic harpoons as the Kinqalatlalas fell upon them. Scores of the Kinqalatlalas collapsed dead and did not turn into birds.

The original Kinqalatlala standing behind me let out a bloodcurdling scream that turned the blood in my veins into ice water. My body convulsed with shivers. She pushed past me and charged toward the melee waving the steel blade that had been her hand.

Red Tara commenced rapid fire release of arrow after arrow, each striking a laxsa's head squarely between his eyes. A laxsa raised a lance and prepared to sling the spear at the original Kinqalatlala. Blue Tara heaved her battle axe before the laxsa could fling his lance. The battle axe whistled through the air and lopped off the laxsa's head. The skull of another laxsa stopped the blade. He collapsed to the floor.

"Come on!" I yelled at Michael and Jean. "What are we waiting for?"

Michael dropped to his knee and pointed his magic harpoon at the ghouls. I started pacing forward, firing a shot with every step, my hand jumping into the air with each recoil. I was thrilled to see that most of my shots hit their intended targets, blowing the laxsa backwards. In a few instances, I saw a couple of laxsa go down from one bullet. After ten paces and ten shots I began to wonder just how many bullets these clips held. Four more paces and four more shots gave me my answer. I took a fifteenth step and heard the firing pin click on empty.

I stopped to fiddle with the pistol when I realized Jean forgot to tell me how to change clips. As I bent over to examine the gun an excruciating pain in my thigh dropped me to my knees. I dropped the pistol. Looking down I realized a lance stuck through my thigh. I heard Jean scream behind me. Several laxsa rushed at me to administer a coup de grâce. A shotgun blast from behind me nearly punctured my eardrums and blew off the heads of two of the charging laxsa. As two other laxsa raised their lances to try to spear me, a black dervish, Black Tara, whirled past me and separated their heads from their shoulders with her flashing steel claws. Thank God for black cats I thought to myself as I suddenly felt very lightheaded. Jean dropped to her knees at my side and put her hands on my shoulders. "Try not to move," she told me. "Everything will be okay," she reassured me.

"Whatever you say, sweetie," I replied, as I faded out of consciousness.

ΔΔΔ

I came to just as Blue Tara yanked the lance out of my thigh. She had sheared off both ends of the lance with her battle axe. Someone tied my belt around my thigh as a tourniquet. I'd be hard pressed to say which hurt worse. The lance going into my thigh. Or Blue Tara yanking the lance out of my thigh. Needless to say, I immediately passed out again.

I awoke to find Jean cradling my head in her lap. "You okay now, hon?" she asked me.

Groggy and disoriented, I reflexively ran my hands over my thigh. No lance. No tourniquet. I sat up and ripped my pants leg open. Blood soaked the pants, but I found no lance. No wound. Not even a scar.

"What the hell happened?" I asked Jean.

"White Tara fixed you up. You were lucky. The lance missed any major artery, so you didn't bleed out."

"Can I get up now?" I asked.

"Don't see why not." Jean scrambled to her feet and helped me up. Other than feeling slightly dizzy I seemed to be no worse for the wear. Better off than my pants anyway.

"Don't mind me," I said, as I pulled my Swiss Army knife out of my pocket, stepped out of my pants, and cut the legs off below the tear.

White Tara alighted on my shoulder and rubbed her beak on my chin. "You do not need to undress now, sweetie," she said. "You can thank me later when this is all over."

"What happened?" I asked, looking around the ruins of the crystal pavilion as I pulled my new shorts back on. Only a pile of crystal shards remained of the exterior wall. Many of the crystal structures within the city lay in ruins. Bodies of dead laxsa and dzonoqwa, interspersed with severed heads, littered the surface of the pavilion.

"Earthquakes have been rocking Dluxulaxa," Jean replied. "Ever since the battle ended.

"Not earthquakes," Michael clarified. "Dluwulaxa quakes. Seattle is most likely rocking and rolling. I'm guessing Mount Rainier is erupting and shaking Dluwulaxa to its core. Don't know how much more we can take here. Don't know what keeps this world up here to begin with. But I'm pretty sure we need to get off this place as quick as possible before we drop into the volcano."

I looked around for Kinqalatlala. She stood chanting a lamentation over the bodies of her dead warriors. A flock of black birds flew circles over her head. "What did I miss?" I asked.

"We killed most of the laxsa and dzonoqwa," Michael replied. "Or I should say Kinqalatlala's people killed most of the laxsa and dzonoqwa. But at the cost of about half their numbers. Some of the ghouls were killed by falling crystal shards. Some escaped and ran back out onto the plain."

"Then the earthquakes started," Jean added. "That brought down the wall and many of the structures within the crystal city."

Blue Tara saw me standing. She darted to my side. She put her arms around me and pulled me to her.

She placed her lips on my lips and kissed me. Hard. I let her. After a few moments I could hear Jean clearing her throat. Hands on my shoulders, Blue Tara stepped back and fixed her one gleaming yellow eye squarely on my face. "I am pleased to see you up and well again, thanks to my sister White Tara. You gave us quite the scare. Your lady friend was very concerned for you. You are a lucky man to have such a friend."

"Yes I am," I replied. I turned to smile at Jean. "Is Hamatsa going to try to strike at us again?"

"All business," Blue Tara responded. "I like that in a man." She smiled. "We must be prepared for any contingency. Thanks to the laxsa we have a large arsenal of magic harpoons at our disposal now. The odds in our favor have improved dramatically."

"Shouldn't we be trying to get off this world before Dluwulaxa blows apart?"

"Hamatsa controls the gagits. They are our only means to get back down to your world. But we still have to complete our mission. To leave now would doom this world to destruction. Leaving would doom your world to destruction."

"Are you kidding me? In case you haven't noticed, this world is doomed to destruction anyway. Apparently we're realizing an ancient prophecy. If we don't get off this world we're going to be doomed to destruction along with Dluwulaxa."

Red Tara placed one of her four hands on my head. "Everything has a way of working out if you are

245

patient," she said. "Hasty action can be just as destructive to our cause as the forces of evil we face."

Her lamentation concluded, Kinqalatlala joined us. "Your ancient prophecy seems to be coming true," I told her. "Shouldn't we be trying to get off your world before Dluwulaxa is completely destroyed?"

"My people will not abandon our home," Kinqalatlala replied. "And neither will I."

"Your people fought valiantly," Blue Tara said, putting a hand on Kinqalatlala's shoulder. "My sister Taras and I are so sorry for the losses your people suffered."

"I thank you for your kind words," Kinqalatlala replied, placing her arm across Blue Tara's arm. "This world literally hangs by a thread. A crystal thread. If that thread is cut my world will be lost. And if my world is lost then your world will soon be lost as well."

A loud rattling noise above my head caught my attention. I looked up. The others looked up. The rattling seemed to descend out of the sky and settle onto the floor of the crystal pavilion. The floor commenced to shake. First gently. Then violently. With nothing to hold onto, we all sat down on the floor to keep from falling down. Clouds of crystal dust billowed into the sky as several more crystal structures within the city collapsed.

"I don't think we have a lot of time left," I said. "We need to get off this world."

"We might be able to surprise Hamatsa's ghouls," Red Tara said, "and capture the gagits. Hamatsa will not be expecting an attack from us. The Yagis may not be watchful."

"We need to try something," I replied. "We're doomed if we stay here."

"I will not leave my world," Kinqalatlala repeated. "But I will help you return to yours."

"Before Hamatsa's attack," I said. "you said you knew who the tlogwala is."

"Yes, I did say that," Kinqalatlala replied.

"Is there still time to find the tlogwala? Or has he been killed by Hamatsa?"

"The tlogwala is still alive," Kinqalatlala replied. "As long as this world survives there is hope to find the tlogwala."

"Then I will stay and help you find the tlogwala. But we need to get the rest of my people back to my world while we still can."

"What?" Jean cried out. "You can't stay. That's what this witch has wanted all along. You'll be killed."

"I have to stay. My destiny seems to be to find the tlogwe. Isn't that right?" I asked, looking at Blue Tara. She nodded her head.

"Then I'm staying with you," Jean replied. "Someone needs to teach you how to use that damn forty-five."

Chapter Eight
Part One

"Nobody is going anywhere, silly man," Blue Tara said. "We either succeed together or fail together."

"That's a noble sentiment," I replied. "I'm sure Davy Crockett told George Russell the exact same thing at the Alamo."

"This ain't the Alamo," Michael replied. "And that's not the Mexican Army out there. And you better find a better analogy than Davy Crockett. I sure as hell don't want to go into a fight with someone who thinks they're going to be dead."

"Anyway, going after the gagits would be too risky," Blue Tara added. "If the Yagis discovered us we would be. . ." Blue Tara pinned her lone gleaming yellow eye at me, "What is that analogy you like so much? We would be burnt bread?"

"Toast," I replied. "We would be toast."

"Please. And can we not talk about food," Michael added. "I'm hungry enough."

"Well then," I said. "What are our options? We can't stay here. We're totally exposed. There's no wall between us and Hamatsa." I pointed out across the crystal plain to where we could just make out the fog rolling up over the rim.

"We move into the city," Kinqalatlala replied. "There are still structures where we can hide."

"What's the point? If Hamatsa or the Yagis don't get us first, an exploding mountain below us may just blow us to kingdom come."

"We must stay alive so we can keep fighting," Blue Tara said. "As long as we fight we have a chance of finding the tlogwala."

"Is the price worth Kinqalatlala's people getting wiped out?" I asked.

"We must prevent that from happening," Kinqalatlala replied. "Dluwulaxa can not exist without my people. And the people of Dluwulaxa can not exist without my world."

"Then I say we go after Hamatsa and drive him off this world," I said. "And capture the gagits while we're at it."

"We'd be exposed crossing the crystal plain," Michael pointed out.

"We're caked in crystal dust," I observed, looking over my clothing. "That can only mean one thing."

"We fly!" Michael exclaimed. "We're birds."

"Bingo." Margarita growled, twirled off the floor and transformed into a small black bird. Wings flailing, the bird screeched and tumbled back to the floor, transforming back into a black cat. "You need to flap your wings to stay airborne," I remarked.

"Bit of a problem if you don't have arms," Michael replied. Margarita got to her feet and brushed her body against Michael's ankles.

I stretched out my arms and visualized myself as a bird. My feet drifted off the floor and I found myself weightless, hanging in the air. "You're a bird!" Jean exclaimed.

"What do you see?" I asked.

"You look like a raptor. A hawk," Jean replied.

Moving my arms gently, I settled to the crystal floor. I turned to Kinqalatlala. "So what was that about needing to take our clothes off?" I asked her, annoyance coloring my voice.

Kinqalatlala smiled at me. She stretched out her arms and morphed into a large black bird. She darted into the air. Blue Tara and Red Tara raised their right feet, placed their feet on their left knees, extended their arms and twirled. They dissolved into pulsating blue and red orbs that coalesced into macaw parrots. I looked for Jean. Instead I saw a large raven flapping into the air.

"I'll stay me," Michael said, "and keep Margarita company. I'll bring the magic harpoons and the shotgun and ammo and we'll catch up to you. Don't start the party without us."

I stretched out my arms again and found myself rising off the floor. I banked toward the rim of the crystal plain to chase the others.

ΔΔΔ

We landed undiscovered in the safety of the fog bank at the edge of the giant fungi forest on the rim of the crystal plain. I settled to the surface near Jean. I cleared my mind and visualized me. "You're getting good at this!" Jean exclaimed. "You are you again."

"And you are you," I replied, throwing my arms around Jean's shoulders to kiss her.

"There will be time for that later," Blue Tara, back in her Amazonian goddess form, interrupted us. "In the meantime, be very careful where you step. One false step could be your last."

My eyes searched the fungi forest for the others. White Tara perched on Blue Tara's shoulder, retaining her Goffin's cockatoo form. The red goddess Red Tara flexed her longbow while she leaned against a giant mushroom. Someone was missing. "Where's Kinqalatlala?" I asked, perplexed. She was nowhere to be seen.

"She flew with us," Blue Tara said. "She must have alighted somewhere else. If something happened to her we most assuredly would have heard something."

ΔΔΔ

Kinqalatlala spooked the several dzonoqwa guarding the gagits when she stepped out of the fog. A couple of dzonoqwa turned and fled. One screamed as he ran the wrong way into the fog and plunged off the crystal rim to his destruction, his scream fading into the distance. "Take me to Hamatsa!" Kinqalatlala

251

ordered. A dzonoqwa pointed his club into the fog and motioned to Kinqalatlala to follow. She found Hamatsa caressing one of the pterodactyls.

"Wonderful creatures, are they not?" Hamatsa said, without looking up at Kinqalatlala. "Obedient. Never complaining. Eager to please. Are you these things my slave?"

"Yes, my master," Kinqalatlala replied as she bowed to Hamatsa.

"You are right on schedule, just as we planned. I am pleased. You have earned the right to live another day."

"Thank you, my master. Everything is happening as you foresaw and planned. The witches are gathered in the mushroom forest preparing to attack you."

"They will be crushed by the Yagis. And then I will exterminate the vermin that inhabit this world." Caressing the gagit, Hamatsa could not see Kinqalatlala grimace and clench her hands tightly into fists. "Then I will have an unassailable base from which to attack the world below."

"Must you exterminate my people?" Kinqalatlala asked. A tear rolled down her cheek.

"Let us not get sentimental," Hamatsa replied. "The Dluwulaxa are a worthless race. They must not be allowed to interfere with my plans."

"The Dluwulaxa only desire to live in peace. They wish to harm no one."

"And that is precisely their problem. And their weakness. There is no peace in a time of war. Peace will only come when those that oppose the new order are exterminated. When those witches and the vermin that assist them are wiped from existence. Then we shall have peace. And you shall be my queen."

"Thank you, my master."

"Together we shall start a new race of warrior kings to rule over a new world. A world of masters and slaves. Of swords and chains."

"Of course, my master. As you ordain. But are you not concerned about the ancient prophecy that foretold the destruction of Dluwulaxa should blood be shed?"

"Do you dare challenge me!" Hamatsa exclaimed, turning to glare at Kinqalatlala. "I am not interested in your fairy tales. They are not real. This is real," he said, patting the gagit on the creature's snout. "Get back to your witches. Soon I will release the Yagis and end this nonsense. And we can get on with our work."

"Yes, my master," Kinqalatlala replied as she bowed in submission.

"When my work is done bring the head of the one with the parrot to me!" Hamatsa yelled as Kinqalatlala fled into the fog.

ΔΔΔ

Kinqalatlala emerged from the fog moments after Michael and Margarita found us hiding among the giant mushrooms. I whipped the forty-five out of my waistband and pointed the pistol at her before I recognized her. Red Tara already had an arrow nocked and pointed at her head. "Easy," I cautioned, nodding at Red Tara. She relaxed her grip on the arrow. "Where have you been? We were worried about you."

"Hamatsa is on his way to attack you," Kinqalatlala replied. "He is preparing to release the Yagis for the final assault on Dluwulaxa."

"What?" I said, surprised. "How does Hamatsa even know we're here?"

"I told him."

"That bitch!" Jean screamed. She pumped shells into the barrels of her shotgun. "This witch has been working with Hamatsa all along." I grabbed the barrels of the shotgun before Jean could raise the weapon to shoot Kinqalatlala.

"You told him? Seriously?"

"Let your friend shoot me," Kinqalatlala replied. "I deserve to die. I have destroyed my own world."

"So why are you telling us this now?" I asked. "I am totally confused."

"I have made a grievous mistake. I need to atone for my sin."

"Don't believe her!" Jean insisted. "She's lying. We're being set up for a trap."

"Was your mistake lying to Hamatsa? Or lying to us?" I asked.

"A long time ago I fell to Earth and Hamatsa captured me and enslaved me," Kinqalatlala said. "He promised to return me to my world if I served him. Now I have learned the true cost of my freedom. Hamatsa aims to reward my service by destroying my people."

"And you expect us to believe this? Why?" I asked.

"I do not expect you to believe this at all. I expect and wish you to kill me."

"You must know we will not kill you," Blue Tara interjected. "You still hold the secret to the tlogwala."

"Then let me help you," Kinqalatlala replied. "If we act now we can surprise Hamatsa before he strikes you. He believes I still serve him and will not be expecting an attack."

"She's leading us into a trap," Jean said. "We can't trust her."

"So let's spring the trap," I replied. "We came out here to punch Hamatsa in the face. Knowing Hamatsa is setting a trap for us gives us an advantage."

"And if she's telling the truth and there is no trap," Michael added, "we have the opportunity to give Hamatsa a knock-out punch."

"White Tara will fly ahead under the cover of this mushroom forest," Blue Tara said. "She will scout out Hamatsa and his ghouls. She can warn us if an attack is coming."

"Okay," I said. "Let's go." I grabbed one of the magic harpoons from Michael. "If you're lying to us," I said to Kinqalatlala, "you will rue the time."

"You bet she will," Jean added, patting her shotgun.

ΔΔΔ

Hamatsa stood outside a gigantic crystal box that caged the Yagis. With a wave of his hand one of the four walls of the box vanished. A monstrous winged creature resembling an enormous vulture, with legs and face covered in thick red scales that gave the appearance of armor plating, and a body and wings covered in feathers seemingly painted red with ochre, waddled out of the enclosure. The dzonoqwa serving as Hamatsa's bodyguard stumbled backwards, growling in fright. "Stand your ground!" Hamatsa ordered. "The Yagis will not harm you as long as you stand by me."

White Tara darted out of the fog and alighted on the shoulder of one of the dzonoqwa. Letting out a screech, she dug her beak into the creature's neck and jumped away. The dzonoqwa screamed. Enraged, the demon spun around and smashed his club into the head of the dzonoqwa standing behind him, dropping the dzonoqwa where he stood.

Several dzonoqwa screamed and rained blows with their clubs on the head of the first dzonoqwa. An arrow smashed into the head of one of the dzonoqwa squarely between his eyes, sending him tumbling backwards. Hamatsa yelled a command, but the screams of the enraged dzonoqwa drowned him out. Emerging from the fog, Michael and I dropped to our knees and took deliberate aim with our magic harpoons at the dzonoqwa sparring among themselves. One by one we dropped them dead. The Taras stood by, ready to assist. Jean kept a close eye on Kinqalatlala.

Seeming somewhat panicked, Hamatsa called out several commands to the Yagis which I couldn't make out over the screams of the dzonoqwa. Hamatsa finally pointed a gloved hand in our direction. The Yagis took several halting steps forward. Head raised, the monstrous creature's great wings spread out, the winged demon opened his beak as if to let out one of his terrible screeches.

"Oh shit!" I yelled. "Watch out for the screech!" I pressed my hands to my ears and squeezed my eyes shut.

Instead, haunting silence gripped the crystal plain, as if all noise were extinguished. The Yagis never managed to screech. A majestic and fearsome bird of immense size appeared in the sky above the Yagis. The gold of the bird's body radiated a brilliant light as bright as the sun. The majestic bird's white face and massive beak gave the apparition the appearance of an eagle. An eagle with a golden crown. Blood red wings spread across the horizon. "Lord Garuda!" Blue Tara cried out.

Garuda stretched his enormous talons down and seized the Yagis. Slowing beating his great wings Garuda climbed into the sky with the Yagis struggling futilely in his claws. The wind created by Garuda's flapping wings knocked us off our feet. Garuda banked into the clouds rolling up over the rim of the crystal plain and disappeared. Hamatsa stood alone, exposed on the crystal plain, surrounded by the bodies of dead dzonoqwa. He seemed stunned into silence.

Kinqalatlala stepped to Hamatsa and handed him the fedora that had blown off his head, exposing his long black stringy hair to the wind of Garuda's wings. "I know how much you love this hat," she said. As Hamatsa reached for the hat, she dropped the hat at his feet. She raised her hand to her face. Her fingers turned into a shimmering steel blade. Reaching out, she drew the tip of the blade across Hamatsa's chin, leaving a line of red blood. Hamatsa stood stone-faced. "The best laid schemes o' mice an' men gang aft a-gley," Kinqalatlala said.

"You will pay for your deception!" Hamatsa screamed out in anger and frustration.

With the tip of her steel blade, Kinqalatlala cut a line of blood across Hamatsa's other cheek. "Maybe so," she replied. "But not to you. I was a fool to ever believe you would assist me."

I heard that loud rattling noise again I first heard inside the crystal pavilion. The crystal plain commenced to shake. The shaking grew in intensity, becoming so violent the huge crystal box that had caged the Yagis collapsed in a cloud of crystal shards and dust. Jean and I grabbed each other for support. The others dropped to their knees or sat down on the surface to keep from getting thrown down. Only Hamatsa and Kinqalatlala continued to stand. "You are too late," Hamatsa said. "Your pathetic world is on the verge of destruction. You and the other witches will be destroyed along with your world."

"I thought you did not believe in ancient prophesies," Kinqalatlala replied.

"You are powerless to prevent the inevitable," Hamatsa continued. "I will find another slave to serve me as my queen. But I regret that I will lose these," Hamatsa added, placing his gloved hands on Kinqalatlala's breasts. Kinqalatlala stabbed the steel blade that was her hand through Hamatsa's chest. As he collapsed to the surface, she sliced the blade through his heart.

Part Two

Another quake convulsed the world of Dluwulaxa as Kinqalatlala wiped Hamatsa's blood off her hand across his black leather coat. Just as quickly as the quake started the convulsion stopped. The feathered tips of a gigantic blood red wing fluttered up through the clouds at the edge of the crystal plain. The great white head of an enormous eagle capped by a golden crown rose over the crystal city of Dluwulaxa.

A blue and gold macaw parrot fluttered out of the clouds rolling over the rim of the crystal plain and alighted on Blue Tara's outstretched arm. I recognized the macaw as the parrot named Aboo, the parrot we left to guard my Ballard apartment when we departed on this adventure, the parrot that first directed me to my fateful meeting with Princess Tara at Charlie's Bird Store. "Greetings Ekajati," Aboo said to Blue Tara. "The world of the Dluwulaxa will no longer be troubled by the eruption of the mountain below. Garuda is protecting and stabilizing Dluwulaxa with his wings and will do so until the mountain returns to sleep."

"Thank you Aboo," Blue Tara replied. "Lord Garuda's arrival is timely once again. If I might ask, what of the Yagis?"

"Garuda has encased the Yagis in an unbreakable cage within the mountain itself, sealed by white hot magma. Rest assured, the Yagis will not trouble this world or your world any time soon."

"What happened to my apartment?" I asked Aboo. "What happened to Seattle?"

"Your apartment suffered little damage," Aboo replied. "A few glasses fell out of a cabinet. A window broke, which allowed me to leave. Garuda managed to contain the violence of the eruptions to the mountain itself, and spared Seattle and other cities around the region. Rainier may be without glaciers for some time to come, but that could not be helped."

"We are ever thankful for Lord Garuda's assistance," Blue Tara interjected.

"Lord Garuda is happy to assist," Aboo replied. "You have achieved a great victory over Hamatsa today. Of course, you realize this is not the end of Hamatsa?"

Aboo added, stretching out a wing toward Hamatsa's prone body. "Hamatsa is crippled, but not destroyed. His magic is too great."

"This at least gives us a reprieve and a chance to rest before the day we must face Hamatsa again," Blue Tara replied. "And to consume pizza and beer."

"I must return to Garuda," Aboo said. "The gagits are resting on the rim of the crystal plain, so you have the means to return to your world."

"Thank you Aboo," Blue Tara said, "but we still have unfinished business here on Dluwulaxa. We must find the tlogwe before we return to Seattle."

"And so you will," Aboo said as he jumped off Blue Tara's arm. Flapping his wings, he disappeared into the fog on the rim of the crystal plain.

"I wish I was as confident," I replied.

"I am confident we will not be troubled by Hamatsa anymore this day," Blue Tara said. She grasped her battle axe in one hand and Hamatsa's hair in the other and lopped off his head. She swung Hamatsa's head over hers and sent the head flying into the fog and oblivion.

ΔΔΔ

Blue Tara pointed her battle axe at Kinqalatlala. "Time for this witch to take us to the tlogwala."

"I can not do that," Kinqalatlala replied.

"Why not?" I asked. "Hamatsa is dead. For now anyway, Dluwulaxa is safe."

"For now," Kinqalatlala said. "But we are not done with Hamatsa. Hamatsa will not give up so easily."

"So take us to the tlogwala. Let me receive the tlogwe. Let me save your world. And my world."

"Not that simple," Kinqalatlala stated.

I shook my head. "You keep saying that," I replied, frustrated. "But I don't believe you. If as you say you know who the tlogwala is, what could be more simple? You can just tell me!" I exclaimed, my voice dripping with exasperation.

"The person who receives the tlogwe must first prove themselves worthy of the gift of the magic of the tlogwe."

I could feel my face flush. "I've been stabbed, speared, fucked. . ." I said, glancing to see Jean's reaction, "and did I mention killed? I've helped save you. Helped kill Hamatsa. Helped save Dluwulaxa. I've flown a gawddamned pterodactyl, for chrissakes. What more do I have to do?"

"That is not for me to say," Kinqalatlala replied. "Expecting and receiving this special gift are two different things."

I hung my head. "I give up. Maybe we should leave and return home," I said glumly.

"That would doom both our worlds to ultimate destruction," Blue Tara said. "Until we find the tlogwala we must stay on Dluwulaxa. Unless. . ." My ears perked up. Blue Tara looked at Kinqalatlala, "unless the black witch tells us to search elsewhere."

"Are you suggesting the tlogwala is not here after all?" Jean asked.

"Huh?" I stammered.

"Here's a thought," Jean continued. "What if the tlogwala is in Seattle instead of here on Dluwulaxa? What if this witch is still working with Hamatsa to deceive us? To keep us from the truth. If she keeps us occupied up here with some silly wild goose chase we can't fight Hamatsa on our world."

"We are not chasing a silly wild goose," Blue Tara interjected.

I put my hand on Blue Tara's shoulder. "That's a figure of speech. Don't take her literally. But Jean is right. We could be sitting up here starving to death chasing wild. . . ah, chasing Hamatsa, while he's down in our world building an empire."

"I was Hamatsa's slave," Kinqalatlala replied. "You knew that. That was no secret. But I am free of Hamatsa now. Here. Free to rejoin my world."

"But you can never become Dluwulaxa again yourself," I said, "without the magic of the tlogwe."

"That is correct. Do you not think if I could give you the tlogwe I would? So you would possess the magic to restore me to my people?"

"That's why she doesn't want you to leave," Jean said. "She wants to make you a bird person. She wants to make you Dluwulaxa. She doesn't care about us. She doesn't care about fighting Hamatsa. She wants you."

"I offer you a world of peace and absolute freedom," Kinqalatlala replied. "All of you. But one of you is special. One of you, and only one of you, has the potential to fulfill the destiny of the tlogwe. To receive the gift of special powers that the tlogwala can dispense." Kinqalatlala took my hands in hers. "If you commit to Dluwulaxa, you could use the magic of the tlogwe to help both my world and your world."

"Don't fall for it!" Jean cried out. "She's trying to trick you."

"Your friend is correct," Blue Tara said to me. "Your destiny lies elsewhere than here in the clouds. We have a war to fight. And if we can not find the tlogwe here on Dluwulaxa then we need to return to our world to search for the tlogwe there."

"I never intended to become a bird person," I insisted. "I never intended to stay on Dluwulaxa." Kinqalatlala dropped my hands and backed away from me, a glum look across her face. "But I believe her. What she says about Hamatsa. I'm willing to stay here on Dluwulaxa to search for the tlogwe if you all want to return to Seattle to search for the tlogwala there."

"Dividing our forces is a bad tactical idea," Michael said. "Don't you watch Game of Thrones? We need to stay together. Either here. Or, more preferably, back in Seattle."

"I for one am ready to go home," Jean said. "I feel like I could sleep for a week."

"In a real bed," Michael added.

"I could stand a pizza and a beer. Maybe a couple of beers. You're welcome to come back to Seattle with us," I said to Kinqalatlala. "I'll even buy the pizza and beer."

"But only if she wears some real clothes, for chrissakes," Jean said.

"You can help us search for the tlogwala in Seattle and help us deal with Hamatsa when he shows his ugly face again," I added. "I promise you that when we find the tlogwe I will come back with you to help restore you to your people."

"We should secure the gagits," Michael said, "before they decide to fly off."

"There might still be laxsa and those sasquatch things around," Jean warned.

White Tara hopped off Blue Tara's shoulder and flew into the fog bank toward the giant fungi forest. "White Tara will check for us," Blue Tara said. "We seem to have accomplished everything we can accomplish here on Dluwulaxa. We should return to Seattle if the search for the tlogwala here is fruitless."

"What should we do?" I asked Kinqalatlala. "Should we go back to Seattle? Will you come with us?"

"I will come with you," Kinqalatlala replied, "if that is what is required to secure your future assistance."

"That would seem to be the case. Will we find the tlogwala in Seattle?"

"You will find the tlogwala wherever the search leads you. And right now the search is leading you to Seattle."

"God I hate these riddles," I muttered.

White Tara flew back out of the fog and alighted on Blue Tara's shoulder. She shook her feathers fiercely. "All clear," she said. "No laxsa. No dzonoqwa. No nontsistalal. We are free to return to Seattle."

ΔΔΔ

Thankfully we only needed to pound on Charlie's trap door for a few minutes before the door swung open. Charlie stood above us basked in incandescent light, staring down at us in wonder.

"Lordy! Lordy!" he exclaimed. "What have we got here?"

"Drop the ladder down," I replied.

He did so. He got down on his knees and helped each of us climb up.

"You're a sight for sore eyes, boss," Charlie said to me, shaking my hand. I noticed he couldn't stop staring at Kinqalatlala.

"You got any extra clothes around?" I asked Charlie, nodding to Kinqalatlala. Charlie's frame was slight enough I thought his clothes might fit her.

"'Course I do," he replied. "What with all the bird shit around I always keep clean clothes handy. You really lucked out. I was just about to close up the shop for the day. Let me get some clothes for this lady. I'll be right back," he said as he walked to his storeroom. I looked around the bird shop. Instead of the usual bustle and din of a bird store the place seemed unusually calm as the birds settled down for the night. Many of the birds stood perched on one foot. A few stood perched with their beaks behind their wings. I suppressed a yawn as I realized how tired I was. "Here you go hon," Charlie said, returning with a stack of clothes in one hand and a pair of flip-flops in the other. "Best I can do." Kinqalatlala took the clothes and dressed. She looked good even in blue jeans and a flannel shirt. Charlie noticed his shotgun slung over Jean's shoulder. "Am I glad to see that," he said with a grin.

Jean handed Charlie his shotgun and unbelted the Smith and Wesson from her hip. "Thank you so much," Jean said. "Saved our butts."

"Good to hear."

"You remember what you said about being able to take down a sasquatch with that shotgun?" Jean asked Charlie.

267

"You're kidding?" Charlie replied. He whistled while he inspected the shotgun. "You're alright in my book," he added.

"You wouldn't believe what we've been through," I said.

Charlie took a long look at me, his eyes dropping down to my pants. "What in God's name happened to you, son? Is that blood on your pants?"

"I got speared."

"No shit."

"Thankfully White Tara saved me." White Tara hopped onto my shoulder and rubbed her beak against my chin. "White Tara. This is Charlie," I said, craning my head to look up into White Tara's pink eye. "White Tara's another witch. Just like Blue Tara and Red Tara."

"My word," Charlie replied. "The Tara of healing. And a Goffin's cockatoo parrot at that."

"We couldn't have beaten Hamatsa without her," I said.

"And did you?" Charlie asked. "I'm almost afraid to ask."

"Yes we did," I replied. "For what it's worth," I added, "we're not done with Hamatsa. He has the power to travel between the worlds of the living and the dead."

"What happened with Mount Rainier?" Michael asked.

"You heard about that?" Charlie replied.

"Heard about that? We were right on top of the mountain!" Michael exclaimed.

"That was pretty scary," Charlie said. "All of a sudden the mountain got active. Totally unexpected. Experts didn't have a clue what was happening. A lot of shaking. Seattle rocked and rolled there for a while. My birds were completely freaked out. There was even talk of an evacuation order. And then the mountain suddenly got quiet and went back to sleep. Nobody could understand what happened."

"Much damage around Seattle?" I asked.

"Thank the Lord, not much at all," Charlie replied. "Few broken windows. Some cans knocked off shelfs in some stores. Couple of brick walls fell down around Pioneer Square. Some flooding around the mountain from the melting glacier. Pretty much all."

"Thank you, Lord Garuda," Blue Tara interjected.

"Lord Garuda?" Charlie asked.

"That's a long story," I replied.

"We don't have time for long stories," Blue Tara said, just before she screeched.

ΔΔΔ

I found myself on the floor of my Ballard apartment, my hands pressed to my ears. Blue Tara helped Jean to her feet. Margarita purred and nuzzled Michael's head as he lay on the floor on his back. Red Tara pulled Kinqalatlala to her feet. White Tara sat on Princess Tara's play stand, one foot tucked into her feathers with her beak behind her wing.

Blue Tara bent down, grabbed my arms, and yanked me up. Then she walked into the kitchen and opened the fridge. "This is a problem," she said. "You have no beer left."

"While you all figure out the pizza and beer," Jean said, "I'm going to jump in the bath. Just bring me some pizza and beer when you have any."

"So I'll just run across the street and pick up the pizza and beer," I offered. I looked at Blue Tara. "There's no need to help with your time and space bend. Okay?"

"I will run across the street with you," Blue Tara replied. "Just in case of trouble."

"Ah, no. That would be trouble," I insisted. "There definitely would be trouble if you joined me looking like you look."

"You do not find me attractive?" Blue Tara asked, her face furrowed by a frown.

"Are you kidding?" I said. "Just that getting the pizza and beer will go a whole lot easier if I don't have a naked crystalline blue-skinned Amazon goddess with a battle axe to explain."

Part Three

Half an hour later I returned to the apartment with a stack of pizza boxes and a couple of cases of beer. While everyone else dove into the pizza and beer, I left a trail of dirty and tattered clothes into the bathroom to join Jean in the bath. I did take a box of pizza and a six-pack of beer into the bathroom with me. Once in the bathtub however, I found I had other things on my mind instead of food.

As Jean and I settled back at opposite ends of the bathtub, I popped a beer can open and stretched my legs out across Jean's thighs. The bathroom door opened and Kinqalatlala entered.

"What the fuck!" Jean exclaimed. "Can't you knock?"

"I need to talk with you," Kinqalatlala replied. "Is this a bad time?" Jean and I looked at each other.

Kinqalatlala sat on the edge of the bathtub and stuck her fingers into the water, splashing the water back and forth. She ran her fingers up my leg and rested them on my thigh. Jean grasped Kinqalatlala's arm and set her hand on the edge of the bathtub. "You don't get to play with stuff you don't own," she said curtly.

"I feel we got off to a bad start," Kinqalatlala said.

"No shit," I replied. "Killing me would do that."

"I want to tell you a story," she said. "After you hear this story you can tell me to leave or stay. I will do whatever you command."

I took a sip of my beer and handed Kinqalatlala a can. "Stories always make me thirsty," I said.

"Okay. Here goes," she replied. She popped the beer can open, kicked her head back and guzzled the entire can.

ΔΔΔ

A being from another world, a youngster, grew up in a world without limits. This was a world of winged creatures, of freedom and flying, of sun and peace, of clouds and sky. This youngster had an accident while testing her wings before she fully fledged. As youngsters these beings stayed close to their community until they fully mastered the magic of flight. Only when they became proficient fliers did they venture out to explore the wonders and mysteries of their world. They took this precaution because their world was a world apart, a world in the sky of another larger world. Venturing beyond the safety of their community before they fully fledged could easily result in their falling out of the sky. Falling to their oblivion. These occurrences thankfully were rare, but did happen on occasion. Because their numbers were small the loss of even a single member of this tightly knit world in the sky provided a severe shock to the people called the Dluwulaxa.

There was one youngster in this world who possessed a curiosity and thirst for adventure that exceeded any of her peers. In spite of admonishments to the contrary, this youngster ranged farther and farther out to the edges of her world well before she had fully mastered the magic of flight.

272

One day while testing her flying abilities she stumbled upon the forest of giant mushrooms hidden in the fog on the very rim of her world. While exploring the giant fungi a storm blew up and snatched her in its maw and swept her over the rim. Because this youngster possessed some limited magic of flight she did not fall to her oblivion like most caught in the grip of a storm. She fluttered and fought and flapped her wings until exhaustion overtook her. Then she fell to the earth, spent and helpless.

A tall gaunt man found her lost, hungry, and scared, cowering on a beach, exposed to the elements and on the verge of death. Paralyzed with fear and exhaustion she could not escape this creature. His glowing red eyes set in a face of pallid scalloped yellow skin burned through her soul and destroyed her will to escape. She shrank back from this loathsome creature, the antithesis of the beauty and purity of the beings of her world.

This man knew of the ancient legends his ancestors shared through the ages over lonely campfires of strange winged beings that fell to the earth. He immediately recognized this youngster for what she was. He wrapped this girl in a net and took her to his home. She was too weak to employ her flying or shapeshifting magic to try to escape.

He locked her in a cedar box and only let her out with a chain wrapped around her neck. He only let her out to feed her, just enough to keep her from starving to death. Finally, much later, this man let her out of the cedar box and did not force her to go back in. She had lost track of time, so she did not realize almost a year had passed while she had been confined to the cedar box. By then she no longer was a youngster, but fully grown. The man explained to her that she needed to take a form similar to the humans around him. If she did so, he said, he would free her from confinement in the cedar box. He failed to tell her that the humans around him were his slaves and his meals. For this man was a cannibal called Hamatsa. And the humans that surrounded him were slaves or zombies. He failed to tell her that she would become his slave. But this saved her life. Because by becoming Hamatsa's slave, Kinqalatlala avoided the gruesome fate of the humans that Hamatsa feasted upon. To become a zombie warrior in his army of the dead.

Hamatsa took her into a large enclosure in his compound. A cell packed with human prisoners. He told her to pick one of the humans and to visualize becoming to look like that person. She picked out a scared, naked, tall, svelte, young, dark-skinned woman, an immigrant from North Africa with long flowing black hair and a muscular body. She visualized herself as that woman. And she became that woman. When the woman saw Kinqalatlala transform herself into a spitting image of her, the woman screamed and fell to her knees, pleading for her life. Hamatsa drew a sword from under his black leather frock coat and stuck the point of the sword to the woman's throat. He told Kinqalatlala to put her hand to her face. She did. He told her to visualize her hand to be a steel blade. She stared at her hand. Nothing.

Hamatsa demanded she concentrate. Focus her thoughts on the sword in his hand. Still nothing.

Hamatsa angrily put the point of the sword to Kinqalatlala's throat. She stared at her hand and the fingers transformed into a shimmering steel blade. Hamatsa ordered her to cut off the woman's head. She recoiled. He stuck the point of his sword in her breast and told her that if she did not cut off the woman's head he would slice her up with his sword and feed her to his zombies. She swung her arm out with a strength she did not know she possessed and the hapless woman's head flew off her body. The body collapsed to the floor of the cell, red blood spurting out from the neck like a geyser. Hamatsa's zombies fell on the body in a frenzy of feeding. Hamatsa speared the woman's head with his sword and held the head up to Kinqalatlala. He told her if she ever disobeyed him that too would be her fate.

ΔΔΔ

"Oh. My. God!" Jean exclaimed. I downed the can of beer I held in my hand through Kinqalatlala's story.

"Hamatsa saved my life," Kinqalatlala said, "but he did not warn me that taking human form would prevent me from ever rejoining my people. To repay my debt to him I became his procurer of bodies. My punishment was to bear the responsibility of picking the unfortunates that would become his victims."

"I am so sorry," I said. "I can't imagine the emotional scars you must bear."

"I did save your life, you know?" Kinqalatlala added, almost as an aside.

"What? How so?" I asked with considerable surprise. "I remember you killing me. I sure as heck don't remember you saving me."

"At Red Square. At your university. When we first met at the monoliths. Hamatsa ordered me to cut off your head, like I did with the woman whose likeness I bear."

"I guess you failed," I smirked.

"I disobeyed his order. Instead of killing you I tackled you and let you go."

"That I remember. I dropped the crystal when you jumped me."

"That is when I realized Hamatsa was not omnipotent. That is when I recognized something special about you. I saw you the way the blue witch saw you. I recognized that Blue Tara picked you for the same reason. She recognized you had the qualities that could be deserving of the special gift of the tlogwe. The special magic that could bring me my freedom and restore me to my world."

"Past time for you to get out of the bathroom," Jean said, pointing to the door.

"I could leave," Kinqalatlala replied. She stood up and pulled off her clothing. "Or I could join you." She stepped into the bathtub and slid down into the water next to me.

ΔΔΔ

We all sat around the dining table with glasses of wine in our hands, the table stacked with empty pizza boxes and beer cans. White Tara sat perched on Princess Tara's play stand, one foot tucked into her feathers, her beak behind her wing. Margarita lay curled up like a furry black ball under the table at Michael's feet, purring in her sleep. Jean and I sat next to each other wearing matching checkered terry cloth robes. Jean wrapped a towel around her hair. She leaned back in her chair and rested her legs across my thighs. Kinqalatlala sat barefooted in Charlie's blue jeans and flannel shirt, unbuttoned two-thirds of the way down the front. I knew she wore no underwear under her clothes. Michael sat in a borrowed pair of U Dub purple and gold sweatpants, with a matching sweatshirt, the only clothes I had that would fit him. Blue Tara sat dressed as, well. . . Blue Tara. She did remove her battle axe from the leather belt around her waist and set the weapon against the wall. Red Tara sat resplendent in her brightly colored silken skirts and shawl draped over one shoulder. I suspected there was magic involved that made her clothing seem so fresh, clean, and vibrant.

"I want to thank everyone for making me feel so welcome," Kinqalatlala said, raising her wine glass. I noticed Jean roll her eyes.

"Hear! Hear!" Michael exclaimed.

"What's the plan?" I asked, somewhat tentatively.

"Sleeping for a week is my plan," Jean replied.

"Your apartment seems very crowded suddenly," Michael observed. "Where's everyone going to stay? Say for tonight?"

"I've got a couple of empty apartments in the building," I said. "We can use those. Strangely enough, I had a bunch of tenants suddenly want to move out."

"Can't imagine why," Michael smirked.

"But seriously," I continued. "After tonight. What's the plan?"

Blue Tara drained her wine glass. Not that I've had much experience with goddesses drinking, but she sure could put down the alcohol. I made a mental note to myself never to get into a drinking contest with her. "We must continue to focus on our paramount goal," she said.

"Yeah," I replied. "I know. Find the tlogwe." Blue Tara nodded. "Well, that's a given. But what's the plan to find the tlogwe?" I turned to look at Kinqalatlala.

Kinqalatlala looked back at me. "If you were fortunate enough to receive the gift of the magic of the tlogwe, what would you do with the magic?" she asked me.

"That's easy. Save the world. Destroy Hamatsa. Return you to your world."

"Those are fine sentiments. But how would you do that? Even the magic of the tlogwe would not allow you to simply snap your fingers and bring peace to the world."

278

"Now you tell me." I laughed. "That's how they do magic in those Harry Potter movies." Kinqalatlala stared at me stone faced. "Well, since I don't know what the tlogwe is I couldn't very well know what I would do with the magic of the tlogwe."

"Would you come back with me to my world? To Dluwulaxa?"

"I already said I would. To help restore you to your people."

"What if I said that receiving the gift of the tlogwe could only be accomplished by joining with me in Dluwulaxa?" Clearly agitated, Jean noticeably and loudly dropped her feet to the floor and sat up straight in her chair.

"Then we would have to find another way to defeat Hamatsa," I replied. "I think I was pretty clear when I said I wasn't going to abandon my world and my friends for you and your world."

Blue Tara leaned leaned across the table to put her hand on Kinqalatlala's arm. "We need to separate the issue of finding the gift of the tlogwe from the issue of helping you and your people," she said.

"We're not talking quid pro quo," I added. Blue Tara gave me a quizzical look. I shook my head.

"Before we can even address the issue of helping your world," Blue Tara said to Kinqalatlala, "you need to help direct us in our search for the tlogwala. We have been through the underground city. We have

279

been to the ancient village of the dead. We have been to the world of the Dluwulaxa."

"And each time you told us we were closer to finding the tlogwala than we knew," I interjected. "So tell us. Where do we search next?"

Kinqalatlala rose to her feet. She stepped to me, put her arms across my shoulders and straddled my thighs. She leaned forward to lick my lips with her tongue. She kissed me. "You are as close to the tlogwala as you have ever been," she said coyly.

Jean jumped out of her chair, knocking the chair over. She grabbed Kinqalatlala's shoulders and pulled her off me, throwing her onto the floor. "That's enough!" she cried out. "I want this game to stop. Now!"

"Once and for all," I said, jumping up out of my chair, "please tell us where to look for the tlogwala."

Kinqalatlala climbed to her feet. "The tlogwala stands before you," she said. My jaw hit the floor. "I am the tlogwala."

"No shit!" Michael exclaimed. "Not Hamatsa after all."

I fell back into my chair, my arms hanging limp at my sides. "I don't know whether to believe you or not," I said. "You couldn't tell us this before?"

"You were not ready to receive this knowledge before. I am unsure you are ready to receive this knowledge now."

"Does Hamatsa know you are the tlogwala?" Blue Tara asked.

"No," Kinqalatlala replied. "I have kept this knowledge from Hamatsa. I have only recently discovered this knowledge about myself."

"Once Hamatsa finds out you are the tlogwala he will tear Seattle down brick by brick looking for you," Blue Tara stated.

Chapter Nine
Part One

"I am stunned," I offered, sitting stunned. "We've literally been chasing around the known and unknown universes looking for you, and you never said a word."

"I could not say a word until I was positive you were the chosen one," Kinqalatlala replied with a smile.

"We could have been killed," I stammered. "In fact, I was killed. By you!"

"I had to wait for you to prove your worthiness to receive the tlogwe."

"Why didn't you just tell me that?" I asked, more than somewhat flustered. "Think how much aggravation you could have saved."

"I did just tell you."

"Yeah," Michael interjected, a big grin breaking across his face. "But wasn't flying a pterodactyl worth the aggravation?"

"Not to mention flying, period," Jean added.

"Without clothes," Michael quipped. Jean's face turned beet red.

"So now you're all taking her side?" I poured myself a glass of wine. And chugged the glass. "How about we just cut to the chase and you tell me what exactly I need to do to prove myself worthy of you giving me the tlogwe."

"I wish the magic of the tlogwe was that simple," Kinqalatlala replied. "I really do." I dropped my forehead onto the table. "The tlogwe is not a thing that I can simply pick off a shelf and hand to you."

"Then what is the tlogwe?" I asked.

"The tlogwe is magic. The tlogwe is a power that is acquired. The tlogwe is not a material object. Say like a golden fleece."

"Oh, if only. . ." I muttered. "Jason had it so much easier."

"Jason?" Jean asked.

"Jason and the Argonauts, I presume," Michael replied.

"Can the Taras shed any light on this matter?" Jean asked, glancing at Blue Tara and Red Tara seated at the dining table. Margarita growled and Jean glanced under the table.

"This magic of the tlogwe is not in our realm," Blue Tara replied. "We can not help you with something even we do not fully understand."

"So what do we do?" I asked. "What do I do?"

"Keep searching," Kinqalatlala replied cryptically.

"That's not very useful," I said. "You're right here in front of me. I've found you. Or more to the point, you've found me. I don't get what more is expected of me."

"Unfortunately, I do not know what is expected of you either," Kinqalatlala said. "I only know that if and when you prove yourself worthy of receiving the tlogwe the gift will be bestowed upon you."

"If and when?" I replied. I could feel my face flush. "We seem to be moving backwards."

"No kidding," Jean added.

"Even I do not fully understand this being a tlogwala," Kinqalatlala quickly replied. "This is new to me. I probably made a mistake to admit to you that I am the tlogwala. That I am something I do not fully comprehend."

"Are you even sure that you are the tlogwala?" Michael asked.

"That is probably why you were able to keep this matter a secret from Hamatsa," Blue Tara said. "Once he learns this secret he will come after you with every means at his disposal."

"Is the tlogwe something that Hamatsa could take from you?" I asked. "By force?"

"I do not know," Kinqalatlala replied. "I do not fully understand the scope of my abilities as tlogwala. I do not fully understand the magic of the tlogwe."

"Then how do you even know you are the tlogwala?" Jean asked.

"That was my question," Michael said, waving his hand.

"How do we know you're not just making this all up?" Jean added.

"I wish I could explain to you," KInqalatlala said, reaching across the table and taking Jean's hand in hers. For once, Jean did not pull her hand back.

"Then how do you know you're the tlogwala?" Jean repeated.

"I just do," Kinqalatlala replied. "Ever since I fell to earth, I have sensed that my destiny was to search for someone special. For a long time I never understood who this person was. Or why I was searching for him. Or even what I was to do when I found this person. I even feared that Hamatsa might be that person. When Hamatsa discovered me and enslaved me I sensed that there was purpose in my enslavement. That I was using Hamatsa as much as Hamatsa was using me. I came to understand that serving Hamatsa would eventually lead me to the one I searched for. And so that proved to be." Kinqalatlala took my hand in hers. "I found you."

I pulled my hand away from hers. "I am flattered," I replied. "I really am. But how do you know I'm even the right guy? You sure it's not Michael here? Or Jean?"

"Ask the blue witch," Kinqalatlala replied, nodding to Blue Tara. "Ask her why she chose you."

"Because I knew you were the one to search for the tlogwe," Blue Tara interjected.

"That's great," I replied. "But you still haven't explained how you came to be the tlogwala. You expect us to believe that just happened?"

"In a matter of speaking," Kinqalatlala replied, "that did just happen." She took hold of my hand again. "At Red Square. At your school. At the monoliths. When Hamatsa ordered me to kill you. I knew then that you were the one I searched for. That is why I saved your life. That is why I disobeyed Hamatsa's command to kill you."

"Okay," I replied. "You saved my life. I thank you for that. You still haven't explained what I need to do to prove my worthiness to receive this gift of the tlogwe from you. This magic. Let alone explain what I can do with this magic? If and when I ever get the damn thing."

"Because I do not know the answer."

"Terrific!" I exclaimed. I slumped back in my chair and stuck my hands in my pockets.

"I only know that the tlogwe will belong to the one who proves himself worthy of receiving the magic."

"Is there more than one tlogwe?" Michael asked. Everyone sitting at the table except Kinqalatlala turned to stare at him. "I only ask," Michael continued, "because we should know whether someone like Hamatsa can take the tlogwe? Say, force you to give the tlogwe to him? Could Hamatsa force you to give him the tlogwe if he discovered you possessed the magic? Could more than one person possess the magic of the tlogwe?"

"These are all questions I have no answer for," Kinqalatlala replied.

"What do you think?" I asked.

"I think anything is possible."

"We can not allow Hamatsa to gain possession of such powerful magic," Blue Tara said. "Both of our worlds would be doomed if that came to pass."

"No shit," I added. "Think how much easier our task would be if someone could just tell me what I need to do to gain the tlogwe."

"We have the advantage of knowing who the tlogwala is," Blue Tara replied. "Hamatsa does not. We need to use every advantage we have against Hamatsa."

"Kinqalatlala's understanding of her power as tlogwala seems to be growing with time," Red Tara interjected. "By keeping her close to us, we will benefit when she fully realizes her power and her ability to use that power."

"We just can't sit around drinking wine and eating pizza and ceding the initiative to Hamatsa," Michael said, glancing at Blue Tara.

"Well, we could," I replied. "But I'm not sure that would get us any closer to the tlogwe."

"I'm ready for this day to end," Jean said, jumping to her feet. She grabbed my hands and pulled me out of my chair. "I need to get some sleep," she added. "I think we all do." She pulled me toward the bedroom. "Anyone who wants to stay up and keep drinking wine is free to do so, but I say let's get a good night's sleep and figure this out in the morning over coffee."

"I would like coffee," Blue Tara replied.

"In the morning," I said as Jean and I slipped into the bedroom. "Hasta mañana," I added, pulling the door closed behind me.

ΔΔΔ

When Jean and I stumbled out of the bedroom in the morning, we were pleased to find a tray of relatively hot lattes on the dining table. Lattes from Jean's coffee shop. "They put the coffee on your tab," Michael cheerily informed me.

"I don't have a tab," I replied, grabbing a coffee.

"You do now."

"Don't worry sweetie," Jean said, picking up two cups. "My treat."

As I rolled the coffee under my nose to take in the delectable aroma of hot caffeine, I noticed that the Taras were all back to their parrot forms, Black Tara excepted, of course. Red Tara and White Tara sat perched on Princess Tara's play stand. Princess Tara stood on the table, her long cobalt blue tail trailing over the edge. Her head bopped up and down into her coffee cup, making her look like one of those plastic perpetual motion drinking birds that bop and down until they're stopped.

Finishing her coffee, Princess Tara fiercely shook her beak, spraying milk foam over the table top. She took a couple of steps toward me, flapped her wings, and jumped onto my shoulder.

"That is one damn fine cup of coffee," she said, wiping her beak on my shirt.

"When did you ever start talking like that?" I asked, surprised. I craned my head to look into her big gleaming yellow-rimmed eye.

"I heard a famous man speak those words on your Internet," she replied.

"'Bout time you sleepy heads got up," Michael interrupted. "We've all been up for a couple of hours. This is our second tray of coffee." Michael took a sip of his coffee. "I can't believe how much coffee a parrot can drink," Michael added, pointing to Princess Tara.

"Coffee's not really good for parrots," Jean offered, getting a bark from Princess Tara in response.

"Well, she's not really a parrot," I suggested. "Though she is," I added, turning my head to peer into her face again. "So, what have you been doing for the past couple of hours? You could have woke us up, you know."

"You guys needed the sleep," Michael replied, winking at me. "We've been monitoring the news."

"What's the latest?" I asked, scratching Princess Tara's head while I sipped my coffee. I watched her eyelid droop closed over her eye.

Princess Tara jerked her head up. "What is a frappuccino?" she asked me.

"Frappuccino? What?" I replied, confusion creased across my face.

"Never mind that," Michael said. "There was a Starbucks commercial pop up on the tablet."

"I would like to try a frappuccino," Blue Tara added.

"Okay," I said. "Whatever."

"You promise?"

"Once I get the tlogwe, you can have whatever you want." I noticed a frown cross Kinqalatlala's face. "Well, maybe not whatever you want. So, what's the latest?" I repeated.

"Looks like the Deportation Police have locked down the city pretty tightly," Michael said. "Roadblocks all around the city."

"Good thing we've got Blue Tara to time and space bend us around any roadblocks," I replied.

"No kidding," Michael said. "And they're not throwing up roadblocks just for shits and giggles."

"They're not?"

"They're looking for us." I almost dropped my coffee cup. "Or to be more specific, they're looking for a guy with a parrot. They're looking for you." Everyone turned to stare at me, including the birds and the cat.

"Well, I guess I won't be taking Princess Tara out for a walk," I replied.

"Looks like the mayor is still in hiding," Michael added. "They've appointed an interim mayor, but haven't revealed who that is yet. The feds are rounding up the Seattle police and detaining them for so-called reeducation."

"Brainwashing, you mean," I said. Michael shrugged.

"On top of all that, Dear Leader is coming to Seattle."

"Oh yeah? What would be the purpose of that?"

"To take a victory lap. To demonstrate that resistance is futile."

"To show how scared the regime is by the threat posed by the Taras," Kinqalatlala interjected. She sat at the end of the table studying the latte art in her cup, a depiction of a bird in flight, covering her coffee. She seemed to fear drinking the coffee and disturbing the artwork.

"I don't doubt that for a minute," I replied.

"That is the only reason the Winalagalis would leave the safety of the capital," she added.

"So Dear Leader is the Winalagalis," I said, more a statement than a question.

"Winalagalis?" Michael asked. "The god of war of the north? That Winalagalis?"

"Yes," Kinqalatlala replied. "That Winalagalis. But I do not believe Dear Leader is the Winalagalis. Dear Leader is the pretty face that masks the evil that is the Winalagalis. Evil that would not dare show himself in public. The Winalagalis would not be sending Dear Leader to Seattle if he did not fear the power of the Taras."

"This is some serious shit," Michael added.

"This is probably a dumb question," Jean said, "but why doesn't the Deportation Police just knock on your door?"

"More like kick in the door," Michael replied.

"Probably. . .," I said, pausing to crane my head to look into Princess Tara's eye, ". . . probably because we've kicked their butts. So far. That, and we have the protection of the Taras. Right?" Princess Tara sat unresponsive on my shoulder, her eyelids drooping almost closed. "Well, that's my guess anyway. We should be really careful about going out alone."

"You mean, we probably shouldn't go out alone at all," Michael replied. "However, having Blue Tara beam us into the coffee shop for coffee might draw more attention to us than we want."

"Time and space bend us into the coffee shop," I clarified. "Not beam us in."

Michael smirked at me. "Beam me up, Scottie," he joked.

"We just need to be careful, is all I'm saying," I said. "Not take any undue chances."

"I need coffee," Princess Tara suddenly said. She pressed her claws into my shoulder while she fluffed her feathers out.

"Ouch," I said, reaching for her feet.

Kinqalatlala interrupted us. "There is a special bulletin on your tablet," she said, turning the tablet so we could see the screen.

"What's going on?" I asked.

Michael picked up the tablet and turned up the volume. "The Deportation Police are preparing to introduce Seattle's interim mayor," he said.

A pudgy spokesman in an ill-fitting suit who reminded me of a visit to Soviet Russia decades ago stepped up to a podium at Seattle City Hall. "People of Seattle," he said, reading from a sheet of paper he held in his hands. "There is a new order established here in your city. Obedience to rules will be required. Compliance will be celebrated. Resistance will be crushed. I am pleased to announce that our Dear

Leader will be travelling to Seattle to install your new mayor and reveal his plans for your city. Until then, an interim mayor has been appointed to oversee the transition." He gestured to someone off camera to come to the podium. A tall gaunt man appeared, clad in black leather from his boots to his gloves and fedora. Stepping to the podium, he removed his hat to reveal his pallid scalloped yellow skin.

"Hamatsa!" I exclaimed. I dropped my coffee cup on the floor.

Hamatsa motioned toward the camera and the floodlights snapped off, turning the podium dark. Standing in the darkness behind the podium, Hamatsa's glowing sunken red eyes seemed to focus through the tablet's screen directly at me.

Part Two

"Oh. My. God!" I exclaimed as I jumped to my feet. "We keep killing this bastard and he keeps popping up again. Like geoducks at low tide."

"Don't insult geoducks," Michael replied.

"More than your puny weapons will be required to destroy Hamatsa," Kinqalatlala replied. "His magic is great."

"You don't need to remind me. We need the tlogwe. I need the tlogwe."

"I need a frappuccino," Blue Tara said, jumping off my shoulder onto the dining table. She started to knock

294

over empty coffee cups with her beak. "I am out of coffee."

"Good God," I replied. "How much coffee can you drink?"

"We could walk over to the Starbucks on Market Street," Jean said. "Would be good to get out and get some air. No point in staying holed up in your apartment."

"Starbucks? Why not your coffee shop?" I asked.

"Her highness asked for a frappuccino. We don't do frappuccinos."

"The parrots are going to attract some attention," I replied.

"And we'll have to count on the Taras to deal with any unwelcome attention," Michael said. "And Margarita as well," he added, glancing under the dining table to see the cat arching her back and stretching her two front legs. "We should get out and get an idea of what's going on. How people are reacting to this situation. Anyone up for a walk?"

"Or a flight?" I added.

Princess Tara flapped her wings and darted back to my shoulder. "I am coming with you, sweetie. Kurukulla can ride with your lovely friend if she wishes." Margarita sauntered out from under the dining table, looked up, crouched, and sprang up into Michael's lap.

"Guess we're all set," I said.

Red Tara stepped onto Jean's outstretched arm while White Tara hopped onto Jean's shoulder. We filed down the stairs outside my apartment and out onto the sidewalk. Once outside, White Tara leaped into the air and flew out of sight over the building. Red Tara climbed up Jean's arm and perched on her shoulder. Margarita leaped out of Michael's arms onto the pavement and scampered over to a tree which she used for a scratching post.

Jean and Michael and Kinqalatlala and I looked up and down the street. In place of the usual morning hustle and bustle of myriads of people going out for coffee or shopping or work, we found the street deserted and quiet. I jumped when a siren somewhere in the distance broke the silence. Two or three cars passed through the intersections at the ends of the street without stopping at the stop signs.

"I feel naked without my shotgun," Jean said.

"Charlie's shotgun," I clarified.

"Whatever. Feels strange to be out unarmed."

"I wouldn't mind having one of those magic harpoons with me right about now," Michael added. "Funny how you get used to having certain things with you. Almost becomes second nature."

"Now that would definitely draw attention to you," I replied.

"More than a shotgun?" Michael responded.

"Anyway, we've got Blue Tara's battle axe and Red Tara's longbow." I craned my head to look up at Princess Tara perched on my shoulder. "We do? Don't we?" I asked her.

Michael looked intently at the two parrots perched on Jean's and my shoulders. "How do they do that exactly?" he asked.

"Do what exactly?" I asked in reply.

"Keep their weapons with them when they're parrots."

"Why, magic, of course. Was that a serious question?" I smirked.

"That's magic we need to learn," Michael replied.

We trooped up the street toward downtown Ballard single file without uttering another word. The quiet seemed ominous and foreboding. I noticed that I didn't hear the usual cawing of crows from the trees above us. Storefront after storefront along Ballard Avenue stood empty and deserted. A veritable ghost town. I felt goosebumps under my clothing. The old buried city in underground Seattle seemed livelier than the scene along this street.

The few people we saw on the sidewalks scurried away or hurried across the street to avoid us. I breathed a sigh of relief when we got to the end of the street. Both foot and car traffic picked up as we approached Market Street, the main drag through downtown Ballard. Here more of the shops looked to be open. Across the street I could see people walking into and out of the Starbucks on the corner. The usual cluster of chairs and tables sat on the sidewalk outside the shop. As we crossed the intersection, one passerby even slowed and smiled at us, then said, "I like your parrots."

I parked Princess Tara on an empty table and glanced inside the store. "This looks better," I said. "Grab some chairs and I'll get the coffees."

"Frappuccino," Princess Tara replied, cocking her head to the side to stare up at me with her big yellow-rimmed eye.

"Yes, ma'am. A frappuccino for the princess. Frappuccinos all around?" I asked, pointing a finger at everyone. Jean raised her hand. Michael looked at Jean and raised his hand. "Kingalatlala?"

"Nothing for me," she replied, frowning.

"Frappuccinos all around," I said.

Michael elbowed Kinqalatlala. "Live a little," he smirked, sitting down.

I walked into the store.

ΔΔΔ

I walked back outside about fifteen minutes later with a tray of frappuccinos and an iced americano for myself. Not surprisingly, the coffee shop seemed a bit understaffed, and the customers seemed on edge. Princess Tara jumped on my arm as I pried the cover off her drink. Frappuccino foam quickly dotted the

298

front of my shirt as her beak bopped in and out of the cup. And my iced americano as she alternated between sticking her beak in her cup and in my cup. Curious passersby paused near our table and gawked at the parrots. More than one guy paused to gawk at Kinqalatlala.

I noticed a Seattle Police cruiser pass through the intersection outside the coffee shop. The car made a quick U-turn and slowly drove back. In addition to the usual cop in blue sitting behind the steering wheel, I saw a black-uniformed Deportation Police goon riding shotgun. I kicked Michael in the shin under the table and nodded toward the intersection. "Look up slowly," I whispered. "Don't be obvious." Michael jerked his head up out of his drink and stared at the cop car passing by. The cops appeared to stare back at us. "What part of 'Don't be obvious' don't you understand?" I grumbled. The police cruiser passed out of sight.

"Do you think they recognized us?" Jean asked.

"I doubt there are too many people with parrots out and about the city right now," I replied.

The police car appeared on the cross street and pulled to a stop kitty corner from the Starbucks.

"Just act cool," I said. "Tara?" I tapped Princess Tara on her head.

"I need another frappuccino," Princess Tara replied.

"Oh, geez," I said. "You drank the whole thing? How is that even possible?" She knocked over the empty cup with her beak and tilted her head to stare up at me with a somewhat defiant look on her face, if parrots could be said to present defiant looks.

"Okay. I'll get you another one," I replied grumpily, getting up from my chair. "Don't do anything rash until I get back."

ΔΔΔ

About fifteen minutes later I walked out with another frappuccino for Princess Tara. I froze at the door when I realized the two cops from the police cruiser now stood at our table with their hands resting on their pistols. I took a deep breath and hurried to the table. I leaned over to step Princess Tara up on my arm. I set the drink in front of Jean. "Here you go sweetie," I said. "Everything okay?" I asked, glancing up at the cops. I eased into my chair and put my hand on Princess Tara's feet to try to keep her on my arm.

"Apparently parrots are a problem," Jean replied.

"Oh?" I grunted. Princess Tara struggled to break out of my grasp. She clamped her beak on my hand. "Ouch!" I exclaimed, releasing her feet. She jumped onto the table and sunk her beak into the new cup of frappuccino.

"Sorry citizen," the cop in blue said, a short middle-aged man sporting a noticeable paunch and a Tom Selleck mustache. He wore sergeant stripes on his shirt. He didn't appear to be a laxsa. "You are in violation of Seattle's new order banning dangerous exotic animals." I noticed him looking at the bleeding bite mark on my hand. I took a napkin and surreptitiously tried to wipe away the blood. "Animal Control has been called to confiscate the birds before they injure anyone else."

"I know perfectly well Seattle doesn't have any such ordinance, officer," I replied, pressing the napkin against the bite. "I researched Seattle ordinances before I got the parrot," I lied.

"You are also in violation of orders against unrestrained pets," the cop added. "Is that your bird?" he asked, pointing to the top of the building. We all looked up to see White Tara perched on top of the building.

"She's not harming anything," I replied. *Yet*, I thought to myself. "She likes to fly around."

"Good exercise for the birds," Jean interjected.

"You need to get the bird down," the second cop, in the black Deportation Police uniform, said. Younger. Tall and gaunt, his skin seemed quite pale, even for Seattle. The black hair falling out from under his black wool cap seemed unusually long, stringy, and unkempt. I couldn't see his eyes underneath his black wraparound sunglasses, but I suspected he was a laxsa.

"She's a free spirit," I replied. "She only comes down when she wants to."

"I am giving you an order," the second cop added. "If the bird doesn't come down the bird will be destroyed."

"Let's back up," Michael said, jumping into the discussion. "Let's back up to the part about exotic birds being banned. When did that happen?"

"A new directive from the mayor's office," the first cop replied.

"This isn't a dictatorship," I said. "The mayor doesn't rule by decree. The city council needs to pass an ordinance."

"Maybe you haven't heard, citizen," the second cop said, with a note of sarcasm in his voice. "The city council has been abolished by order of the mayor. Decrees come directly from the mayor now. And the mayor has ordered the police to confiscate all exotic animals." He stepped toward the table and reached his hand out toward Princess Tara.

I squeezed my eyes shut and reflexively pressed my hands to my ears when Princess Tara screeched. I heard a scream. I opened my eyes to see a severed hand laying on the table top. The Deportation Police goon held his handless arm in his other hand. He screamed in pain as blood spurted across the sidewalk. I jumped to my feet. The cop dropped the arm and fumbled with his holster. Blue Tara stood next to me in her naked crystalline blue-skinned Amazonian glory, swinging her battle axe in her hand.

The cop attempted to pull his pistol out of his holster. He toppled over onto his back with an arrow sticking out of his head squarely between his eyes. The arrow split his sunglasses into two pieces revealing lifeless sunken bloodshot laxsa eyes. The sound of people screaming assaulted my ears. Passersby and customers knocked over chairs and tables and coffee cups as they scrambled to get away.

Then I noticed the first cop, the older Seattle cop. He stood next to our table with his hands in the air. "Please don't kill me," he pleaded. "I'm not one of them. I was on desk duty for chrissakes. I'm a Seattle cop. They forced me to join up. Or else."

Kinqalatlala rose from her chair. "Get in your vehicle and leave us!" she commanded. "And do not show yourself again." Margarita walked out from under the table on her two hind legs and growled at the cop. Looking down at Black Tara, the cop stumbled backwards and tripped over the curb. He turned and ran to his car, jumped in, and gunned the engine. Tires squealing, he sped away and disappeared.

I slowly looked around me when I noticed people had stopped screaming and had gathered around gaping at us. Blue Tara stood next to me, blood dripping off the blade of her battle axe. Red Tara stood behind me, an arrow nocked in her longbow. A bloody severed hand lay on the table next to my coffee cup. A Deportation Police goon in a black uniform lay dead, sprawled across the sidewalk with an arrow sticking out of his skull between his sunken laxsa eyes. The crowd of people gathered around us, staring at Blue Tara and Red Tara and Kinqalatlala, quickly grew. Like they'd never seen a naked crystalline blue-skinned Amazonian warrior with a battle axe and one breast and one eye. Or a scantily clad red-skinned four-armed goddess sporting a longbow.

"This is not good," I said to no one in particular. I couldn't keep from staring at the severed hand next to my coffee cup. I badly wanted a drink of my iced americano to sooth my sandpaper dry throat. "Tara. Do something," I muttered under my breath. I covered my ears with my hands. "People are staring." I forced my eyes closed as Blue Tara screeched.

ΔΔΔ

"Are you going to sit down and drink your coffee?" I heard Jean ask. I slowly opened my eyes. Jean and Michael and Kinqalatlala sat around the table sipping their frappuccinos. White Tara sat perched on Kinqalatlala's shoulder. Red Tara sat perched on Jean's shoulder. Princess Tara stood on the table bopping her beak up and down into her drink. I tentatively looked around me as I lowered my hands. No cop car. No goons. No severed hand next to my coffee cup. Customers walking into and out of the coffee shop with coffee cups in their hands. Passersby pausing to stare at the birds. Margarita lay curled up in Michael's lap. I did notice Michael's face seemed unusually blanched.

White Tara spread her wings and hopped onto my shoulder. "Miss me sweetie?" she asked as she rubbed her beak against my chin. "My sister Ekajati fixed things as you asked."

"Blue Tara rewound the clock," Michael added. "Now maybe we can enjoy our coffee without interruption."

I sat down and drained my coffee cup. "How many of those are you going to drink?" I asked Princess Tara. A young woman walked out of the shop with an iced

304

latte in her hand and stopped near our table to watch Princess Tara drinking her frappuccino. "Is your bird really drinking that?" she asked.

"Loves the stuff," I replied.

"Isn't caffeine, like, bad for parrots? That's a parrot, right?"

"Right on both counts," I said. "But I let her have a treat every once in a while when she's a good girl," I added, grinning. "A little coffee never hurt anything." Princess Tara paused from drinking her coffee and took a feint at my hand with her beak.

"She seems to be drinking a lot of coffee," the lady observed.

Princess Tara tilted her head and glared at the woman with her big yellow-rimmed eye. "Mind your own business," she said, loudly and clearly. A look of shock froze across the woman's face. She turned and stumbled away, trying not to drop her coffee cup.

Part Three

"Well, then. That went really well," I said. "How about we not insult the citizens?" Princess Tara glanced at me and went back to drinking her frappuccino.

"So Hamatsa abolished the city council and is ruling by decree," Michael said.

"I'm sure the whole country will be next," I replied.

"The question is, what are we going to do?" Michael added.

"What do you mean, what are we going to do? Why is that our responsibility? Seems we have enough problems of our own, what with the Deportation Police hunting us."

"The only way to stop the implementation of the new order is to fight Hamatsa and the Winalagalis," Kinqalatlala replied. "The whole purpose of finding the tlogwe is to gain the magic to take the fight to the seat of power."

"Sounds like we're going to have the perfect opportunity to strike, what with Dear Leader coming to Seattle to coronate the new mayor," Jean said.

"And isn't this why we signed on with the Taras?" Michael asked. "To help them overcome the Winalagalis? The Taras can't bring down the regime without the tlogwe."

"Sitting here drinking coffee," I replied, "the problems of the world just seem less urgent. . ."

"What the fuck?" Michael interrupted. "We just killed a Deportation Police goon. You think they're going to let up on us?"

"They're going to keep coming after the parrots," Jean added. Margarita growled. "After the Taras."

"Well sure," I replied. "Don't get me wrong. One thing to go after Hamatsa and his goons. To keep the Taras safe. Another thing entirely to go after Dear Leader.

He's going to have the entire police power of the state at his disposal."

"Well yeah," Michael said. "What's the problem?"

"The problem is, dear friend, we're not going to get far with one battle axe and a quiver of arrows against the organized military might of the state. Are we Tara?" Princess Tara paused, fixed her big yellow-rimmed eye on me, and went back to drinking her frappuccino. "No worries," I added.

"I have to say," Jean said. "I'm scared to death." I reached across the table and took her hand in mine. "I don't see what we're going to be able to do even if I had Charlie's shotgun."

"We need information," Kinqalatlala replied.

"What kind of information?" I asked.

"Information about Hamatsa's plans."

"How exactly are we going to get that? We can't just waltz into city hall."

"I can."

"What?"

"I would not believe that Hamatsa would reveal to anyone that I broke with him. I can waltz into city hall and find out the information we need."

"Is this an appropriate time to be dancing?" Princess Tara asked, taking a pause from her drink.

307

Kinqalatlala glanced at Princess Tara. "I can walk into city hall. They will never question me or impede me."

"Are you sure? Could be dangerous. What if you run into Hamatsa?"

"I will need to make sure that does not happen."

"How are you going to get the information to us?"

"Leave that to me. I will work something out." Kinqalatlala stood up.

"Are you going now?" I asked.

"Yes. Now is a good time."

"How do you plan to get there?"

"Simple." Kinqalatlala whistled and waved her hand. A police cruiser appeared seemingly out of nowhere and pulled up to the curb beside her. She leaned into the open window and talked with the cop behind the steering wheel. The cop motioned her inside. Kinqalatlala opened the door and slid onto the seat. The cop activated the cruiser's light bar. He darted through the intersection and disappeared up Market Street.

"Well, that was just too damn convenient," I observed.

"I still don't trust her," Jean replied.

"We still have no evidence that she's even the tlogwala," Michael added. "Beyond just her word that she is."

"We need a plan," I said. "A good plan that won't get us killed. Simply sitting around drinking coffee and bullshitting doesn't seem to be getting us anywhere."

"Coffee makes me happy," Princess Tara said. She climbed up my arm onto my shoulder and wiped her beak on my shirt.

"Well, I'm happy for you," I said. "But what's our plan? Hamatsa has his goons out looking for us. Apparently rounding up every parrot in Seattle. And now we've lost Kinqalatlala."

"We have to take that black witch at her word," Princess Tara replied. "She is the key to finding the tlogwe. But we should take the fight to Hamatsa. For once, we know where he is. He does not know where we are."

"What do you propose?"

"We pay Hamatsa a visit. Catch him off his guard. He will not be expecting us to. . . how do you call it? Dance into his city hall."

"Waltz into his city hall."

"Dance. Waltz. Whatever you say."

"And once we drop in on Hamatsa. Then what? What do we do? Kill him? He'll have a ton of security to protect him."

"His laxsa. We can deal with them."

"And Hamatsa?"

"I am making this up as we go. Unless you have a better plan."

"I have no plan right this moment."

"If we kill Hamatsa and he comes back to life will not the citizens of Seattle realize that something is not right? Hamatsa and his goons hide in dark places out of the light of day. We need to shed light on his plans and schemes. Make your people know who and what Hamatsa really is. What the Winalagalis really is."

"You know what?" Michael said, looking up from his smartphone. "There's a farmers market outside city hall tomorrow morning. We could use that for cover, assuming we haven't heard from Kinqalatlala by then."

"What are we going to do until then?" Jean asked.

"Drink coffee," Princess Tara replied. "Until the time comes to eat pizza."

"Do you ever worry about putting on weight?" Jean asked. "Me. I gain weight just by looking at food."

"She probably just makes extra calories go away with her time and space bend magic," I smirked.

Around the corner and out of sight of the Starbucks where we sat drinking coffee a convoy of armored

SWAT vehicles pulled to a stop at the curb. Squads of black clad Deportation Police goons exited the vehicles and assembled on the sidewalk, large machine guns with short barrels slung over their shoulders. Several of the cops in command carried magic harpoons.

ΔΔΔ

Kinqalatlala walked into the security checkpoint at Seattle City Hall. Black clad Deportation Police waving machine guns stood guard in place of the usual city police. "I am Kinqalatlala," she said to the guards. "Take me to Hamatsa." The guards pointed their machine guns at her. "Take me to Hamatsa," she repeated, "or I will carve you up and feed you to the furies." A cop wearing a standard blue Seattle Police uniform, with sergeant stripes on the sleeves, hurried out of an adjoining room.

"Stand down!" he ordered the guards. They lowered their weapons. Kinqalatlala recognized the cop from the Starbucks. "Follow me," he told her.

Once out of earshot of the guards the cop asked Kinqalatlala, "What are you doing here? You're taking a big risk. I know who you are."

"Why are you here?" Kinqalatlala replied. "I told you to leave us and never come back."

"Someone needs to fight back from the inside," the cop replied. "Not everyone on the force supports the new regime."

Instead of taking the elevator, the two walked to an unmarked doorway and descended a couple of flights of stairs to the SPD's secure command center in the subbasement. Hamatsa found the dark depths of city hall much more amenable to his temperament than the airy mayor's office on the top floor of the building. The cop swiped a pass card through a card reader and pushed the door open.

Just as at the Control compound in the other Washington, a bank of computer monitors along the back wall provided the only illumination across the room. The cop led Kinqalatlala to a solitary figure standing in the shadows to the side of the monitors. The darkness nearly swallowed his tall lithe frame clad in black leather. But the darkness accentuated his glowing red eyes. Kinqalatlala stepped to Hamatsa and bowed. "I am here to serve you, my master."

"Where did she come from?" Hamatsa bellowed at the cop.

"She walked into the building, sir," the cop replied.

"Where are the others?"

"She came in alone, sir. There was no one else with her."

"You are either showing off for your new friends," Hamatsa said, "or you are very stupid."

"I am here to serve you, my master. This officer is not who he appears to be," Kinqalatlala added, pointing at the cop. "He is part of the resistance."

Hamatsa seized the cop by his throat with a gloved hand and lifted him off his feet. He opened his mouth and bared his fangs. He bent over to rip the man's neck open. Before Hamatsa could do so, Kinqalatlala raised her hand to her face and watched her fingers turn into a shimmering steel blade. She stabbed her hand through the cop's chest. Hamatsa released the man's neck and the cop's body crumpled to the floor. Blood seemingly as black as the room pooled around the body.

"I have been expecting you," Hamatsa said. Pulling Kinqalatlala away from the dead cop, Hamatsa motioned to a couple of attendants standing nearby. "Clean up this mess," he commanded. His sunken red eyes scanned Kinqalatlala's body. "Where did you get this ridiculous outfit?" Hamatsa grabbed her flannel shirt with his gloved hands. He ripped the shirt off her body, flinging the torn shirt to one of the attendants. "Much better," he said. He placed his gloved hands on Kinqalatlala's breasts. "I missed these. Bring my slave some real clothes!" he barked at one of the attendants. "You will find them in my quarters."

"Yes sir. Right away," the attendant replied as he turned to run out the door.

"How did you know the officer was part of the resistance?" Hamatsa asked.

"He fell across the path of the witches at a coffee shop in the part of the city where the man with the parrot lives. The witches killed his partner. A laxsa."

"How did this one escape?"

"I allowed him to escape. I would have killed him then if I had known he was part of the resistance. I killed him now to prove my loyalty to you."

"That is a shame you did so. I would have feasted on him to make him a warrior. To replace the laxsa I lost to the Taras."

"There will be many more to take his place once you complete the subjugation of this city."

"So tell me, slave. What do the witches, the Taras, plan to do next?"

"They know that Dear Leader is coming to Seattle to install you as mayor. Most likely they will plan an attack on you and him."

"Precisely as we have foreseen," Hamatsa said, gleefully rubbing his gloved hands together. Hamatsa's attendant reentered the command center with a stack of Kinqalatlala's clothing in his hands and presented them to her. "Put that on," Hamatsa ordered.

Kinqalatlala stepped out of her shorts and slipped on a pair of skin tight black leather pants, a black leather vest, and a black leather jacket. She pulled a pair of black leather boots onto her feet. "Are you done staring?" Hamatsa asked the attendant. "This slave belongs to me." The attendant stumbled backwards and disappeared into the darkness.

"Much better," Hamatsa said, his bloodless scalloped lips breaking into a lecherous grin as he admired

Kinqalatlala's sveldt body. "When Dear Leader comes to this city to install me as mayor I will have the entire police power of the state at my disposal. I will be able to destroy that coven of witches and crush the resistance once and for all."

"Why wait until then, master? Why not crush them now?"

"I am preparing a strike against them," Hamatsa replied. He could not see the surprise on Kinqalatlala's face in the darkened room. "Unfortunately, I do not yet have complete control over the Deportation Police. And the Seattle Police are yet too unreliable. They have not been completely cleansed of seditious officers as you have discovered yourself. The Taras are still too powerful to eliminate with the forces I have at my command."

"What are your intentions?" Kinqalatlala asked.

"I will harass these witches with whatever forces I can muster. Keep them on the defensive. Prevent them from striking the regime."

"You are striking them now?"

"Does that concern you? Where do your loyalties lie, my slave?"

"With you, my master."

Hamatsa's gloved hand darted out and grasped Kinqalatlala's throat. "You know what your fate will be if you disappoint me."

"Yes, my master," Kinqalatlala managed to reply.

"You need to insure that the witches carry through with their plan to strike at our Dear Leader. What a shame that would be if they succeeded and I was forced to take Dear Leader's place."

"That would be your destiny, my master."

"I would be forced to use the power of the state to crush those witches and those that serve them. To crush the resistance. To wipe the vermin from the face of this world."

"Absolutely, my master."

"And you would take your place at my side as my queen. Together we would start a new race of warrior kings to rule this world for all time. A world of slaves to serve me."

"That would be my duty and my honor, my master."

"What of the tlogwala?" Hamatsa asked. "Do the witches believe your story that you are the tlogwala?"

"I believe so, my master. The man with the parrot believes himself to be ordained to find the tlogwe. The blue witch has him sucking at her breast."

"What a fool. When I am coronated I want to see his head mounted on the wall of the mayor's office of my city hall."

"Your wish is my command, my master."

"And the heads of the Taras will be displayed on pikes at the front door of my city hall."

Chapter Ten
Part One

Around the corner and out of sight of the Starbucks where we sat drinking coffee a convoy of armored SWAT vehicles pulled to a stop at the curb. Squads of black clad Deportation Police goons exited the vehicles and assembled on the sidewalk, large machine guns with short barrels slung over their shoulders. Several of the cops in command carried magic harpoons.

The crowd of people running up the street past the Starbucks gave me the first indication something was wrong. Several stragglers at the back of the crowd stumbled and fell to the pavement and lay motionless as goons with magic harpoons came into sight. Michael jumped to his feet. "What the fuck!" he exclaimed.

"Something is not right," Jean said worriedly. The sound of a machine gun firing gave me reason to believe something was not right. A string of bullets pockmarked a car passing through the intersection. The vehicle veered into oncoming traffic, smashed into another car, and sent the car spinning into a cluster of newspaper boxes on the opposite corner. Several pedestrians knocked down like bowling pins screamed in pain.

White Tara bolted off my shoulder and darted to the top of the building. Red Tara launched herself off Jean's shoulder. Furiously flapping her wings she climbed into the sky. Feathers fluffed out, Princess Tara stood erect on the table.

The first squad of black clad Deportation Police goons appeared along the sidewalk, running directly for our table. Customers at other tables scattered and fled, knocking over tables and chairs in the panic. This slowed the goons down long enough to give us a few extra critical seconds to react. Jean leaped to her feet, upending our table, sending our coffee cups and Princess Tara flying. "Sorry sweetheart!" she yelled.

I jumped to my feet. Outright fear made my skin crawl like nothing had since the time I went to see the first Alien movie. By myself. A goon with a magic harpoon appeared on the opposite side of our sideways table. His pale skin and gaunt frame screamed laxsa, although his eyes hid behind black wraparound sunglasses. He leveled his magic harpoon to aim the death stick at me. Jean's hand appeared next to my head holding a pistol. Jean pulled the trigger. The gunshot nearly burst my eardrum. The goon's sunglasses split in two and the two pieces flew off his face. A hole appeared directly between his sunken bloodshot laxsa eyes. He flew backwards as if someone with a stage hook yanked him off the stage. The magic harpoon flew forward directly into my hands. I spun around to face Jean. "Where the hell did you get that gun?"

"Took the gun off that dead laxsa during all the confusion," she replied.

"I love you," I said. A feeling of calm settled over me.

"Give me that thing, gawddammit!" Michael exclaimed. He grasped the magic harpoon and yanked the weapon out of my hands. "If you're not

319

going to use it. . ." He kneeled next to our overturned table and pointed the harpoon at a couple of Deportation Police goons. "Die you fuckers!" The goons crumpled to the sidewalk.

A burst of machine gun fire shredded our table, showering us in metal shards. Michael pointed the magic harpoon at the goon with the machine gun just as he squeezed the trigger to fire another burst of bullets. As the goon fell dead the recoil spun him around, his finger stuck on the trigger. The burst of bullets cut down half a dozen Deportation Police goons behind him.

Another crowd of people running up the center of Market Street dodging horn blaring cars alerted us to the squad of Deportation Police goons trying to flank us. A goon with a magic harpoon stopped at the door to the Starbucks. He turned his magic harpoon toward me. *Oh shit*! I thought to myself. I heard a heavy thud. I realized an arrow pierced the center of his forehead. The force of the impact flung his body backwards through the glass door. I turned to see Red Tara, the four-armed Amazonian witch, standing next to Jean and Michael. She smiled at me as she calmly nocked an arrow into her longbow.

The sound of machine gun fire reverberated along the brickwork facing the street. I ducked and slapped my hands over my ears as Jean raised her pistol at another target. Thankfully my hands muffled Princess Tara's screech. I looked up to see two goons with machine guns standing over me. One raised the butt of his weapon to smash my head. I heard the swoosh of a battle axe whirling through the air and caught the glint of a steel blade in the sunlight. The goon's weapon flew up into the air, along with his head. The body toppled backwards onto the sidewalk. As the body fell the gusher of blood from the severed neck sprayed the second goon. He looked down at the blood sprayed across his uniform. He looked up. I heard another heavy thud. An arrow pierced his skull and threw him backwards. His machine gun fell onto the sidewalk at my feet and bounced into my hands.

Two more goons dashed to the two bodies sprawled across the sidewalk and dropped to their knees. They lifted their machine guns to their shoulders. A battle axe whirled past my ear and split the head of one of the goons neatly in half. The second goon hesitated. He tried to stand up. A black dervish jumped over my head, knocking me to my hands and knees. I caught the flash of steel claws as Black Tara separated the goon's head from his shoulders.

Behind me I heard Jean scream "Damn it!" I heard the sound of a pistol clicking on an empty clip.

"Jean!" I yelled, spinning around. I flung the machine gun up to her. She dropped her empty pistol as she caught the gun. She racked the charging handle, aimed the machine gun, and pulled the trigger.

Blue Tara dashed past me. I saw her battle axe sticking out of the windshield of a parked car. Deportation Police goons blocked the sidewalk, machine guns in their hands. Blue Tara skipped into the air and knocked two goons down with her feet. She grabbed the handle of the battle axe and yanked the blade out of the windshield. Flinging the axe around her she planted the blade in the skull of a laxsa goon. Another goon swung his machine gun

321

toward her. Before he could pull the trigger the black dervish that was Black Tara whirled between the two of them. I saw a flash of steel claws and the goon's head flew off his shoulders. Blue Tara kicked the headless body backwards as she yanked her battle axe out of the laxsa skull in which the blade was buried.

I realized I was still on my hands and knees. I saw a magic harpoon laying on the sidewalk next to Starbucks' busted door. I scrambled to grab the death stick. As I struggled to my feet a burst of machine gun bullets laced the sidewalk behind me. Jean screamed. I spun around, fearing the worst. Jean pointed up the sidewalk. "Tara!" she cried out. "Tara's been shot."

I turned to look for Blue Tara. She lay on her side on the sidewalk, her battle axe in her hand. Blood covered her legs. She struggled to push herself up with her elbow. A Deportation Police goon pointed his machine gun at her. I pointed the magic harpoon at him. He collapsed to the pavement.

Two other goons ran to Blue Tara and aimed their machine guns at her. The black dervish that was Black Tara jumped between Blue Tara and the goons. Black Tara lopped off one of the cop's heads with her flashing steel claws. The other scrambled backwards. He attempted to aim his machine gun at Black Tara. I pointed the magic harpoon at him. He crumpled to the pavement.

Sirens blaring, armored SWAT assault vehicles drove into view and pulled to the curb, smashing between parked cars. I ran to Blue Tara's side. Blood spurted out of several bullet holes in her legs. "Hang in there,"

I pleaded with her, putting my arm around her shoulders. I pulled her upright.

"Take my blade, honey," Blue Tara said. She gave me a weak smile as she pushed her battle axe to me. I grasped the handle put for all my effort I couldn't life the weapon.

Jean joined us. "We need to get out of here!" she cried out, telling me what already was painfully obvious to me. "Now!" she insisted. She stepped to my side and fired a burst from her machine gun at one of the SWAT vehicles.

"Tara," I said. "We need to get out of here."

"I would like a frappuccino right now," Blue Tara replied. A pained grin creased her face. I couldn't tell if she winked at me, or winced from the pain.

"Please," I pleaded. "Get us out of here." Blue Tara pressed her one big yellow eye closed and grabbed hold of my arm. I moved her hand to the handle of her battle axe. "Please Tara." I pressed my eyes closed. Blue Tara screeched.

ΔΔΔ

I opened my eyes. I found myself kneeling on the floor of my Ballard apartment. I cradled Blue Tara in my arms. My head throbbed like I had been thrown against a wall one too many times. I struggled to focus my eyes. Blood pooled across my hardwood floor from the bullet wounds in Blue Tara's legs. Jean kneeled next to me, her hand on my shoulder.

Michael stood behind her cradling Margarita in his arms. "We've got to stop the bleeding," Jean insisted.

"We need White Tara!" I yelled. I looked around me. The apartment seemed like a blur. Red Tara stood in the bay window looking up the street.

"You don't need to yell," Jean replied. "We're right here."

"Where's White Tara?"

"She didn't come back with us," Michael replied.

"What do you mean she didn't come back with us? What happened?"

"My sister White Tara must have flown away from where we stood," Red Tara said. She stepped to my side and knelt next to Blue Tara. Blue Tara placed her hand on Red Tara's arm.

"Hopefully she's not hurt," Jean said.

"Or worse," Michael added.

Red Tara turned to look up at Michael. "Ekajati and I would sense if anything happened to White Tara."

"We've got to stop the bleeding," Jean said, visibly concerned. "Before she bleeds out. She's lucky. Looks like the bullets passed cleanly through her legs. I don't see any bone matter in her wounds."

"We've got to find White Tara," I insisted. I motioned to Michael. "Mike. Go down to the street and take a look. Prop the front door open." Michael headed toward the door. "Take your magic harpoon with you. Just in case."

"We need tourniquets to stop the bleeding," Jean said. "You guys give me your belts." I pulled off my belt and handed the belt to Jean. "Michael! I need yours too!" Jean yelled before Michael got out the door. He stopped, pulled off his belt, and tossed the belt to Jean. Jean quickly wrapped the belts around Blue Tara's thighs.

"We need to do something until White Tara shows up," I said.

"I am doing something," Jean replied, cinching the belts tight.

"What else do you need?" I asked, my voice cracked from panic. To my eyes, Blue Tara's crystalline blue skin seemed to be slowly turning black. "Sheets? Hot water?" I blurted out.

"What are you talking about?" Jean asked.

"That's what they do in the movies," I replied lamely. "They're always sending people to get all the clean sheets and hot water they can."

"Seriously?" Jean replied, staring at me. "They do that to get the people out of their hair. However, you might want to get some hot water and towels to start cleaning up this mess," she added, nodding toward the blood pooling on the floor.

"I'm not worried about that," I replied. "Red Tara," I called out, pointing into the kitchen. "There's some towels in the cabinet above the fridge." Red Tara retrieved the towels and placed them on the floor next to us.

"We should maybe call for an ambulance," Jean said. "Before Blue Tara goes into shock."

"Blue Tara reached over and took Jean's hand. "No ambulance. I can not fall into the hands of the regime."

"Please hang in there Tara," I said. "I can't lose you."

"You won't lose me honey." She smiled at me. "We yet have much to do before I am done."

"The bleeding's pretty much stopped," Jean observed.

"Oh thank god," I said to Jean. "Don't know what I'd do without you. I couldn't believe how you handled that machine gun."

"A firearm is a firearm," she replied. "You and Michael did pretty darn good with those magic harpoons."

I glanced around the room. "Did I lose it?" Jean pointed toward the corner by the door. Couple of magic harpoons, a machine gun, a battle axe, and a longbow leaned stacked against the wall. "We're building a nice arsenal," she said.

"Bet Charlie can get us more ammo."

"I grabbed some clips from some dead laxsa," Jean replied.

"Damn, you're good."

"I didn't think they'd mind."

"Wonder how long the magic harpoons last? Hate to have to find out the hard way when they run out of juice."

"Let's not worry about that now." Jean put her hand on Blue Tara's leg. "How do your legs feel?" she asked.

"I can not seem to move my legs," Blue Tara replied.

"Hang in there sweetie," I said. I squeezed her shoulder. "I love you."

"Hey," Jean responded. "How about me?"

"Do you need to ask?" I said. I leaned over and kissed Jean. "You know I love you."

"Where's my kiss?" Blue Tara asked. She grasped my arm and pulled me to her. I kissed her. Her lips felt cold.

"Gawddammit!" I cried out. "Where's White Tara?"

I heard footsteps pounding up the stairs outside the apartment. Michael burst through the door. White Tara sat perched on his shoulder. "I found her!" he screamed.

"Calm down," I said, my heart pounding. "You don't need to tell us the obvious."

White Tara leaped off Michael's shoulder and alighted on Blue Tara's thigh. "I apologize for my delay in returning, my sister Ekajatia. I had not realized you were so badly injured."

"Where have you been?" I asked. "We've been frantic."

"I knew you would arrive in due course," Blue Tara replied.

"Please do something," I pleaded. "Talk later."

White Tara cocked her head and pinned a pink eye on me. "Of course, sweetie. I have every intention of doing something." She stepped down Blue Tara's leg and rubbed her beak across the wounds. Blue Tara closed her eye and groaned.

"What's happening?" I pleaded. I stared at Blue Tara's thighs. The wounds closed and disappeared before my very eyes.

Part Two

"Thank you. Thank you. Thank you," I told White Tara.

White Tara hopped on my shoulder. "That was nothing sweetie. That is what I do."

Blue Tara opened her eye. She struggled to stand up. "Hold on there," I said. "You lost a lot of blood. You should probably stay horizontal for a while and rest. I can get you some pillows and blankets."

"I thank you for your concern, sweetie, but I will be fine." Blue Tara reached up to Red Tara. "Help me get up, sister." With her four hands Red Tara gingerly pulled Blue Tara onto her feet. Blue Tara swayed, her eye closed. I put my arm around her shoulder to steady her.

"Jean. Grab a chair. Please," I said. Jean pushed a chair to me and we eased Blue Tara onto the seat. "Damn, you had me worried."

Blue Tara looked up at me with her one big yellow eye. "I do not desire to worry you."

"Well, I couldn't help being worried," I replied. "This is the worst possible news."

"What?" Jean responded. "What are you talking about? White Tara saved her."

"Learning that our Blue Tara is mortal. The hard way. Which I'm guessing means all the Taras are mortal. I thought goddesses lived forever."

"Come here," Blue Tara said to me, patting her knee. I stepped to her and she took my hand. "Only our visible form is mortal. Our spirit is eternal. The form can be killed. But not the spirit."

"If one of the Tara forms is ever killed," Red Tara added, "another will take her place. Eventually."

"I am not a goddess," Blue Tara continued. "Being a god or a goddess implies omnipotence. We Taras each possess our own powerful magic, but we are far from omnipotent. There are some like the Winalagalis who would have his followers believe he is a god. But in truth he simply only possesses a special magic. A special magic that gives creatures like him and Hamatsa the ability to act as if they were gods."

"They don't have snakes in their heads? Do they?" Michael asked.

"Never mind him," I said. "I can't believe there could be another Blue Tara like you. I don't want to ever have to find out."

"There are many others like me," Blue Tara replied. "They just have not mastered the magic that I possess. I am not the first Blue Tara that ever was. I certainly will not be the last. But I possess the memories and knowledge of all the Taras that have come before me since the beginning of time."

"Oh my god," Jean said. "What a burden."

"A burden and a duty," Blue Tara replied. "But one that I have gladly accepted."

"It's hard to be a god," I quipped.

"Not a god," Blue Tara replied.

"I know. I'm joking. But still, I can't deal with the thought that I might lose you."

"I explained that to you. Would you like me to explain again?"

"No need," I replied.

Blue Tara grabbed the collar of my shirt and pulled me onto her lap. She kissed me. Her lips felt warm and moist." "You are the one I worry about," Blue Tara said.

"Me?"

"There is only one of you. That is the weakness of your kind."

"Until you are reincarnated," Red Tara interjected. "But that might be some time."

"Whatever did I do in my last life to be the one to suffer in this life?" I quipped.

"Me," Michael interjected. "I want to be reincarnated as a bird so I can shit on all the people I don't like."

"Be careful what you wish for," Blue Tara replied. "You might get your wish."

"I don't know about anybody else," Jean said, "But all of a sudden I feel really really hungry. And thirsty."

I walked into the kitchen and retrieved a six-pack of cold Rainier from the fridge. "A beer would taste good right now," I agreed. I passed out the beers. We all stared as Blue Tara popped the tab open and chugged the entire can. I handed her another.

"You don't suppose the pizza place is open?" Jean asked. "After all that's happened today, I am starved."

I stepped to the bay window to look across the street. "I see people entering the shop. So I think we're good." I retrieved my tablet from the kitchen table to look up the online order form. "Oh shit!" I cried out.

"What now?" Michael asked. He and Jean scrambled to my side to peer over my shoulders at the screen. I turned the volume up to maximum.

"Effective immediately," a familiar voice stated, "a state of emergency exists within the city of Seattle. The mayor authorized me to state that a bloody insurrection in the Seattle neighborhood of Ballard this morning has been crushed by the authorities. But not without the cost of a great number of our brave Deportation Police. All citizens of Seattle are hereby required to wear black arm bands in mourning of their sacrifice."

"That can't be," Michael said.

"That was hardly an insurrection," I replied. "And we were the ones who were attacked."

"Not that. Look at the speaker. That's Kinqalatlala."

A svelte dark-skinned woman clothed in black leather, with long black hair flowing over her shoulders, stood at a podium inside Seattle City Hall. "My god!" I exclaimed. "I thought that voice sounded familiar."

"That fucking bitch!" Jean exclaimed. "I'm going to kill that bitch the next time I run into her."

"She set us up for a fall," Michael said. "She led us right into a trap."

"And conveniently stepped out right before all the trouble started," Jean replied. "That fucking bitch."

"Listen," Michael interrupted. "She's talking about us."

". . . per order of the mayor, all citizens of the city of Seattle are hereby required to be on the lookout for a small band of rebels led by a criminal coven of witches that possesses the magic to confuse people's minds. A criminal coven of witches that possesses the magic to make people see things that are not as they really are. . ."

"We're fucked," I said.

"This band of rebels is armed and extremely dangerous," Kinqalatlala continued. "If any citizen encounters these criminals, do not approach them under any circumstances. Alert the authorities immediately. Let our brave Deportation Police deal with them."

"Well, thank you very much," I replied to the screen.

"This concludes this emergency broadcast," Kinqalatlala added. "The citizens of Seattle will be notified when there are additional updates. The mayor commands that you stay vigilant and that you stay alert. If you see something, say something. Report your observations to the authorities immediately. That is all." The screen went blank.

"Oh shit," I said. "Now what?"

Blue Tara emptied her can of beer. "Pizza," she replied.

ΔΔΔ

We ate our pizza in silence. Afterwards, I poured glasses of wine for everyone. "This kind of changes things," Michael finally said to break the quiet.

"What do you mean?" I replied.

"About trying to sneak into city hall tomorrow, is what I mean. Kinqalatlala would spot us."

"Maybe. Maybe not. We talked about that after she left our little coffee klatch this morning. So she's not privy to our plans. She wouldn't necessarily be looking for us."

"What exactly would be the purpose of our visit then?" Michael replied. "What's your plan?"

"I'm making this up as I go. I don't know. Take Hamatsa out."

"Take Kinqalatlala out," Jean interjected.

"Shock and awe," I added. "Shock and awe. We could strike a meaningful blow at the regime if we actually did something."

"We seem to be losing sight of our original plan," Jean said.

"What was our original plan again?" I asked.

"To find the tlogwe," Blue Tara said.

"Precisely," Jean responded. "To find the tlogwe."

"And how well is that working out?" I smirked.

"Without the tlogwe we can do no more than harass Hamatsa," Blue Tara added. "We need the magic of the tlogwe to stop Hamatsa and the Winalagalis. Right now, Hamatsa's power is greater than ours."

"So what are we going to do?" I asked. "Kinqalatlala was our only lead to the tlogwe. We can't just sit here and drink wine."

"I am still your best lead to the tlogwe," a familiar voice interrupted us from across the room. We jumped out of our chairs, knocking over glasses and spilling wine across the table and over the floor.

"Jesus Fucking Christ!" I yelled. "How the fuck did you get in here?"

Kinqalatlala stood in the doorway to the apartment. "Your front door was wide open," she replied. "I walked in. Your apartment door is unlocked. I thought maybe you were expecting me. I promised you I would be back when I had information to share."

"You fucking bitch!" Jean screamed. She ran across the room and picked up the machine gun. She racked the charging handle and pointed the barrel at Kinqalatlala. "And I promised I would kill you if you ever showed yourself again."

"Jean. Wait!" I cried out. Jean pulled the trigger. The firing pin clicked on an empty clip.

"Shit!" Jean exclaimed.

"You would be doing me a favor if you could kill me," Kinqalatlala said. "Can I come in? We have much to discuss."

"Oh shit," I replied. "Why not?" Jean put down the machine gun and reached for one of the magic harpoons. "Jean. Wait. Please," I pleaded. "Let's hear her out. Then you can kill her."

Kinqalatlala walked across the room to join us at the dining table. Margarita growled and jumped out of Michael's lap, trotting to the bay window. I toweled up the spilled wine as best as I could. "A glass of wine, please?" she asked. I poured her a glass and pulled a chair out for her. She looked resplendent clad in her skin-tight black leather.

"How dare you come back here," Jean stated vehemently. "You lying piece of shit."

"Tell us how you really feel," I quipped.

"We saw your performance on the news broadcast," Michael said. "So you are still serving Hamatsa."

"A performance is precisely what that was," Kinqalatlala replied. "Nothing has changed. I am still working against Hamatsa. I needed him to believe I am still his slave. I yet want to help you find the tlogwe."

"I no longer believe you are even the tlogwala," I replied.

"I am sorry to hear that," Kinqalatlala said. "But I know that I am the tlogwala."

"Let's cut to the chase," I said. "Tell us what you have to tell us."

Kinqalatlala drained her glass of wine and reached the empty glass up to me for a refill. "Hamatsa plans to assassinate Dear Leader when he comes to Seattle for the coronation. Hamatsa's megalomaniacal narcissism rivals Dear Leader's. He ultimately plans to challenge the Winalagalis himself."

"What?" I replied with some astonishment in my voice. "Why would he do that?"

"To take his place as ruler of the New American Order. I am to be his queen."

"Lucky you," Jean responded.

"Well, that's good," I replied. "One less bad guy to deal with."

"Not so good," Kinqalatlala responded. I looked at her quizzically. "Right now the regime has two centers of power. The Winalagalis. And Hamatsa. If one is eliminated all power falls to the survivor. That would be a disaster. Both for your world and for mine."

"What does Hamatsa know about us?" I asked.

"He knows you plan to strike when Dear Leader arrives in this city."

"And how would he know about that?"

"Because I told him."

"The fuck!" I exclaimed. I could see Jean growing visibly angered. "Why would you do that?"

"To save you."

"The fuck," I said again.

"Without the tlogwe you do not have the power to strike the regime. Such an ill-considered action would result in disaster for you. And that would allow Hamatsa to consolidate his power beyond anyone's capacity to resist."

"I say we kill her now," Jean whispered angrily.

"Does Hamatsa know you're here?" I asked.

"Yes he does."

"What the fuck!" I exclaimed, thinking to myself I needed a new word. Jean raised the magic harpoon in her hands. I grabbed the shaft to stop her.

"Hamatsa believes I am here to encourage you to attack Dear Leader. His plan is to eliminate both the Winalagalis and you at one fell swoop. What is the saying? To kill two birds with one stone?"

"And what do you plan to do?"

"I can best help you from inside city hall. Passing information to you about Hamatsa's activities and his plans. By connecting you to the resistance."

"What resistance?"

"Hamatsa depends upon the Deportation Police to protect his regime. The Seattle Police Department and city hall are yet infested with resistance cells."

"Infested?"

"Hamatsa's word. Not mine. I have also learned that the deposed mayor has organized a shadow city government to coordinate the resistance."

"Good luck with that," I replied. "We seem to be the only ones doing much resisting these days," I added, waving my hand around the apartment.

"You are not the only ones. But you are the ones Hamatsa fears most. Your cause may be lonely. But you are not alone," Kinqalatlala replied. "I must return to city hall to report to Hamatsa that you are still planning to strike Dear Leader."

"We need weapons and ammunition," I said. Kinqalatlala nodded. She drained her glass of wine, pushed her chair back from the table, and stood up. She turned and walked across the apartment and out the door.

ΔΔΔ

"Maybe you shouldn't have said anything about needing guns and ammunition," Jean suggested. "Just shows her how weak we are."

"On the other hand," I replied, "that might just be one way to find out which side she's really on."

"Wouldn't surprise me if she's on her own side," Jean replied. "She may be playing Hamatsa against us. While she's playing us against Hamatsa."

"Wouldn't be at all surprised. In fact, I'm counting on that." I looked at the Taras. Blue Tara and Red Tara sat at the end of the table, glasses of wine in their hands. Margarita lay curled up in the bay window underneath Princess Tara's play stand where White Tara sat perched on one leg, napping with her beak behind her wing. "What do the Taras make of all this?" I asked.

"The black witch underestimates our powers," Blue Tara replied. "We are stronger than she knows. I do not doubt her word that she is the tlogwala. But she has not yet learned that being the tlogwala constrains her actions. We can use her to our benefit just as she may believe she is using us to hers."

"So, what do we do?" I asked.

"We strike at Hamatsa before he consolidates his power," Blue Tara replied. "We have the element of surprise on our side. If we delay, Hamatsa's magic and his grip on power will only increase."

"So you're saying we raid city hall?"

"Hamatsa will not be expecting us. The black witch believes we will wait to strike when Dear Leader arrives."

"I say we take out Hamatsa and Kinqalatlala," Jean added.

"Some rise by sin and some by virtue fall," I quipped.

Part Three

The weekly farmers market on the plaza in front of Seattle City Hall looked like any of the other farmers markets around the city. Scores of vendors sold everything from cut flowers to veggie starts. Bins of apples, onions, cherries, and peas sat shaded by big white canvas canopies. Ice cream and sandwich vendors competed with homemade doo dads and printed T-shirts. Instead of the families with baby strollers, students pushing bicycles or carrying skateboards, and young urbanites walking countless yapping dogs that populated most other farmers markets around the city, office workers, lawyers, and other professionals crowded the city hall farmers market looking for a particular heritage tomato or chipotle pepper for their guacamole or garden salad.

I drove my truck directly into the city hall parking garage. No one talked on our drive across town. The cab was a tad crowded, what with three people, three parrots, and one black cat. Me. Jean. Michael. Princess Tara. Red Tara. White Tara. And Black Tara. Not to mention two magic harpoons and one machine gun stashed behind the seat. We would work out getting the arsenal into city hall when the time came to get the arsenal into city hall. Once parked, the parrots flew out of the parking garage. Jean, Michael, and I walked out. Margarita scampered along behind us.

I stopped at an expresso cart and ordered three lattes. As we stood and sipped our coffee I half expected Princess Tara to swoop down out of the sky and snatch the coffee out of my hand. I knew that somewhere she sat perched watching me drink my coffee. I smirked to myself knowing she could only futilely watch me drink my coffee. I knew I would pay for my gloating.

We sat on the retaining wall lining the plaza's central fountain. Margarita hopped onto Michael's lap. Several passersby stopped and admired the cat. She is a particularly attractive cat. Especially when her reddish black fur shimmered in the spring Seattle sunlight.

I studied the crowd around the plaza. The farmers market exuded an air of tranquility that belied the tension that roiled my gut. I watched people chat with coworkers. People laugh at private jokes. Coworkers smile at each other as they passed. Security seemed lax, even by normal standards. A couple of black clad Deportation Police officers stood at the ice cream booth eating cones. A couple of Seattle cops in blue stood on the other side of the plaza chatting with each other, holding coffee cups in their hands. However, they did all sport machine guns slung over their shoulders.

"How's this going to go down?" Michael asked.

"Margarita is going to slip inside and find a safe spot for us to time and space bend in. Blue Tara can't just time and space bend us in without knowing the layout. We don't want to materialize between floors. Or in an elevator shaft."

"Then what?"

"Margarita alerts Blue Tara to her location, like a homing beacon. Blue Tara does her magic. We end up inside safe and snug."

"I still don't get how Margarita communicates her location to Blue Tara from inside the building," Michael said.

"I don't understand either, completely. But somehow Blue Tara can hear Margarita, even from the depths of city hall."

"Parrots have acute hearing," Jean replied. "Macaws can hear each other from miles apart in the rainforest."

I reached over and rubbed Margarita's head. "Showtime," I said. Margarita stretched out, arched her back, and sprang off Michael's lap. She meowed and trotted off around the fountain toward the front door of city hall. We watched her stop at the entrance to wait for someone to open the door. Once someone opened the door she scampered between their feet and disappeared into the lobby. "Wait here," I said to Jean and Michael. "I'll be right back."

"What the. . ." Michael said, startled. "Where are you going?"

"I'll be right back," I repeated. "Just going to check on Margarita." I entered the lobby just in time to see Margarita run past the security checkpoint.

"Hey!" one of the black clad Deportation Police guards yelled. "Who let the cat loose?"

"What cat?" another guard replied.

"A cat just ran through here," the first guard responded, pointing to the bank of elevators across the lobby. I caught a glimpse of Margarita slipping through a closing door leading to a stairway to the basement.

Without thinking about the consequences, I ran through the security checkpoint. "My cat escaped!" I yelled. "Did anybody see which way the cat went?"

"God damn!" the first guard exclaimed. "Why in the hell did you bring a cat to city hall? The fur ball went into the basement." He stepped to the door and swiped the door open with his pass card. "Follow me." He took a step down the stairway.

I heard a screech, like fingernails dragged across a chalkboard. "Somebody grab that parrot!" someone cried out from the lobby.

The guard stopped and turned back to the lobby. "What the fuck is going on?" he yelled. "Where are all these damn animals coming from?"

With the guard's back to me, I slipped through the door, but not before catching a glimpse of White Tara

344

flying through the lobby. I raced down the stairs. I burst onto the basement level. Two black clad Deportation Police cops stood at another doorway at the other end of the hall looking down another flight of stairs. "Anybody see my cat?" I yelled as I ran down the hall. "I lost my cat." The cops pointed down the stairs to the subbasement. I ran through the door and down the staircase. "Thanks!" I yelled as I passed the cops. I quietly thanked the laxsa for being so dimwitted.

I found the door at the bottom of the stairs propped open. I grabbed the handrail to stop myself from running out the door. I took a deep breath and peaked around the corner. Margarita stood on her hind legs midway down the hall studying a set of doors. She growled when I appeared out of the stairwell. Upon recognizing me, she dropped on all fours, arched her back and purred.

I dashed to her and leaned down to rub her head. "Do we open Door Number One? Or Door Number Two?" I asked her. I counted six doors, three on each side of the hallway. "Or Doors Three, Four, Five, or Six?" Margarita stepped to the farthest door and meowed. "You picked Door Number Six." I walked up to the door. *It can't be this easy*, I thought to myself. I heard one of the other doors swing open. I grabbed the handle of Door Number Six and pulled. The door opened and Margarita and I slipped in. "This works for me," I quietly told her.

We found ourselves in a storeroom. Not an ordinary storeroom with tools and mops and lightbulbs, brooms and paper towels. This was a storeroom with machine guns and shotguns and magic harpoons. With stacks of cases filled with stun grenades and clips of ammunition. With rack upon rack of Deportation Police uniforms. "Bingo," I said to Margarita. "Time to muster the troops."

Margarita rose on her hind legs, forelegs stretched above her head, and growled. Not her typical growl. A growl that grew in pitch and intensity until I thought my eardrums would burst. I slapped my hands against my ears and fell back against the wall. My butt slid down to the floor. A searing blue light burned through my closed eyelids.

Several hands grabbed my arms and pulled me to my feet. I opened my eyes. Jean, Michael, and the Taras surrounded me. "You freaked me out when you ran through the lobby," Jean said. "Please don't ever do that again."

"That was a spur of the moment thing, I assure you," I replied.

"How did you ever find this place?" Michael asked, running his hands over the magic harpoons.

"You can thank Margarita for that. She found the storeroom." I started taking off my clothes.

"What the fuck are you doing?" Michael asked.

"Watch," I replied. I picked out a Deportation Police uniform I thought would fit me. I started putting on the uniform. "The perfect cover," I said. "Pick out a couple of uniforms," I told Jean and Michael. Michael started to take off his clothes.

"No fucking way am I wearing one of these uniforms," Jean insisted. "I haven't seen any lady goons around. I might draw more attention to us than we want."

"Suit yourself," I replied.

Michael tucked the black shirt into his black pants and pulled on a black bullet proof vest. He selected a magic harpoon from a rack stacked with magic harpoons. "Okay. We're armed and dangerous," he said. "Now what?'

ΔΔΔ

"Now you come with me," a familiar voice responded. We spun around. Kinqalatlala stood in the doorway. Michael reflexively aimed his magic harpoon at her. I grabbed the shaft and pointed the death stick at the ceiling.

"How did you know we were here?" I blurted out.

"How do you think you got in so easily?" she replied. "I have been expecting you."

"We've been set up," Jean said, picking up a machine gun. She racked the charging handle. She checked the clip. Empty.

"Clips are in the end cases," Kinqalatlala said. "You have not been set up. I am here to assist you."

"Does Hamatsa know we're here?" I asked, fearing the worst.

"He does not. He is preparing a press conference to announce the details of Dear Leader's coming visit to Seattle."

"So he's in the mayor's office on the top floor?" I asked.

"Hamatsa is in his command post on this level. At the end of the hall. The darkness of the depths suits him better than the light of day."

"Nothing is ever this easy," I said. "Something is wrong."

"I say we kill this bitch," Jean said. "Then worry about Hamatsa."

"You would be doing me a favor if you could kill me," Kinqalatlala replied. "I grow weary of the burdens of your world. But you would only be hurting yourself if you do so. I am the only friend you have in this situation."

"How many attendants does Hamatsa have with him?" I asked.

"Just his usual command staff. Mostly computer jockeys and flunkies. Lightly armed. I have dispatched his security detail on an emergency call."

"That's convenient," I replied.

"They believe they are going after you."

"Well then. What are we waiting for?" I selected a machine gun and popped open a case of clips.

"Careful with that sucker," Jean warned. "Those machine guns have a wicked kick."

"Thanks for the warning," I replied. I copied Jean as she loaded a clip and racked the charging handle.

"Stick extra clips in your pockets," Jean said. "Eject the clips as they empty and slam in new ones."

"Let's mount up" I said.

"We are not riding into battle," Blue Tara replied quizzically, swinging her battle axe in her hand.

ΔΔΔ

We followed Kinqalatlala to the end of the hall. She waved her hand and a door appeared that I had not previously noticed. She entered the room beyond. We followed. Hamatsa stood in the center of an otherwise empty chamber, lit only by the florescent light flooding in from the hallway. I aimed my machine gun at him. "What the fuck is this?" I asked, glancing sideways at Kinqalatlala. She stepped to Hamatsa's side.

"You did well, my queen," Hamatsa said.

"Capturing them proved easier than even you expected, my master."

A door opened at the back of the chamber and a squad of black clad Deportation Police decked out in black body armor filed in. "Kill them!" Hamatsa ordered. The goons lined up in front of Hamatsa and Kinqalatlala. They aimed their machine guns at us.

"Wait!" I cried out. "You can't do that."

Hamatsa repeated his order. "Kill them!" The goons pulled the triggers on their weapons. I closed my eyes. Nothing. I waited a few moments. Still nothing. I had been dead. This did not feel like being dead. I opened my eyes. "Shoot them down, you fools!" Hamatsa screamed.

The goons looked at their weapons, racked the charging handles, and pointed the barrels at us again. I could see their fingers pull the triggers. Nothing. Maybe this was my lucky day.

Hamatsa grabbed one of the goons and spun him around. "Damn you. Give me your weapon!" Hamatsa snatched the machine gun out of the goon's hands. He racked the charging handle and pointed the weapon directly at me. I saw him pull the trigger. Still nothing. He ejected the clip, examined the clip closely, and smashed the clip back in place. He pointed the barrel at my head. I watched him pull the trigger. Nothing.

"What the hell?" I finally said. I turned to look at Blue Tara standing behind me. "Are you doing this?"

"This is not my magic," Blue Tara replied. "I do not know what kind of magic is in play here."

"This is your magic," Kinqalatlala stated. I turned to stare at her, my jaw at my feet. Hamatsa turned to stare at her, his jaw at his feet.

"Whose magic?" I asked, as astonished as Hamatsa seemed to be.

"You have been given the gift of the tlogwe."

"I have?"

"Your destiny lies in your hands now."

I looked down at my hands.

"The tlogwe is a gift of magic and power that you must master," Kinqalatlala said. "If you fail to do so the magic will consume and destroy you. Hamatsa once grasped the gift of the tlogwe, but failed to master the magic. The power of the tlogwe corrupted and twisted him."

"You fool!" Hamatsa cried out. "You really are the tlogwala." He pointed his machine gun at Kinqalatlala and pulled the trigger. A burst of bullets shredded her chest and flung her backwards into the dark room.

I pulled the trigger of my machine gun. Hamatsa's head exploded into a cloud of blood red pulp. One of the Deportation Police goons pulled a bayonet from his gun belt and charged at me. A battle axe whirled past my ear and struck his head squarely between his eyes, flinging him backwards onto the floor. The other goons dropped their machine guns and drew their bayonets. An arrow pierced the skull of first one, and then another goon, knocking them on their backs. Jean opened fire with her machine gun and cut down the remaining goons.

I ran to where I saw Kinqalatlala fall. Even in the darkness I could see blood on the floor. But there was no body to be found. Jean dashed to my side. "You okay sweetie?" she asked.

"Yeah. I guess so," I replied. I took a deep breath. I felt thoroughly exhausted. And scared.

"Where did she go?" Jean asked. "Hamatsa shot her at point blank range. No way in hell could she have gotten up from that."

"Yes he did," I replied. "I assume she's gone back to her world."

"What do you mean gone back to her world?"

"Because I wished that for her. Call me crazy, but I visualized her flying free on Dluwulaxa the moment Hamatsa shot her."

"It isn't as easy to go crazy as you might think," Jean replied.

I dropped the machine gun and put my arms around Jean. I pulled her to me. I pressed my lips to hers. My tongue found her tongue. "I see us spending the rest of our lives together," I told her. "I love you."

"I love you too, sweetie," she replied. She wrapped her arms around me and squeezed me to her chest.

###
Not The End

More From Princess Tara and Me

You can never keep a good witch down. Stay tuned for future episodes of the continuing saga of the Princess Tara Chronicles. More witches. More monsters. More daemons. More pterodactyls. More parrots. And more coffee. We promise to make it worth your while.

From an Amazon Customer

★ ★ ★ ★ ★ Caffeine fueled fantasy ride

Blue Tara grabbed my interest immediately! I couldn't put it down, as it rushed me headlong into a supernatural world that is a mix of history and fast paced fantasy. The characters are so believable I felt that I knew them. What a fun read for a parrot owner!

Be sure to read the gripping spine-tingling caffeinated conclusion of the Blue Tara Trilogy, *Parrots and Witches; Or, Love. Desire. Ambition. Faith. Without Them, Life Is So Simple, Believe Me*, available from Blue Parrot Books.

If you haven't already, read the introduction to the Blue Tara Trilogy. *Blue Tara; Or, How Is a Hyacinth Macaw Parrot Like a Tibetan Goddess?* available from Blue Parrot Books.

Follow the continuing saga of Princess Tara and her friends and villains in the Kālarātri, or Black Night Trilogy. Part One of the Kālarātri Trilogy, *She Was Not Quite What You Would Call Refined*, Book Four of the Princess Tara Chronicles, available from Blue Parrot Books.

Part Two of the Kālarātri Trilogy, **She Was Not Quite What You Would Call Unrefined**, Book Five of the Princess Tara Chronicles, available from Blue Parrot Books.

How do you defeat a goddess who controls death and time? Can you? Find the answer in the third and last installment of the Kālarātri Trilogy, **She Was the Kind of Person That Keeps a Parrot**, Book Six of the Princess Tara Chronicles, coming 2020.

Princess Tara thanks you for your support!

Michael Ostrogorsky is a parrot, word, and coffee
bean wrangler living in Seattle, with his two parrots,
the Hyacinth Macaw Princess Tara, who really is a
princess, as well as a witch (but in a good way), and
the Blue and Gold Macaw Aboo. Like the protagonist
in this story, Michael boasts two Ph.D.s, in History
and Archaeology, is retired from an academic career,
and currently roasts coffee.

Connect With Princess Tara and Me Online

About Me: https://about.me/michaelostrogorsky

Blog: www.thezenparrot.com

Twitter: https://twitter.com/BlueParrotBooks

Facebook: https://www.facebook.com/The.Zen.Parrot

Instagram:
https://www.instagram.com/michael_ostrogorsky/

CPSIA information can be obtained
at www.ICGtesting.com
Printed in the USA
BVHW041342041019

560259BV00015B/1213/P

9 781087 801261